Also by John F. Rooney

Nine Lives Too Many
The Daemon in Our Dreams
The Rice Queen Spy
Clawed Back from the Dead

LAST PASSAGE TO SANTIAGO

a novel by

John F. Rooney

Senneff House Publishers
Fort Lauderdale, Florida

Senneff House Publishers
P.O. Box 11601
Fort Lauderdale, FL 33339
www.senneffhouse.com

Cover design by Kevin Stawieray

Inside book design and formatting by Dawn Von Strolley Grove

Manufactured in the United States of America

ISBN-13: 978-0-9752756-5-8
ISBN-10: 0-9752756-5-8

"A Good Man Is Hard to Find."

1

That Saturday it was an oppressive setting as hundreds of recent luxury cruise ship passengers wandered around the huge, gloomy, eerily-lit convention center in Santiago, Chile. The sprawling building was hot and stuffy, though it had been touted as being air-conditioned. It was beginning to take on the odor of hundreds of unwashed, sweating, flu-ridden, flatulent elderly bodies.

Some of the hapless beings were sprawled out on three or four of the cushioned banquet chairs they had pushed together into makeshift cots. Others, some in house slippers, shuffled up and down the wide corridors, meandered in and out of the enormous high-ceilinged meeting rooms, while a few could be seen through the upper windows patrolling dispiritedly around the second floor of the center.

Impatient and anxious to do anything to relieve the boredom, some tourists stopped for juice or coffee at one of the hospitality tables, chatted briefly with friends they had met on the ship, then wandered back to areas they had staked out as their territories. It was a world of constant hacking and coughing, red eyes, roiling stomachs, sour urine smells, dry throats, and loose bowels. People headed purposefully back and forth to the toilets. For the last four or five days on the ship there had been an outbreak of some flu-like illness.

These lost souls, who were now waiting for their late night flights, had been on a two-week cruise around the lower half of South America. Their trip aboard the *Global Quest* had begun in Buenos Aires, and it was ending on a sour note there in Santiago, Chile's capital. It was difficult to believe these unfortunates were the same individuals who had looked so self-possessed, so sophisticated, so classy, so haughty in their finery on the formal nights aboard ship.

Looking at them now, one would be hard pressed to

1

differentiate them from the bag ladies, vagrants, and homeless who wandered in and out of Manhattan's Grand Central Station. Air travel is a great leveler and tyrant; long-delayed international flights sweep away dignity, gentility, good grooming, and class distinctions.

Most of the travelers had been on all-day tours of Santiago originating that morning at eight at the ship's berth in Valparaiso, the Chilean seaport. The cruise line had planned for the fact most flights left for the States late at night from Santiago.

The cruisers had boarded tour buses and had been driven to the capital while guides gave commentaries during the ride. Most had remained on the buses for a tour of the capital, had been served lunch with Pisco Sours at a restaurant in a park high above the city, and had continued their tours after lunch. Eventually, they had been dropped off at the convention center where they were told they would wait in air-conditioned comfort.

The former passengers were overwhelmingly older people, their skins grayish, pasty, and lined. Their footfall seemed leaden. Who else but old retired people could afford the time and money to fly all the way to Buenos Aires and take a two-week cruise around South America?

It was to be a long wait for the late night flights, waiting first in the convention center and later in the airport. Here they were hacking, shuffling aimlessly about, sneezing, passing gas, trying to rest, killing time, and scurrying in and out of the toilets. Most had given up reading. They were very bored in this half-lit, depressing place.

A bowed old man with a walker, sweating, was slowly making his way through the long central hall accompanied by a gnarled old crone with a cane.

The old man snarled, "This fucking place was supposed to be air conditioned. It's so goddamn stifling."

The old lady with him crinkled her nose. "It smells like B.O. City in here. Everyone is sweating and farting. All this hacking."

The old man coughed up sputum and spat it into a Kleenex. "Most of us have this flu stuff we picked up on the ship. When will our goddamn flight be called?"

A signal was given a little after five-thirty, and the doors were opened to a spacious banquet room. Tables were set with linen, candles glowed on each table. The room was blessedly air-conditioned. It almost had the feeling of a festive occasion, and people felt somewhat restored.

The dinner itself was disappointing, certainly not up to their cruise-ship standard. It consisted of wilted salad, tasteless chicken (they had already suffered with indifferent chicken for lunch) and six vegetable balls fashioned like melon balls (two each of beets, carrots, and potatoes). The whole thing looked distinctly unappetizing and was barely edible. Stale cottony rolls and pitchers of flat Coca Cola added little to the presumptive banquet.

One large group of passengers was supposed to line up and go by bus to the airport at 7:30 for a United Airlines flight to Miami, but the line started forming outside the convention center at 7:00, well before the dinner was over.

A young couple in their mid-thirties were talking to a couple in their mid-forties. Beside the four, a flamboyantly dressed elderly couple danced together slowly, mechanically. The woman was counting out steps as they moved. A muffled voice came over the loudspeakers.

"Good evening, ladies and gentlemen. This is Sue Swanson, your land tour director. We hope y'all enjoyed your day. The bus trip up from the port of Valparaiso was fascinating. All those vineyards and orchards. Gosh! Our tour of Santiago was a real eye-opener, wasn't it?"

She cleared her throat and said, "We'd like to apologize for the lack of air-conditioning in this building. We had been assured it would be a comfortable place for y'all to wait for your flights, but the airport terminal is worse. It's very crowded, and seating there is limited."

The PA crackled, failed, then came on again with Sue's voice. "When you hear your flight called out, please line up in front of the building. All right, will those folks on United Airlines Flight Nine-Nine-Six bound for Miami, please line up for bus transportation now."

The young couple said their goodbyes to the forties couple. The older couple stopped their robotic dancing to embrace the youngsters. Hugs and handshakes were exchanged all around.

The line for the airport bus stretched down the central walkway outside the building. To the left was a line of tour buses, their doors closed. The drivers were chatting in a group near the second bus in line.

To the right of the walkway was a line of eight hire cars. Drivers were calling out loudly in heavily accented English, vying for attention.

"Taxi to the airport."

"Car for hire to the airport."

"Get ahead of the lines in the airport by taking fast cab."

"Fast trip. Take private limo."

"Car for hire to airport."

Already scores of people were in line for the buses when the man and woman in their mid-thirties headed for the queue. The couple seemed to be arguing about something. The man kept gesturing toward the hire cars and was obviously pleading with his companion. She seemed to be resisting his imprecations, then finally, they broke away from the crowd and headed toward the line of hire cars. The young man and woman were each carrying a small carry-on bag; in addition, he had a camera bag over his shoulder, and she had a large over-the-shoulder pocketbook.

The driver of the first car inexplicably directed them to the third car in line. This driver, avoiding eye contact, opened a rear door of the black car, and they got in the back seat.

The car sped away at a fast pace, headed along the main road toward the international airport, but at a certain point, the car took a side road through what looked like an industrial area and started traveling down a bumpy, deserted unlit road.

As the car rounded a curve in the road ahead, a line of traffic cones blocked its passage. A dusty disreputable van was parked halfway in the road beyond the cones. The hire car approached the cones. At first, the driver didn't seem to slow down, but finally he eased up and brought the car to a stop.

The rear and side doors of the van flew open, and the people in the hire car were facing four men in ski masks with automatic weapons. The disguised men hurried to the hire car and threw open the doors.

A man's voice ordered, "Vamos! Out! Hurry up! Get out!"

The armed men pulled the driver and the two passengers out to the roadway and forced them to lie down while they stood over them, their weapons pointed. The protests of the driver and the two passengers were the only sounds that could be heard.

The three people had cloths thrust over their mouths and noses. They quickly sagged, and their bodies drooped onto the roadway. The woman was half-carried, half-dragged to the side door of the van, and thrown inside, unconscious, like a sack of grain. The van sped off, leaving the driver and the woman's male companion lying lifeless in the street next to the car's open doors.

2

Four days later, in the American Embassy in Santiago, Chile, a group of six men and three women gathered around a conference table. At the head of the table, a man with an impressive white brush mustache was speaking. He was Thomas Garand, the CIA head of station for the embassy.

"Guys, I've asked Greg Pearce from *Newsweek* to join us for this briefing. Greg was a close friend of Stephanie Ably Ranier and her husband Ben. He saw them in Buenos Aires before the sea voyage. Before I ask him to fill in some background, let me recount the details as we know them about this situation to the new people in the room.

"A young couple in their mid-thirties, the Raniers, decided to take a three-week trip to South America. The woman is Stephanie Ably Ranier, and her husband is Benjamin Ranier. They both work in Washington. Stephie works for the National Security Agency, usually referred to in the media as a hush-hush U.S. intelligence agency. Ben is an investigative reporter working for *Newsweek*.

"On their way to the airport in Santiago, the hire car they were traveling in was stopped. Armed men forced them out of the car and onto the pavement. The driver and the couple were rendered unconscious by chloroform or some fast-acting substance, and Stephie was kidnapped. It is a complete mystery as to why this happened to her. Her husband and the driver gave us an account of what transpired.

"From Valparaiso the passengers came in tour buses here to the capital, and most remained on the buses for a tour of the city and lunch at a restaurant in Metropolitano Park.

"The tour continued after lunch, and eventually they were dropped off at the big convention center where they waited for their airline flights. They had their dinner, and the Raniers were among those who lined up for buses. At the last minute, as they were about to board one of the buses to the airport, Ben decided to hire one of the cars.

"The car took a circuitous route to the airport down a couple of back streets. Ben reported to us he had told Stephie if they took a hired car, they would be able to get to the airport ahead of the others and check in faster.

"Why the driver chose that route, we aren't quite sure. He claims it was a shortcut. A few other drivers say they use that route sometimes, but only when things are really backed up on the main highway. Traffic wasn't heavy or backed up that night.

"Believe me when I say we have questioned Ben and the driver intensively. They both stick to their stories. Are one or both involved? That's something still unresolved.

"The NSA in Washington has assured us Stephie could not compromise any American secrets even though she handled highly classified material. Whether they are leveling with us completely, we don't know. She was not at present in any highly sensitive position, they say.

"No one has claimed responsibility for the kidnapping. No ransom has been demanded. It doesn't seem to be the work of terrorists. The husband's magazine, as well as the Chilean and U.S. governments, are investigating very diligently.

"One very strange twist to all of this: in April of 1997, Stephie's uncle, Lee Ably, was gunned down with two other people in the lounge of a London hotel. He had been a lecturer on this same cruise ship, the *Global Quest*, on a voyage from Singapore to Bombay with a land portion to the Taj Mahal. The other two people killed had been passengers on the same vessel.

"The British police said they solved that case. An assassin was apprehended and killed in a raid, but in the media and even in the government itself, there seem to be deep suspicions about whether he was the right man.

"Now, Greg, would you tell us about Ben and Stephie's background?"

Greg was a tall handsome man with sparse straw-colored hair.

He began, "Stephie and Ben are a couple in their mid-thirties. Both have good positions. Since they had no children, they had more disposable income, more time to spend at gyms, restaurants, movies, and on long vacations. Each had their own personal life, going to separate gyms, bonding with different friends, etcetera. They did not cling to one another. Often she would lunch with or have a night out with her girlfriends. Supposedly, he would be dealing with colleagues or sources some evenings as part of his *Newsweek* job. Quite a hit with the ladies is Ben.

"He frequently had to travel for story assignments, and her work sometimes called on her to travel. But they always planned to go on at least one major trip together each year. She had once traveled alone with her uncle, Lee Ably, on a Singapore to India trip, on the *Global Quest*. Not his fatal one though.

"Since they traveled so much, they gave up the idea of having children or pets. They didn't want to be tied down. They always talked about major trips to Argentina, South Africa, and Australia. Both liked cities, the theater, urban life.

"They were *with it*, busy young people with a circle of mutual friends, as well as independent friends. They were not shallow vacuous people, but at the same time, both were self-centered. There seemed to be something missing in their joint lives, not necessarily in their separate lives.

"I've known Stephie and Ben for a number of years. Ben began working for the Tribune Syndicate in 1986 at the age of twenty-three. A few years later, he started working for *Newsweek*. From the start, he did incisive reporting and was often doing investigative stuff.

"Occasionally, his assignments would be in South America. He had been in Venezuela, Columbia, Brazil, and Ecuador, but he told me he had never been in Argentina or Chile before this trip. Neither had Stephie.

"Ben had probed and investigated a rogue operation in the Pentagon and the White House that began sometime in 1988 in the Reagan and Bush administrations. He started investigating in 1994 and wrote some important articles about it in 1995. He was seriously considered for a Pulitzer Prize, had worked on a book called *Rogue Elephants Loose in the White House*, but he didn't complete it. He has done some reporting on various CIA operations. He has pissed off some important people over the years."

The telephone on the table behind Garand rang. He rose, answered it, talked for a few moments and said to the group, "Pardon me. I have to meet with one of the Chilean police authorities. I'll be back, and we'll continue at two o'clock."

3

The South American trip began for Stephanie Ably Ranier and her husband Ben with a United Airlines flight at midnight Friday, January 16, from Miami. After eight hours they were in Buenos Aires on Saturday morning, standing in a slow-moving line at an immigration counter; it took a half-hour before they were processed.

After they picked up their baggage, they were met by an attractive dark-haired young woman who had a sign with the name of her travel bureau and Mr. and Mrs. Ranier written on it.

"My name is Maria, and I represent the Campos Travel Bureau. Welcome to Buenos Aires, my city, my hometown. We are going to be your transfer agency for the trip to the hotel, your liaison during your stay, and at the end of the stay, your transfer to your luxurious ship, the *Global Quest.* Tomorrow, we shall be picking you up at 1:30 for your afternoon tour of our beautiful city. Please follow me."

Both Stephie and Ben spoke fairly fluent Spanish, but with Maria it was best to stick to English since she spoke it so well. She escorted them to a waiting van and driver. On the way in from the airport, she busied herself juggling her cell phone, pen, and clipboard of voluminous papers.

She explained some of the areas they were driving through. They saw some small cattle farms.

Maria said, "These are tiny farms, not like the enormous estancias out in the pampas. Cows are raised for dairy, and steers for beef and leather. Throughout Buenos Aires there are stores selling everything made of leather including jackets and handbags. I can give you the names of the ones with the best bargains."

As they closed in on the central city, Stephie commented to Ben, "I'm impressed. It looks nice. No slums or run-down areas so far. And no tall buildings dominating the sky. I like the scale of the city. The buildings don't seem drab. A little style. A European flavor. It seems more upscale than I had imagined."

It was a warm sunny Saturday. Traffic was fairly light. They passed a high obelisk in the median between two very wide streets.

"This is the Ninth of July Avenue," said Maria, "one of the world's widest avenues. That obelisk is one of the signature sights of the city, and you will often pass it as you head to various destinations. We, the people of Buenos Aires, call ourselves Porteños. A well known saying here is 'An Argentine is an Italian who speaks Spanish, wishes he were English, and behaves as if he were French.'

"This is a very late city. The dance clubs don't really get going and swinging until one or two o'clock or later. In some places, if you show up at midnight, you may be watching the bartenders setting up. Young people here have late dinners, go to the movies, take strolls, go to the cafés, then hit the clubs. Everything should be well underway by three or so."

Stephie asked, "Will we have to wait until ten to eat dinner? I'm kind of an early riser. I like to take long morning walks."

"Don't worry about restaurants being too late for you. Most of the good restaurants are used to tourists and start serving earlier for them. I can arrange tickets for some good tango dinner shows for you. While you're in Buenos Aires, you must see a couple of tango shows, eat our great steaks, and you'll probably want to see Evita's grave.

"I bet you are thrilled about your two-week cruise—all around the tip of South America, ending up in Chile. I wish I was going too. You live in Washington?"

Stephie answered, "Yes, in Georgetown, a nice section of Washington. Like a village within a city."

Maria responded, "Wonderful. Don't forget, if you'd like, I can be your guide to the best tango clubs."

Stephie said, "Thank you, but my husband has a friend

from his magazine who's stationed here in Buenos Aires. He's going to show us around."

Ben said, "Steph, I'll call Greg as soon as I have a chance."

The van pulled up in front of their hotel.

Maria commented, "You'll like this hotel. A great location right down the block from Calle Florida, the main pedestrian shopping street. *Global Quest* uses this hotel for its pre-and post-cruise bookings, so you're sure to meet some of your fellow passengers here."

Ben had chosen, indeed insisted upon, the Claridge Hotel in downtown Buenos Aires, and it was an impressive looking fifteen-story white building with high columns and a pediment at its entrance.

After a fast registration, the bellboy took them up to their room. The room was standard but pleasant with a large bathroom. It had a television set, but the furniture and accessories were not modern. The twin beds had heavy oak headboards. Whenever they reserved a hotel room, Stephie and Ben always made sure the room had twin beds.

The one large window had wooden slat blinds that were raised or lowered by pulling on a fabric belt beside the window. Stephie tried raising the blinds, but it took quite a bit of physical strength to raise and lower the shutters.

She said, "It's going to take a gaucho to raise and lower these beauties."

After they had unpacked and freshened up, Stephie said, "It's one o'clock. I'm not tired yet. I got some sleep on the plane. How 'bout some preliminary reconnaissance of the area. We have the whole afternoon before us."

Ben answered, "Okay, but not too long. I'm kinda beat. I want to get in an early nap. I'll grab my camera."

On the elevator, Stephie pointed to a sign that read, "Health Spa and Pool, Second Floor."

She said, "Let's take a look."

On the second floor was a health club overlooking an outdoor pool. People were lying in chaises sunning themselves. One beautiful full-breasted young woman, wearing a skimpy bikini, was stretched out on a lounge chair. She had a deep tan and looked sleek and fit.

She looked casually at Ben and Stephie. Ben, behind Stephie, nodded almost imperceptibly to her and smiled. Had Stephie caught the look, she might have detected her husband's pride-of-ownership look.

Stephie turned, the look vanished, and she said, "I'd like to spend some time relaxing out there while we're here."

When they reached the lobby, the couple looked in the restaurant and lounge area off to the side. The clubby-looking lounge was definitely an inviting area for their pre-dinner cocktails. Buffet breakfasts were part of their hotel package deal. The barman told them their buffet breakfasts would be provided in the large restaurant behind the lounge.

Stephie said to Ben, "You were right to choose this hotel. It has a real charm and ambience. The staff seems friendly. It doesn't feel like one of those characterless chains."

"Hey, babe, do I ever lead you astray?"

Stephie did not react, but she would have loved to make a telling crack.

They walked out of the hotel, took a right onto Calle Tucuman and in less than half a block were at the corner of Calle Florida, the central downtown pedestrian street.

They saw a Citibank branch with two ATM's. Each went to a machine and used an ATM card to draw out Argentine pesos. Argentina kept the dollar and peso on a par so one dollar equaled one peso. Ben drew out two-hundred pesos from his account, and Stephie drew the same from her account. This was typical of them, their independence in marriage; each managed his or her own money.

Across the street from the bank, a beautiful old ornate building in Beaux Arts style had been restored into the Galerie Pacifico shopping center. The old architecture had been kept, and the interior was replete with romantic rococo touches: murals, domes, and a central atrium. Marble balustraded balconies and terraces surrounded the atrium area.

They strolled around the balconies, browsing in the upscale shops and boutiques. In wide halls kiosks and carts augmented the fashionable shops. Perhaps the extravagant excesses of the building invited extravagant spending in the stores.

Stephie said, "God, what a great location for a Bloomingdales."

All sorts of independent food places were located in the basement food court of the atrium. One could get coffees, pastries, or complete dinners and lunches. They weren't branches of American chains, but classier local businesses.

As they wandered around the food court, Stephie couldn't resist. "God, look at these terrific desserts. Let's stop at this place and get a coffee and some pastry."

They sat with their cups of rich strong café con leche, she with her creampuff covered in chocolate sauce, he with his apple strudel.

Stephie commented, "Look at these people. Fashionably dressed. Men in suits and ties. Women dressed to the nines. Every other person seems to have a cell phone."

Long-time students of married couples viewing Stephie and Ben quietly eating their desserts would detect in their body language and behavior some insights into their relationship. It had indications of being an old shoe relationship, also a certain coolness and detachment.

They were certainly not lovers stealing furtive romantic moments from spouses. They hardly looked at each other. He avoided eye contact as much as possible. There was a distance between them not so much physically but evocatively, a spiritual and emotional distance. An unkind observer might label the distance a chasm.

One might wonder about their lovemaking. If it existed, would it be cool and mechanical? It would be hard to imagine a spirited thrusting stallion and an active willing mare, a mad, devil-may-care kind of wild lovemaking.

A well-dressed couple in their fifties a few tables away were far different. One of her feet had been freed from its high-heeled shoe. She moved her chair in a position so she could gently caress his calf with her toes. Their eyes were fastened on one another; their talk was spirited and lively; their laughter rang out, a vivid contrast to the cool politeness between Stephie and Ben.

The detachment seemed to be more on Ben's part than Stephanie's. She was too much the avid tourist and observer to notice much about her husband's behavior.

Out again on Calle Florida they saw a shabby Harrod's, apparently a branch of the London store, but looking like a run-down Walmart. They wandered down Florida, which dead-ended at a park across the street.

It was Saturday; traffic downtown was light. Ben and Stephie crossed over to a park, San Martin Plaza. At one end of the park, a slope ran down to a lower street level with the harbor a few blocks away. They walked down the hill to the bottom where two soldiers in camouflage garb guarded a wall memorial dedicated to the Argentinean servicemen who had died in the Malvinas War.

Stephie said, "Here they call the Falklands the Malvinas. For them it was a war to reclaim lost territory; for the British and for Maggie Thatcher, the iron mistress, it was a war for British soil. Her prestige was at stake."

Ben said. "We'll be in the Falklands on the cruise in a few days."

Across the street from the memorial in another square was a high ornate tower that looked like a combination bell tower and lighthouse.

Stephie read from her guidebook: "This says it used to be called the British Tower, a gift from the British people a long time ago. It has been stripped of its name because of the 1982 Falklands War. It's now called the Monumental Tower."

They walked back to Calle Florida. Traversing Florida, they wandered into mini-malls and saw a number of con-fiterías and galleries.

As they passed one street corner, a dwarfish man peered around a building at them, then hurried to a doorway. He was intensely interested in Stephie. He raised a camera with a telescopic lens to his eye and snapped a couple of shots of her. When Ben happened by chance to glance back in the man's direction, he quickly ducked back into a doorway.

Their first encounter with tango in Buenos Aires came on that first morning. Some of the music stores were piping tango music out to the street, recordings with vocals by well-known male and female tango artists.

Stephie had been determined to experience tango as part of their trip to Argentina. She and Ben had tried dancing it several times, had succeeded somewhat, but the fancy foot-work had deterred them. Neither was an adept dancer; they weren't as technically proficient or dexterous as the tango demanded.

Finally, after a couple of hours of walking, sightseeing, and browsing, Ben said, "I'm beat, Steph, let's head back."

4

Back in their room in the Claridge, Stephie said, "I'm really tired now. I'm going to take a nap."

Ben said, "I'm going out for a little while. I forgot some shaving stuff. I also want to get an English language newspaper. I'll be back in a jiff unless I see something worth photographing."

"Okay, take your time. I want to rest. We'll get up whenever. There's no rush. We can always find a good restaurant open when we decide to eat. After our cocktails, of course."

Stephie stretched out on her bed. Ben turned out the light and left Stephie in the darkened room with only a few thin chinks of sunlight seeping in through the wooden slats.

He went down to the front reception desk and asked, "Which room is Ann Glidden in?"

The clerk smiled, remembering him checking in a few hours before with his wife. "She's in 806."

Ben got back in the elevator, went up to the eighth floor and knocked on the door of 806. The door opened a crack. Ann was wearing only a man's extra large jersey that had a big emblem for the Baltimore Orioles.

They hugged, tightly embraced. Ben covered Ann's face with kisses. They kissed for a long time, pressing, mouths open, tongues probing and flitting against each other, sexually charged hungry kisses. His thigh was between her legs urgently pressing against her sex.

He slipped the shirt over her head. Her breasts were large, beautifully formed and poised, erotically white against her deep tan. He leaned his head down and kissed them, lapping nipples that became erect, and fondled her sex between her thighs. Quickly he threw off his clothes.

They were soon on the bed in a tight embrace, her hand around his erect penis. His hand explored her opening, lightly caressing in a circular motion. Above her, he entered her slowly. At the beginning, their motions were gentle, unhurried, and the rhythm was graceful.

These were two people who had made love many times, who were capable of urgent, frantic love, furtive love; more insistent and satisfying because it was a covert love. They knew each other's needs and desires, responded to subtle signals and gestures. They touched each other tenderly, exploring anew each other's sensual zones. His lips went from nipple to nipple and then to her open mouth. Hungry kisses. Their motion gradually intensified and quickened. He was penetrating her fully and deeply.

She used the same scent as Stephie. To him it seemed as if he were making love to both of them simultaneously. The coming for him was an enormous burst of light, a flooding of blood to the head, a quivering, then a spent collapse. Ann moved her body persuasively and skillfully against his, and soon she was thrilled with multiple organisms.

Ben had been gone from his room for about an hour. He kissed Ann and walked to the bathroom, then used a wash-cloth to wipe his body off carefully.

When he came out of the bathroom, he donned his Calvin's. Ann thought, *What a hunk he is. My hunk, uh, and still hers too. A marriage license is more overwhelming than a hotel room key anytime. Marriage can trump adultery any day of the week, but adultery's more fun.*

Ben, all business now, said, "We've got to talk about some logistics. Timing things. Getting our acts together. How was your flight? Were all the tickets and the hotel, everything the way I arranged?"

"The flight was all right. I got here yesterday morning. This whole thing must be costing you a bundle."

"Stephie always pays for her share of travel expenses out of her uncle's inheritance. We've always had separate accounts. She never gets into my accounts."

Ann said, "I brought along plenty of novels. And I've met an older American couple, the Lewises, here in the hotel.

We're going to dinner tonight. They're going to be on our cruise. I found a great restaurant on the corner, a few doors down.

"The Lewises and I have a date to go to a tango theater Tuesday night. Maybe other nights too. I'll have plenty of company. I've already set up some sightseeing tours. I'll make sure I'm not in your way on any of your tours. I'm going to see if I can meet some of the ship's passengers in advance.

"Ben, hon, this whole thing is so insane. How many women could you ever talk into doing something so completely bizarre and off the wall? We'll be having sex in the same hotel as your wife and on the same ship on a two-week cruise."

"Ann, honey, after the cruise, this will all be over, and we'll be together for keeps. I absolutely promise."

"Well, a three-week vacation isn't exactly torture. I've always been able to be comfortable by myself, and I always find plenty to do. These Argentinean guys are handsome. I get ogled by the cute barmen and all the bellhops. I took your advice; on the street, I dress very conservatively.

"Most of the guys are so busy with their cell phones they don't have time to bother me. And the steaks here are delicious. So far it seems like a great city. I've heard there's a very good Italian restaurant I'm going to try with the Lewises. We'll have to coordinate our restaurant going so we don't meet."

"Stephie has no idea what you look like. She doesn't even know you exist."

"Oh, wow, Buster, how lucky for me!"

"I didn't mean it like that."

As he walked down to his own floor, he realized how exhausted he was. He'd hoped to get in a few more hours of sleep, but it would be a long night ahead with a rested Stephie to escort.

5

Ben stole quietly into the darkened room where Stephie was still asleep. She looked like a child, curled up and vulnerable lying there in the dim light. He had a sudden unexpected twinge of guilt, but it quickly passed. He had long ago learned to compartmentalize his feelings, rationalize his infidelities.

He crawled onto the adjoining bed, exhausted, grateful to be able to rest for a while after the long flight, the initial burst of sightseeing, and his satisfying bout of lovemaking. A little after eight, Stephie got up. Ben was relieved when she went in to use the bathroom first, giving him an additional half hour of sleep.

After they had both showered and dressed, they went downstairs to the lounge for pre-dinner cocktails. Drinks before dinner were a daily ritual for the Raniers. Usually they each had two martinis.

The Claridge lounge was a high-ceilinged space adjacent to the lobby, an inviting place with comfortable leather arm chairs, some love seats, and a sprinkling of high-backed Windsor chairs.

Stephie said, "An ersatz hunting lodge adrift in an elegant restaurant and awash in a British private club."

Near the door was a grand piano that might occasionally be commandeered by hotel guests or a resident pianist. A rack by the door held a supply of daily newspapers. A sign announced that tea was available in the afternoon at four.

Stephie said, "That's a British touch. This is a very male, clubby bastion. I think we're going to find a lot here in Argentina favoring men. The heavy-fisted male touch."

The two welcoming bartenders introduced themselves as Joey and Renaldo. They looked to be barely out of their teens. They didn't seem to take their jobs too seriously; it was a game they were playing and enjoying. Why would people with hairs growing out of their noses and ears, insane foreigners, pay to drink some of those horrible-tasting cocktails like Manhattans?

They were handsome, with short cropped black hair. They liked to joke around and banter. To them, the computer for making out the bills was a toy they loved to operate, making quick jabs at the keys, quickly reacting to and anticipating its every prompt as if it were a game rather than a business tool.

Stephie's cocktail drink preference was a gin martini up with an olive; Ben's was a vodka martini on the rocks with a twist. Both were to be made extra dry.

When Ben asked for two very dry martinis, this got big smiles. Joey juggled glasses, threw gin and vodka into shakers like a mad chemist and giggled as he passed a vermouth bottle over the shakers allowing a drop or two to filter in.

Both martinis were substantial. Renaldo arranged small plates of snacks in front of them containing homemade potato chips, diminutive sandwiches, very crisp little pretzel-like poppy and sesame biscuits, and a plate of huge luscious cashew nuts, big brown ones. They could almost make a meal on the bar snacks.

After the two bartenders were sure their two customers were completely satisfied, they huddled around the computer where their fingers darted over the keys, making entries as they laughed and whispered.

Stephie sipped her drink and purred, "They make great martinis."

At cocktail hour, they nursed their drinks, savored them, and liked to snack while they drank. They drank to relax, to get a minor buzz on, but not to get drunk.

Stephie carried the conversation. She now felt rested and ready to go. Ben seemed tired, detached, and quiet. Probably the long flight had gotten to him. If only they could coordinate their moods, she thought. Maybe if he had started his nap when she did, he'd be raring to go now.

Stephie had done her homework on the city. They had decided they would try some of the famous steak restaurants in the city.

"Tonight let's start with La Chacra," Stephie suggested.

Ben agreed; he was famished for good reason. It was not easy being a stud to a woman years younger than himself, but it was deeply satisfying.

After they had taken their time enjoying two martinis and become slightly toasted, they went outside and caught a cab that took them to La Chacra, with a stuffed steer guarding the entrance. Inside by the front door was an open grill where men tended big steaks over the flames. All of the wait staff were male in starched white coats. Stephie and Ben studied the menu and ordered a bottle of the local rosé.

First they were served small meat pies and hearty crispy bread. They ordered de loma steak because they had been told this would appeal to them. The waiter suggested they order one steak between them. They asked for medium-rare. They would split an order of French fries.

The restaurant looked like another male bastion with Teutonic trappings. A group of twelve middle-aged men and women in the middle of the restaurant spoke and shouted German, sang German anthems, and stood and toasted each other. Amid the heavy Germanic decor of the restaurant, this large group, full of hearty laughter, stoked with hearty food, was apparently celebrating some event.

Ben couldn't help but think that perhaps this group might slip and issue a Nazi "heil." Maybe unreconstructed Third Reichers, he mused. But reason told him most of Argentina's large German population weren't of that persuasion. At least they were having fun.

The steak came out, two enormous pieces that looked to be more than a pound.

Ben tasted and said, "This steak is sensational. Very tender and tasty. It's really rare, but it's delicious. The quality of the meat is better than I've had in years."

Stephie agreed. Ben seemed to have an enormous appetite,

really chowing down, voracious, feeding his engine. Stephie, too, had a good appetite, but she marveled at her husband's.

That night they ordered the same dessert they would order at other restaurants, a Macedonian, scoops of vanilla ice cream topped with fresh cut fruit. It became a tradition of their trip.

As they were getting ready to leave, the boisterous German contingent marched around the restaurant, having a wild time, saluting everyone as they passed. One older man with a monocle bowed in courtly fashion as he passed Stephie, and a busty woman patted Ben on the shoulder. In an unexpected British accent she said to Stephie, "He's a movie star, my dear."

From their friend Greg Pearce they had the name of a trendy place to go for people-watching and drinks, which he said was close to their hotel. Outside La Chacra, they hailed a cab and gave the cabbie the name of the place, Café Memorabilia. He drove around a series of blocks and landed them in front of the door.

Memorabilia had a circular bar in the room right off the street, and a big area in the back with a restaurant and a large dance floor for shows. As they entered the second room, they were greeted by a tarot reader who had a small table to herself.

The place was crowded with young people, mainly men who seemed to be wearing stylish and expensive casual clothes. Ben and Stephie decided to sit at a table near the front bar.

The decor of Memorabilia was an eclectic bag of modern decorative styles; it was a blending of bright colors, industrial light fixtures, glossy tiles, designs that looked *in*, modern, cutting edge, and trendy. Male mannequins in plexiglass cases advertised boutique clothing.

They ordered beers and people-watched. The place wasn't particularly welcoming or friendly, but rather off-putting, and too cliquish for tourists. The help and clientele ignored them.

After a time, referring to her guidebook, Stephie said,

"What do you say we try a sidewalk café on Sante Fe, just to get a feel for different parts of the city? It's Saturday night after all."

"I'm game."

Neither one was desperately tired, though Ben was far more in need of sleep. He knew Stephie was not a late-night type so he'd give her a little more leeway before they decided to head back to the hotel.

They took a cab to Sante Fe Avenue, a thoroughfare busy with people strolling, bright lights, and teeming sidewalk cafés.

They chose a thriving sidewalk café, the Cinema, at a strategic corner of Sante Fe and Callao. It was a major gathering place for young people. Since all the outside tables were full, they sat inside in a two-story atrium loaded with black-and-white poster-size shots of old movie stars, including Charlie Chaplin and Rudolph Valentino. They ordered beers, and the waiter brought them seven hors d'ouvre dishes with French fries, peanuts, ham, crackers, cheese, and other snacks.

After their huge steak dinner, they could only stare at the bountiful offering. Stephie reminded Ben of a favorite watering hole of theirs in Georgetown where they had their martinis. The bartender would bring them snacks, which he called "kibbles and bits."

Later, they took a walk by El Olmo Café on Sante Fe, which was jammed with young people. The Saturday night revels were just beginning for these youngsters. As they walked along the avenue, a dark blue van passed them, cruising slowly. The driver and passenger checked out the couple.

A few more blocks of walking, and Ben surrendered to his fatigue. "Steph, we've got a whole week ahead of us. Let's take a cab back and hit the sack."

As the cab let them off in front of the Claridge, the dark blue van passed them again.

By 1:30, they were back in bed. Stephie thought at dinner

and in the cafés that Ben seemed withdrawn, hooded. He looked exhausted. Long ago she had given up trying to figure out what was on his mind. As far as she was concerned, he liked being secretive. She thought they should switch occupations; he should work for the NSA enmeshed in its clandestine spying, and she should work for a magazine whose job it was to reveal secrets to an expectant public.

Ben's thoughts were for Ann who was nestled in bed sleeping soundly on a floor above him.

6

At nine on Sunday morning, Stephie and Ben went down to breakfast in the large Claridge dining room adjacent to the lounge. A buffet table had been set up, laden with all sorts of pastries, fruits, juices, cereals, cold meats, cheeses, and several chafing dishes of hot food. The couple piled their plates with various samplings. Both liked the crispy little lunettes, baby-sized glazed croissants, an Argentine specialty.

A tradition had been established over the years for most of their mornings on vacation. Stephie would take one of her long vigorous walks, and Ben would either go to a gym or take a more leisurely walk. When he walked, he usually stopped frequently for photographs. At times, his focusing and use of light meters exasperated Stephie. On her own, she would sightsee, windowshop, and explore, but she would usually walk long enough to get in her daily exercise quota. From what she had read of Buenos Aires, she did not feel insecure or wary of morning walks.

Stephie said, "I'm going to take my walk. I'll be back by twelve-thirty or so. We have the tour at two."

Ben answered, "I've checked; the gym is open. I'm going there and work out. I'll see you when you get back. I may even go out part of the time and walk around as well. While you're gone, I'm going to give Greg a call. He said he'd meet us for cocktails tonight and join us for dinner and bar hopping. Okay with you?"

"Fine. He's sure to know his way around the city."

Ben watched her as she strode out of the dining room. She was wearing her Rockport trainers, jeans, a cap, and a dark green nylon windbreaker. He had no intention of going to the gym. He already had a semi-erection in anticipation of his meeting with Ann.

26

Stephie stepped outside of the hotel. When she reached the corner, instead of taking a right on Calle Florida, the broad pedestrian street, as she and Ben had done the day before, she headed down to the left. Even at this early hour the street was busy with strolling people. She passed a few record shops playing tango music, a policeman with a non-threatening Labrador on a lead, and several people talking on cell phones. One man had Walkman headphones, a cell phone to his ear, and a beeper on his belt.

Many tourists and locals were wandering up and down the street. Few of the locals paid any attention to her as she blended in with the other tourists. She was a busy purposeful individual who occasionally wrote a brief comment in her notebook about things she had seen. Her baseball cap shielded her upper face, and her sunglasses masked her eyes.

Had she been more attentive, she might had seen watchers at a distance. The dwarfish man and others were taking turns shadowing her. She was unaware of anyone watching; she was preoccupied with everything new to her.

She noticed at practically every corner the newspaper and magazine kiosks, which carried a large selection of books, maps, and postcards. The newspapers had big headlines about President Clinton giving a deposition in the Paula Jones sexual harassment case. Photographs showed her big nose and made her look unattractive.

Stephie thought, *This is just beginning. Soon the shit is going to hit the fan. This is a story that has legs; it isn't going to go away. A hanky-panky scandal. Clinton, like Ben, seems incapable of not fooling around. Too bad a President has to get involved in a civil case during his term in office. That was a stupid decision by the Supreme Court, a bad precedent.*

She and Ben were Clinton backers, and she admired Hillary, whom she had met a few times at big functions. She had an affinity for what Hillary had to go through, because she, too, had caught Ben rummaging in the cookie jar, various cookie jars, over the years.

For the past few months, he seemed to have turned over a new leaf, but the distance between them had been widening. Each time an infidelity happened, it left scar tissue that never really healed; her love for him diminished, and she had become more hardened toward him.

Eventually, she thought, the marriage would self-destruct from lack of real caring. She knew a break-up was coming, but she hated change. She resisted any alterations in her pattern of life. Was she taking the easy way? Was it laziness, fear of an unknown future without a putative man, an inability to cope with uncertainty? Their troubled relationship over the years had had too many lows to survive much longer.

Right now, she was fascinated by the scene around her. It was an inviting warm morning, pleasant for walking. She passed beautiful old ornate buildings with elaborate stonework, statuary, rococo detail, and decorative elements reminiscent of late nineteenth, early twentieth-century buildings in Europe.

Everywhere were interesting architectural details, little fanciful decorative touches that delighted the eye. Not the modern day flatness and boring look of endless dull planes. The highly ornamented old buildings had a charm lacking in most American cities. No tall monster structures jutted up to destroy the sense of scale. What she judged to be political graffiti and sloganeering on walls were quite common.

She noticed the Chelo Café with its special promotion for breakfast with café con leche, three media lunas, those half-moon pastries, and a glass of juice for two-and-a-half pesos.

When she got to Corrientes, the movie industry street, she continued on to the corner of Avenida de 9 de Julio to look at the obelisk, the symbol of the city. The central, enormously wide avenue had smaller side avenues with medians in between. The huge lanes of the avenue were almost devoid of traffic on Sunday morning.

As she walked around, she saw many ads for hair removal and lots of businesses providing depilation services. *Why is hair removal such a big deal here? Are they very hairy people or what? There seems to be a huge industry for getting rid of unwanted hair. Maybe the popular media and advertising have made silken smooth unhairy skin the ideal. Ben carefully shaved his chest and legs—a trait he had picked up from the younger guys at the gym. Well, as long as he didn't go in for tattoos.*

She made a joking comment in her little notebook: "Hair removal fetish. Are we dealing with a hirsute race here?"

Back walking along Florida, Stephie came to Avenida de Mayo. She headed down the fourteen blocks to where the Congress met. She was still unaware she was being stalked; her shadows remained at a guarded distance.

7

After breakfast Ben stopped in their room to brush his teeth and use the Listerine. He took the elevator to Ann's floor. He knocked, and she opened the door. She was wearing jeans and a sweatshirt, no footwear. He hurried in to avoid being seen by a maid and held Ann in his arms.

Ann said, "I went down to breakfast about seven so I wouldn't run into you and Stephie. Met some more people. Last night was fine. So far, time has whipped by."

"She's out for a long walk, and I'm supposed to be at the gym. She won't be back until after twelve."

"Great, honey. Ummm."

They embraced. Clothes came off. They were naked on the bed, groping, caressing, kissing, probing. His hands were busy in preparatory moves. He kissed her breasts, ran his tongue over first one nipple, then the other, until they were tensed. His hand was urgent at her vagina. She lovingly ran her hands along the clefts formed by his buttocks. He entered her, slowly, inched forward, rotated, swayed side to side, then slowly, masterfully, penetrated her.

Their bodies were meshed tightly together, and her hips gyrated slowly, meaningfully, moving in rhythm to his gentle thrusts. Undulating, she was stimulated and delighted by his skillful and satisfying penetrations. She thought gratefully, *This man knows how to do it, how to take care of my needs and desires. He knows instinctively what a woman craves.*

Once in a Washington Best Western, she had asked him about Stephie's sexual proclivities and had gotten the reply, "She's really not into much. Whenever I suggest something different in our sex life, she says, 'Let's not start getting kinky.'"

They had a long lovemaking session together. The first

30

bout was insistent, necessary, urgent. The second was more gentle, more patient, more loving.

They took a long erotic shower together. He had time to lie down and close his eyes briefly before he left Ann's room.

If an Olympian director that morning, supplied with two invisible camera crews, had shot a montage of the wife and of the husband and his paramour, he would have captured a series of shots: Stephie walking briskly along opposite the obelisk, Ben on top of Ann briskly and energetically grinding away, a curiosity-seeking and content Stephie strolling in a shopping gallery cul de sac off Calle Florida, Ann astride Ben, Stephie sitting in a sidewalk café having a café con leche, writing in her notebook while some distance away a dwarfish man was observing her, and Ben and Ann, sated, lying together, panting, eyes closed, restoring themselves.

Stephie came back at 12:45. Ben was lying on his bed. She told him of some of the places she had been.

She said, "The city is quiet today. It'll be a good day for the tour without all the traffic." She went in the bathroom and took a long shower.

They relaxed for a time before going down to the lobby to join their tour. Stephie looked at Ben lying on the other bed. She thought, *He still hasn't gotten over the long flight. He's losing his staying power. Maybe with age will come stability and fidelity. That would be a welcome change, but too late for me to care.*

8

That first Sunday afternoon, as Stephie and Ben waited outside their hotel for the tour bus to show up, they had a diversion. A couple in their seventies, spry and agile, hotel guests, were waiting with them. They were dressed like a couple much younger in years. She was trim, with bright blonde hair, probably a wig, wearing a red slack suit; he wore a dashing double-breasted blue blazer with a crest, paisley ascot, and two-tone wing tip shoes. He had a moustache, apparently waxed. They looked like a theatrical act wearing stage make-up.

In a small circle, they danced a fox trot to imaginary music, rather mechanical in their steps. Ben and Stephie couldn't help smiling at them, and they smiled back, in a world of their own making, probably in the center of some imaginary ballroom, showing off.

Stephie was thinking, *Here was a real couple joined by a love of dance. Loving and united. Enjoying each other's company. Truly interdependent. Wasn't this what marriage should be all about?*

When they took a break, they came over and introduced themselves. He said, "We're the dancing Rilleaus, Marge and Terry. We're passengers-to-be, not entertainers, on the *Global Quest.*"

The Raniers introduced themselves. Ben said laughingly, "We're going aboard the *Global Quest* too. When I watch you two pros, I keep thinking of Ginger and Fred."

Terry replied, "We've often been compared to them, but I rather think they suffer by comparison because of our virtuosity."

Stephie asked, "Are you looking forward to the cruise?"

Terry said, "You bet your life! Tickets in order. The ship's band is getting warmed up. Tea dances, cocktail dances, evening soirees, dances day and night."

32

They began their dancing again, slowly moving in a small circle. Only the arrival of the tour bus brought their dancing to an end.

Once on the bus, Stephie noticed the large number of hotels and bars with British names: Liverpool, Trafalgar, Pickwick, Shakespeare, Old Bailey, Covent Garden, and Big Ben. The Argentineans supposedly hated the British for the war, but they were still enthralled by things English from their past associations.

The tour guide was a woman named Sophia in her early twenties. She said, "On this Sunday trip, we will be making four stops: our central square, Plaza del Mayo, and then the districts of San Telmo, La Boca, and Recoleta. You're lucky it's a Sunday, because three fairs will be going on in our last three stops."

The bus made its first stop. Sophia said, "Here we are, Plaza Mayo, the central governmental square of the country where the executive offices of President Menem are located in the Casa Rosado. Here in Plaza del Mayo in addition to the Pink House, are the Casa de Gobierno, executive offices, museums, and our national cathedral."

Sophia led them across the plaza until they faced the Casa Rosado. Ben took pictures of the grenadier sentries in their colonial uniforms and shakos.

Stephie remarked, "The Pink House is really a kind of pale beige. Up there is the balcony where Juan Peron and Evita stood."

Ben countered, "Arms outstretched to her people, that's where she sang 'Don't Cry for Me Argentina.'"

"Wise ass!"

In the plaza opposite the Casa Rosado, Sophia pointed to the white-painted outlines of bodies on the sidewalk. The life-size outlines were of supine corpses, like the chalked outlines of victims of a homicide investigation.

Sophia said, "These ghost bodies are reminders. They are meant to be burning, searing symbols of the disappeared ones in what was called Argentina's 'Dirty War.' Many people were kidnapped in the middle of the night, taken away by the army and the secret police to God knows where. Questioned, tortured. Many of them, probably all of them, were brutally murdered. Their bodies hidden and done away with without even a prayer.

"Every Thursday, the widows, mothers, grandmothers, aunts, sisters and fiancées of these disappeared ones somberly march around out here on the plaza to remind the government questions haven't been answered, that the torturers, the murderers of thousands have not been brought to justice. They are saying, 'Don't you dare ever forget our loved ones.'"

Her voice broke and tears ran down her cheeks. Perhaps she had lost a loved one to the atrocity. The tour group stood looking at the grim reminders of those who had been abducted, tortured, murdered, and perhaps had their bodies dumped in the River Plate or in some desolate place without ceremony or funeral rites.

Ben and Stephie wandered over to the cathedral. The plain pastel facade was not like that of the big European cathedrals, was not heavily ornamented or imposing. Mounted on its front wall, a perpetual flame burned in a huge sconce shaped like Aladdin's lamp.

When they went in, they found the traditional nave with many side-chapels around the perimeter. One chapel-tomb was guarded by two grenadier sentinels of the same regiment that guarded the Pink House. In it was the tomb of the country's revered hero, San Martin.

Back on the bus, Sophia lectured to her flock, "As you get used to Buenos Aires, you will see how important the neighborhoods or districts are. Each one has its own distinct personality. San Telmo, our next stop, is the home of the tango with its tanggerinas.

"Later, we'll go to La Boca with the bright multi-colored metal buildings, then finally the more upscale Recoleta where there are the beautiful parks. A crafts fair will be in progress while we are there. The cemetery where Evita is interred is in Recoleta. Your hotels are located in the Monserrat or Micro Centro areas, the central downtown."

In San Telmo, the bus let them off on a wide boulevard, and Sophia led them down to a side-street which in two blocks would take them down to the Plaza Dorrego and its Sunday flea market.

Sophia explained, "San Telmo is full of tango, in night spots, in the streets. It also has antique shops, courtyard gardens, and beautiful churches."

They headed down a street that had been turned into a pedestrian thoroughfare. Their first encounter was with a mime, bathed entirely in white, with ivory skin, flowing robes, and hair made to resemble the Statue of Liberty. He stood in frozen positions for some minutes; many took his picture, including Ben.

An old faded tango queen in her late sixties who had seen better days, wearing a tango outfit with a red scarf tied at her waist, was dancing provocatively by herself to the tango melodies on her little tape player. She, with a bittersweet look, was living in her own world of the past expressed in the tango. As she danced to the tango strains, she occasionally inveigled a passerby to dance with her. Ben took her picture, and she pointedly indicated a little tip cigar box next to her tape player. Ben dropped a dollar in the box.

At the corner of San Telmo Square, a tall male tango dancer with a fedora had gathered a crowd around him. He was dancing to a live combo. He chose women from the crowd and danced the tango with them.

Sophia was beside them, "He is made up to look like the great Gardel, an international superstar, the greatest tango singer of all time, a national icon. Gardel made many recordings beginning in 1917. He was in movies, five for Paramount. Sadly, he died in a plane crash in 1935."

As Stephie stood there, the Gardel-lookalike searched the crowd and deliberately seemed to zero in on her. He grabbed her, pulled her into the center of the ring of spectators, and they danced the tango together. She did a serviceable tango.

The Rilleaus, born show-offs and participants, used the opportunity to get in the circle and do their own tango—to considerable applause.

Ben was proud of Stephie and took pictures of her and the Rilleaus. When the dance finished, her partner kissed Stephie's hand, and she thanked him. Off to the side, the dwarfish man and a man in a leather jacket stood staring at Stephie.

She and Ben walked to the center of the square, which had scores of stalls set up for an outdoor antique and curio flea market. People were tightly packed into the small square as they jostled their way through the rows of tiny stands. On the outskirts, people sat in sidewalk cafés eating and drinking.

Stephie and Ben wandered around the perimeter of the square. They were not interested in any of the items, which seemed to cover a wide range of categories. Some antique musical instruments were piled on one table. After an hour of sightseeing, they reboarded the bus and were on their way to the next stop.

At the street known as Camelita in La Boca, were more white living statues. Ben said, "Remember how many of them we encountered in Paris; they were everywhere. Skin, clothing, everything white. This has become a worldwide novelty with a lot of people earning a living as the frozen white people. That one's made up to resemble Gardel."

One of the living statues all in white—clothes, skin everything—was a Gardel giving a jaunty tip to his white fedora.

At the corner, in a small plaza in the midst of a street fair, a tango band had set up speakers and a microphone, and a few couples danced. Not missing any opportunity to perform, the Rilleaus did some polished tango turns. Further down the street, another white mime of Gardel stood transfixed.

Along the street were the brightly colored tenements, each wall or section of corrugated metal a different vivid color. La Boca had been one of the poorer working-class areas of the city. Sophia said the early Italian immigrants worked in paint factories, brought home leftovers, odds and ends, and painted their houses in various colors. Not enough of one color to paint a whole house so one wall would be one bright color, another wall of a different strong color, not pastels, but bright strong primary colors. It was a street that duplicated what a kindergartener might create.

One house had a front yellow wall, a startling red outside staircase, corrugated metal window overhangs of blue and purple, and a shiny black roof. Each window had curtains with different patterns. The houses were actually lived in; a woman leaned out of a window, languidly watching the tourists.

At the end of Carmelita was a busy area full of locals, a park square, with soccer games, modern music blaring, real life going on. At the other end of the street was an abandoned port area.

Ben said, "It's the Rio Plate, the silver river, the widest river in the world."

On board the bus, they headed for the last stop, Recoleta, the fashionable district with museums, upscale shops, and Evita's cemetery. Another open-air fair, a crafts show, was in full swing with stands spread along the sidewalks beside the large gentle sloping park. The arts and crafts displayed were of less interest to them, so they wandered onto the grass itself where hundreds of Porteños were enjoying the Sunday sun, lying on blankets or stretched out in beach chairs, some sipping maté.

Stephie and Ben had their fill of sightseeing and decided to head back to the hotel on their own in a taxi. The cab took off, and at a distance of about a block, it was followed by a beat-up van in which two of Stephie's shadows rode.

9

After their long tour, Stephie and Ben had taken naps and risen at eight that night. At nine they were in the lounge where they received hellos from the barmen, Joey and Renaldo. Their friend, Greg Pearce, rose from a Windsor chair near the front windows. He gave them both hugs as he greeted them. He was slightly over six feet tall and carried his two-hundred pounds well. He was a fairly fit thirty-eight year old with slightly receding blond hair.

He said, "God, it's good to see you guys. It's been more than two years."

They exchanged small talk. Joey brought them their drinks and five small plates with all of the cocktail goodies as before. Ben described the day's tour to Greg.

Greg commented, "While you're here, I would recommend the Rio Plata combination bus, train, and boat tour that takes you to the Parana River where you board a small boat and see a pretty part of the country. I suppose you'd also like to see Evita's tomb. Everybody does."

Stephie asked, "Is Evita still revered here?"

Greg answered, "Adored by some, hated by others. To foreigners, Buenos Aires is tango, steaks, and Evita. To most Argentineans, it's President Menem, psychoanalysis, and rage about the way everything gets fucked up here. You come here and want to see the past, but the locals are more interested in the present. It's like tourists everywhere, myopic, unable to see the here and now, stuck in the past of a place. Believe me, many Porteños are much more cosmopolitan and sophisticated than the average person living in Washington, D.C.

"You asked me for a restaurant find nearby so I have chosen a place that couldn't be any closer, the posada next door, just two doors away. Very economical and good food."

Greg was right about the steak restaurant next door. The Posada 1820 was very reasonable. Stephie had tenderloin steak smothered with a delicious thick gravy with mushrooms and a plate of French fries. They had two bottles of red wine, salad, and crisp bread.

After dinner, Stephie said, "Memorabilia advertised tango for tonight. Now that we've found out it's only a few blocks away, let's walk over there for dessert and tango."

When they got to the café, they found the place thronged with a young trendy crowd. Stephie noticed they were mostly young males, successful and fit looking young men. She picked up on the fact it was a gay hangout.

Greg, seeing some friends across the room, walked over and greeted two young men accompanied by a willowy attractive young woman. As was usual in Argentine social life, everyone had to do some near-miss kissing on the cheeks, first one cheek, then the other. Greg conversed with his friends in Spanish.

Stephie and Ben had often speculated as to whether Greg was gay. Ben had weighed in heavily that he thought he was; Stephie wasn't so sure. She had voted for bisexual.

Ben had said, "I'm not positive. He never tried anything with me." Knowing Ben's sexual appetites and preferences, she wasn't sure he wouldn't accede to anyone offering to service him, be it male or female.

The maitre d' gave them a table next to the dance floor in the room beyond the bar. Ben and Greg were soon talking about the Washington office of *Newsweek*. The night before in the Chacra, Stephie and Ben had enjoyed their Macedonian dessert, so she ordered it, and the two men followed suit. Plates were served with large scoops of vanilla ice cream smothered in fresh fruit pieces.

Stephie cooed, "Umm. This is delicious."

Ben was guzzling his drinks, Stephie noticed. Greg pointed to the tarot lady who was sitting at a table by herself, a big overweight woman wearing a bright multi-colored muumuu.

"Steph," Greg said, "why don't you get a reading from her? She's good."

"Hey, good idea. I'm a skeptic, but what the hell?"

She went over to the woman and asked for a reading. The tarot reader, serious and businesslike, spread her cards before her. After some concentration, she began with some innocuous predictions, then she became somber and said, "You must be very careful. You are being watched."

"Watched by whom?"

"People who do not wish you well. And a beautiful woman will come into your life and will be a threat to your happiness."

Stephie laughed and said, "So what else is new? Sorry, go on. Will I meet her?"

"The cards do say you will—just by chance. She will play a role in your fate. She is very beautiful, just as you are. The cards do say you do not want babies in your life."

"No, not now. Maybe later."

"Do not wait too long. It will help to heal the rift in your marriage. Be very careful. Look about you and be aware of everything and everyone around you. Everyone. You must learn to trust only yourself and your own instincts."

When the woman finished, Stephie returned to the table, disconcerted. The woman had stirred up something her boss had said to her before the trip.

Ben asked, "How'd it go?"

"She said to keep my eyes open."

She grinned at Greg. "And she said watch out for my husband's friends."

The lighting changed, and a tango melody filled the café over a spectacular sound system. A tango team came out. Both dancers were tall and slim, immaculately garbed in formal outfits. Their backs were ramrod straight. They danced one number in a very effective, very mannered, and poised style. It was explosive when they came to the brilliant foot movements, male feet darting between female feet in rapid precision.

It was attitude personified, with controlled pyrotechnics,

fiery bursts of energy and simulated passion. With their whole bodies and especially their feet, they were dramatizing sexual encounters and sensual ambiguities. Stephie thought they were like two giant insects performing a sex act, a sensual ritual.

She loved the stylized gestures. Passions were on fire within, but a controlled exterior was belied by the sudden outbreaks expressed in almost violent foot explosions, the rapid passing of legs. Passions erupted into brief bursts of stylistic, ritualistic violence. Foreplay soon became consummation.

The three of them were mesmerized by the dance. Ben was thinking of his couplings with Ann; Stephie was thinking of her matings with a younger, less problematic Ben, and Greg, having seen so many tango shows, was merely being entertained by the stylish footwork and posturing.

The dancers acknowledged the applause of the audience and hurried off through a door by the deejay booth.

The second set took place a half hour later. Ben had drunk three vodka and tonics. Stephie thought, *Along with his two martinis and his share of the dinner wine, he's well on his way to being sloshed.*

Greg looked at his watch and said, "It's twelve-forty. How would you guys like to see something really different? Are you into seeing an arty male and female strip show, done with showmanship and theatricality, Tango Especiale?"

Stephie wondered if Greg was ready to drop his beads, come out of the closet.

She said, "Sure. I'm game. I'd love something different."

Ben was slurring. He looked glassy-eyed. He croaked, "Bring it on."

They took a cab to a club called Especiale. Greg paid the admission fee. It was a showroom with a series of tables surrounding a runway that jutted out into the audience. They arrived at 1:15. Greg said they would have a long wait. Drinks were very expensive. A crowd was starting to form, ninety percent male.

They killed time talking about the past, their lives in

Washington. At 2:10, the club lights dimmed to almost total darkness. Music filled the room: loud dramatic portentous beginning-of-the-universe music that announced the birth of worlds and gods and goddesses.

The stage lights came up slowly. Fog jetted up from the edge of the stage. There stood four magnificent nude male bodies in different poses. They were titans, oiled, pumped, flexed, with enormous muscles everywhere: calves, thighs, abs, pecs, shoulders, biceps, like Arnold Schwarzenegger in his prime. Two of the godlike creatures had long hair, the other two short hair. As the music altered, they changed their poses.

After the opening number, there were a series of strips. Each dancer had a different costume: a construction worker, a gaucho, a sailor, a policeman, a fireman or some other macho costume gimmick. They stripped slowly, but some-what robotically. When they finally stripped all off, they had huge, engorged penises. The penises stayed erect. Stephie was astounded by the size of them.

Greg whispered, "They're wearing cock rings." Greg seemed fascinated by the show, while Ben's eyes were glazed over from his alcohol intake.

Two males and two females with magnificent bodies, clad only in leather bikini straps and boots, took the stage. Tango music erupted, then they began their dancing as couples, a male paired with a female, the men very muscular, the women with firm bodies and large jutting breasts. Ben con-tinued to gulp his drinks.

The music changed to a more sensuous tango rhythm. The couples danced along the runway in a tango that quick-ened and intensified. The tango music altered slightly; first one woman then the other removed her bikini bottom. Next one male and then the other removed his bikini briefs to reveal a thrusting penis.

They continued dancing erotically, nude but for their boots. In a sudden shift the two men were dancing with each other; the two women were dancing together. At the climax, the four were wrapped in an erotic ménage à quatre.

After another set, Ben's interest waned, but then he became more attentive when the two girls came out, stripped and simulated sex acts. In one comic interlude, a stripper kneeled and leaned over a ringside table and beat his huge member against the top of a girl's head. Ben was working on his third drink while Stephie and Greg still nursed their first.

Stephie became bored by the constant parade of male penises, huge or not. It was a clever show with theatrical values and an athletic and gymnastic flavor as well as the nudity, but she wasn't into it. It was hard for her to endure too much of it. The show ended with all the cast on stage in a grand finale.

While Greg was in the men's room before they left Stephie said, "I think I'd rather have gone to a straight disco rather than look at naked titans for an hour. Greg seems to have enjoyed it; maybe it's his way of letting us know his proclivities. Who knows?"

* * *

The three were outside the Claridge saying their goodnights as a taxi waited for Greg.

A well-lubricated Ben hugged his friend and said, "Thanks for everything. I'm beat."

"Get some sleep, Bro."

Stephie added, "I'm wiped out. Goodnight Greg."

Greg said, "How about I meet you in your hotel bar tonight at eight-thirty, and we go see a real tango show in the city's oldest coffee house?"

Ben and Stephie agreed.

Greg exhorted, "Get some sleep, you guys."

Minutes later, the couple were in their room, getting ready for bed. Ben, sitting on his bed, clad only in his briefs, reached out to Stephie as she passed. He guided her toward him. Reluctantly, she sat next to him.

She said, "It's very late, hon. I'm exhausted. Get some sleep. You need it."

Ben smoothed her hair, leaned over, kissed her, began fondling her breasts. She wasn't responding. He kept working on her. Her responses were tepid at best.

Ben coaxed, "C'mon, Steph, it takes two to tango."

Ben was becoming more persistent.

Stephie protested, "Ben, I'm so tired . . ."

Ben implored, "Please. Those dancers were so hot."

Stephie was passive, like a mannequin. Tears filled her eyes. She whispered, "I can't. I'm exhausted. I can't help myself. I . . ."

Ben was angry. "You can't! Well, goddamn it, I can. I'm ready, willing, and able."

Stephie, in barely a whisper, said, "I'm sorry."

Ben forced Stephie down onto the bed using all his strength, the strength and willfulness of a drunk.

Stephie flailed out. "No, no . . . Stop . . . Please, Ben."

Stephie was a strong woman. She didn't use some of the moves she had been taught, but would if she had to.

Ben was very forceful; he held Stephie's arms back. Finally he relented, held her still for moments, then let her up.

"You're my wife, goddamn it."

"And I stayed your wife after all those times you had your women on the side."

"Don't start. You have to play the bitch at the wrong times. Well, go screw yourself. No one else can."

He pulled on his pants, stuffed the room card in his pocket, rushed from the room and slammed the door. Stephie wept, her body heaving with sobs. With tears streaming down her face, she stared at the moonlight peeking through the window slats. She was desolate as she cried uncontrollably.

Ben, barefoot, ran up the stairs to Ann's floor. He pounded on her door. She came to the door clad only in her big tee shirt. She was half asleep.

"Ben, what the hell are you doing here?"

He pushed her inside. He kissed her roughly like a crazed person. He pulled the tee shirt over her head, threw off his clothes and pushed her onto the bed. He was crude, reckless. He forced her into position and had desperate forceful sex with her.

Minutes later, Ben was lying on the bed, spent. Ann, very angry, was sitting in a chair facing him. It was not love in her eyes, rather, hate and revulsion.

"Ben, that was rape—plain and simple—not making love. I was scared to death. If you ever do that again, ever again, I'm warning you, we're history. You're toast. And you're a dead man!"

"I'm sorry. Ann, really . . ."

He crept over and knelt in front of her. He pleaded, "It was Stephie. She wouldn't . . ."

"No, Stephie didn't rape me. You did. And if I hadn't been here in the hotel as a convenient lay, what would you have done then? I pity what might have happened to Stephie."

10

The blinds had been raised, and sunlight was streaming into the room. Stephie was staring at Ben lying in his briefs atop the duvet. He woke up, looked at her like a death row inmate awaiting his fate, feeling crestfallen, guilty.

"Steph, I'm sorry about last night. I was so drunk."

"Drunk is no excuse for what you tried to do to me. Believe me, it'll never happen again. Ever! Don't talk about it. Don't ever mention it again. We have a lot to do in the next couple of weeks, but don't ever try that again. Ever!"

"Stephie, I . . ."

"No more. Just shut up about it! I don't want to hear any more about it. Where did you go last night?"

"I stayed in the stairwell and cooled off. I'm so sorry . . ."

"We came here to see Buenos Aires and take a trip around the Horn, and that's what we're going to do."

At eleven, they realized they had missed breakfast in the hotel.

Stephie said, "I don't want to miss any more breakfasts. They're good, and they're included in the bill. Besides, I want to get early starts in the morning for walks. I'm going to pass on the late night entertainment. I realize Buenos Aires is a late town, but it's not for me. If you and Greg want to go bar hopping on your own, fine. Just watch your drinking."

"No, I want my early mornings for gym workouts just as you want to be able to enjoy your walks."

And my morning sex . . . if Ann will have me, Ben thought. In advance, he had explained to Ann that some mornings he might be late in case he and Stephie stayed out late. He knew Stephie well enough to know there wouldn't be any more late nights.

They went in a confiteria a few doors from the hotel and had café con leche. Each was brought a small glass of freshly

46

squeezed orange juice with their coffee. They ordered lunettes to go with the rich coffee.

After the small breakfast, Stephie announced she would take her walk. "Since it's so late, I'll be back around one or so. Then we'll plan our afternoon if it's okay with you."

She was all business, trying to make it seem as if nothing had happened.

Outside the confiteria Ben made a left turn and headed back to the hotel. He took the elevator to Ann's floor where he knocked several times on her door. No answer. *Oh, oh, she's pissed.*

Stephie began her walk. This time, instead of making a turn at Florida, she continued on Tucaman Street four blocks to the broad Ninth of July Avenue, crossed over, and found herself at the opera house, Teatro Colon. A fumigation truck was outside. A sign announced "No tours today."

She had seen pictures of the stunning interior. She went around the entire block that encompassed the building, then walked along Ninth of July for quite a distance.

She found the city easy for walking. Even though there were many wide avenues, she found good pedestrian walk-lights and was able to cross the busiest and widest streets easier than she could in almost any other city.

She felt more aware, more on guard than she had been on previous days. The past night's experience made her squir-rely, edgy. Once she thought she saw someone shadowing her. No, it must be her imagination. But she thought of the tarot card reader's warnings.

Before her NSA posting, she had taken a short course in surveillance procedures. The instructor had made her aware of techniques used by people following you. Wasn't that man in the next block the same one who had been behind her at Teatro Colon? She became more alert as the morning went on. She thought a dwarfish looking man had shown up more than once, but then had disappeared.

She was an attractive young woman, but she blended well into the scene. Other women on their way to work or shopping were smartly dressed. She was the tourist in casual wear. Men did not ogle her, and she did not inspire the Latino displays of machismo.

She could take care of herself, and her walks were almost always on busy streets. She looked around but was not aware of anybody tailing her then. *Such nonsense. What an imagination.*

A few blocks east, and Stephie was again back on Calle Florida. The downtown location of the hotel was ideal for her. She loved urban walks in New York, Georgetown, and London. Tango melodies emanated from music stores. Several tables of popular tango CDs and tapes were in front of each shop, and older Porteños and tango-fascinated tourists browsed through the selections.

Young people were selecting the latest international pop group, music worlds removed from tango. They were probably oblivious to tango, perhaps sick of it, having heard it all their lives. It represented the older generation, the past, the old fogies.

After the late night and Ben's assault, Stephie decided she needed another coffee fix. She entered a confiteria, sat down and ordered café con leche from a handsome young waiter. He brought, as a matter of course, a glass of orange juice, a tiny foil-wrapped ingot of chocolate, and some poppy and sesame cookies. As she sat at the table, her mind wandered, and she thought about her dead uncle, Lee Ably.

The whole thing had been so strange and heart-wrenching for her. Months before, an Indian or Pakistani, a man named Ramesh, had walked into the lounge of a hotel in London and had shot and killed her uncle and two others. The three victims were in London on a stopover before returning to the States from a cruise on the *Global Quest*.

The trip had included brief stops in India and visits to the Taj Mahal and New Delhi. Ironically, it was the same ship she and Ben were due to take on their cruise in a few days. She had also sailed with her uncle on the ship before his fateful cruise.

On the ship, Uncle Lee had been a lecturer and was returning from a series of cruises. The British police claimed they had shot the killer in a raid, but she had never been convinced. In her heart, she didn't believe they had caught and killed the right man. Police were always in an almighty hurry to "clear" cases, she thought. It seemed too convenient a solution, especially when the police ended up with a dead man who couldn't be questioned.

After the murders, there had been suggestions her Uncle Lee had been a CIA agent. This was utter nonsense to Stephie; she couldn't imagine her uncle as a secret operative. He was secretive and a very private person, but not the type to be engaged in spying.

He had written numerous books about India, even written novels about the country which she found perceptive and cleverly plotted. He had corresponded with her regularly, interesting witty letters that recounted his impressions of the passengers or eccentric characters he met on his journeys.

Stephie had flown to London to learn more about Lee's death from investigators. They could give her no further satisfaction about his death. It was still a subject that came up from time to time in the British tabloids as a sensational mystery. Infrequently she would get a call from some prying reporter trying to breathe new life into the story. The British tabloids tried repeatedly to discredit the police account of the identity of the killer. There seemed to be no way to unearth the motivation for the killing.

Stephie thought, *I feel I'm the same type as Lee. Self-sufficient. I love to travel, to see and hear, to experience, and record.*

At the hotel her randy husband had tried Ann's room several times, calling by phone and knocking at the door.

The last time a maid materialized and said, "Sir, madam went out earlier."

He hadn't wanted to be seen by the maids in case they also worked his floor.

Around twelve-thirty, Ben tried Ann's door again. She

opened the door, a sheet partially wound around her body. Her face was grim. She was still furious.

"You're awfully late, Buster."

"I'm really sorry about this morning."

"Sorry? That's it? You shit. I'm warning you. That is never going to happen again, is that clear? Never again! I mean it!"

"I was completely out of line."

"You were out of control. It was criminal."

"I'm sorry, hon."

"Your apology is not accepted. Not for what you did. And while I'm here, I'm not going to play Little Miss Patience and wait in this room for you to show up. I'm here to see the city too."

Stephie was walking along a street. She stopped and looked in a window, glanced back, and thought she saw the dwarfish man about a block behind her. Later, she looked in another window, glanced back, but there was no one behind her.

11

That afternoon, Ben and Stephie took a cab to Puerto Madero, a newly rehabbed and gentrified area where new condos and businesses had been built from old brick warehouses. It had once been a booming commercial port on the Rio Plate. A series of wide canals and locks ran along the strip of waterfront. Huge five-story gantries that had once run along the waterside on tracks, positioned to load and unload ships, now stood at intervals and had been made stationary emblems, hallmarks of the port, merely decorative.

The tracks had been cut out except beneath the monster cranes. Alongside the port was a broad walkway running in front of a series of substantial warehouses that had been converted into condos on the upper floors, with balconies and large windows providing expansive views of the harbor.

In one of the locks, a big three-masted schooner was berthed. At night, the high masts and rigging were lit up and could be seen for quite a distance, a come-on to the area. Puerto Madero stretched for at least a mile. On the ground floors of the well-spaced condo buildings were large restaurants, some quite toney with some retail stores to make the area a magnet during the day, and night spots for the evening crowd.

In the afternoon and evening, strollers promenaded along the quay with its benches, and diners sat on patios or inside.

They had asked the cab driver to take them to the end of Puerto Madero near Recoleta so they could walk the whole length of the harbor promenade.

Ben was still trying to mend fences and smooth the waves so he made small talk. "There's a Bice restaurant. That's a very exclusive chain with a branch, I think, in Palm Beach. Oh, look, Freddo's ice cream. They have outlets everywhere in the city. Notice on the other side of the canal they are

51

starting to work on those old buildings over there, rehab them."

They walked almost to the end. Ben took pictures of the sailing schooner. They decided to have lunch at another parada, La Caballeriza.

Ben said, "While we're here, let's freak out on steaks. They're so good, and we may never get back here or to any other place where the steaks are so tender and tasty. The hell with cholesterol for a week."

The day was pleasant. They did a lot of walking, unwinding, and peace-making. When later they returned to the hotel, Stephie went out to do some shopping (actually she wanted some time alone), and Ben snuck out to see Ann. In the beginning, Ann had a lot of "issues" she wanted to thrash out. There were recriminations, anger, some forgiveness, and a smoothing over of the difficult situation. Ben was on a trip with a very unhappy wife and now a less malleable lover. Not a good situation for a philanderer to be in.

Ann declared, "Look, Ben, I'm going to be a tourist too. I'm here to see the sights. Thank God I've met some people I can eat with, see tango shows with. Try to see me in my room around nine. Set your clock if you have to. Tell the little woman you have to work on your abs. But be here."

A chastened Ben was soon thrashing out some libidinous issues on the bed with Ann.

12

On Monday night, Stephie and Ben walked in the Claridge lounge and were greeted by Greg. The three friends had martinis, but Ben carefully nursed his drink. Better to be cautious than sorry. Greg told them he was going to take them to a tango show that catered to true lovers of the genre. Greg noticed his friends' coolness toward one another.

Later, when Greg, Stephie, and Ben piled out of a cab on the Avenue de Mayo, Greg explained, "This is the Café Tortoni, the oldest café in Buenos Aires, dating back to 1858. Down the street is the Capitol, and in that direction is the Casa Rosada, so this is the equivalent of Pennsylvania Avenue."

They entered the high-ceilinged café, which seemed frozen in time, looking like a sepia photograph from the mid 1800s. Some of the customers looked creaky enough to have been around at the café's opening. The trio walked through the café slowly, studying its many wall exhibits. They ended up in a smaller performance room at the rear left.

People were seated at long tables perpendicular to the stage. The three took seats near the front. On the small stage three musicians were warming up. The bandoneon player was a fat man dressed all in black. The piano player seated at an upright piano was like a beanpole, while the guitar player was gaunt and sullen.

Shortly after the waiter had served them drinks, the show began. The trio played two popular tangos. Stephie's attention was riveted to the bandoneon player whose rubbery face, undulating brow, and pop eyes were very expressive. As the tango had developed over the years, the bandoneon, a squeezebox concertina-like instrument, had become central to the music. adding a plaintive somber sound.

His pursed lips and rolling eyes were coy, flirty, campy. His face, full of gestures, mirrored the sounds of the instrument, as if the face itself was being played along with his bandoneon.

A tango dance couple came out, tall and slim, immaculately garbed in formal outfits. Both had gleaming black slicked-back hair. Their backs were ramrod straight. Proud in their bearing, they danced, rather slinked in a mannered and poised style with explosive foot moves, a male set of feet darting between a female set in very rapid motion. When they finished their dance, the audience burst into applause.

A barrel-chested man sang two tearful tango numbers full of woe. Then a male tango dancer in an undershirt, cocky and rooster-like, came out with his prop cup of maté and strutted imperiously like a bull fighter; his female partner joined him, proud and disdainful. Their dance was fiery, athletic, and sexy.

The star of the show was a famous Argentinean singer named Silvia Martine. She announced, "My first number is sado-machista so watch out."

As she finished her set of famous numbers delivered with real feeling and expressiveness, the audience members, devout, attentive and worshipful acolytes, tango aficionados, broke into a flurry of applause and cheers.

At intermission, Stephie talked with Greg while a whipped Ben listened, sometimes uncomfortably.

Greg said, "Tango is attitude personified. The stylized gestures have become traditionalized over the decades. Without attitude, tango would be unimportant; attitude gives it gravitas."

Ben wasn't anxious to talk about an art form so sexually charged, but he edged into the conversation. He asked, "Tango started as a disreputable dance for the lower classes, didn't it?"

Greg answered, "Yes, it was like jazz or ragtime in America. In a sense, it started in whorehouses and ended up in palaces. Strictly déclassé at first. Then over time, the whore that was tango became a duchess."

Stephie, with more on her mind than a discussion of tango, addressed Greg. "The male plays the role of a controller in the tango, doesn't he?"

"Oh, yes. The male is the dominator. Like the Parisian apache dance. Often his gestures are cruel. He acts like he is trying to break the woman's spirit."

"But she gives as good as she gets while he's saying, 'Look at me, I'm special. I'm cock of the walk.'"

As she talked about the tango with Greg, Stephie gave furtive glances at Ben, talking about one subject while implying a subtext.

Greg was on a roll. "Tango is controlled violence and pent-up sexuality. A lot of dangerous stirring, upheaval beneath the surface."

Ben was listening, but he wasn't participating. He seemed progressively uneasy, discomfited.

Greg expounded, "Sexuality explodes in the wild exchange of feet zipping in and out of the partner's legs. The shooting in and out of the other's legs is a metaphor for the courting and copulating ritual. It's sexual probing and eventual coupling, the sex act."

Ben got up. "While you two tango nerds are at it, I'm going to have a look at those neat old photographs in the café."

He walked into the main room.

After he had gone, Greg asked, "How is it going with you two? I know you've had your troubles in the past."

"You mean his straying off the reservation now and then? Presently I'd say we're not doing well at all. On the surface, we might look okay, but he has a habit of always pushing the envelope. I've taken a couple of hits, and my feelings about him have done a nose dive. This trip may well be the swan song. Yes, sooner rather than later. Pretty definitely at an end, I'd say."

"I'm sorry to hear that."

"I am too, but only because I hate change. I used to say he was a low-maintenance husband because he was so self-sufficient, but now I'd call him a high-risk husband, a high-maintenance spouse."

They saw Ben coming back and changed back to their tango mode.

"You two get along so well you should partner a TV show. Call it Ably and Pearce and the Psychology of Tango. It could be sponsored by Florsheim. But what about tango's effect on the young people here? Aren't they like kids everywhere with their own music? Isn't tango just for us tourists, the real enthusiasts and the old folks?"

Greg replied, "Oh, sure. The young people are into the newest stuff, but tango is endemic too, part of the social and cultural fabric of Argentina. The younger generation has its own music, its modern sounds, but beneath it all is the rich tradition of the tango. Even the youngest have heard a great deal of tango melodies in their lives, so it's embedded in their psyches whether they like it or not."

The trio of musicians were back on stage, and the tango music began again. More explosive dances, more solos, and the haunting refrains of melancholy and stolen love affairs. Ben thought, *What a country to come to for a sub rosa affair, to a place that had so deeply enshrined jealous lovers and sexual hanky panky into its musical heritage.* And at the same time, he thought, *Clinton, back in the States, is having to fess up about his peccadilloes. I can sympathize with the poor guy.*

After the show, the three took a cab. The driver had been a sheetrock worker in Mineola on Long Island for three years. He took the long way around and drove by Puerto Madera where all the masts and lines of the old sailing ship were lit up. The rehabbed buildings were brightly lit as well, giving the place and the city a festive lively feel.

On arrival back at the hotel, Ben said to Greg, "Come on in for a night cap. We're really early for this town."

The three entered the Claridge lounge. It was a busy energized place. A young woman was playing a spirited tango at the grand piano. The Rilleaus were dancing in their inimitable fashion. Quite a few tables were taken, mostly with future cruisers on the *Global Quest.* Ben, Stephie, and Greg took a table near the bar. The couple at the table next to them smiled a greeting.

The woman, mid-forties, was tall with a long face, short brown hair, something of an overbite. She seemed eager to meet people. Her husband, also mid-forties, was handsome, outgoing, but he had an obvious toupee. It had a rather lopsided, slapdash look to it, and it failed to blend in with his own hair.

Ben, at first, failed to see Ann seated in the far corner with an older silver-haired couple, the Lewises. Joey and Renaldo were so busy at the bar they had little time to wait on tables. Greg offered to fetch drinks, so he walked over to the center of the bar.

As he was waiting for one of the bartenders to serve him, he looked around the lounge. He glanced beyond the Rilleaus to the back table where Ann was seated. He did a double-take when he saw her. She was looking at and talking with her companions and did not see him. He was almost sure he knew her. Yes, it was a woman he recognized from when he and Ben had worked together in the Washington *Newsweek* office. A woman that Ben had lusted over, he remembered.

A whole series of insights hit Greg at once. If this was what's-her-name—her name escaped him at the moment— then this was just too much of a coincidence for her to be in the same lounge without Ben knowing about it. *What the hell was she doing here? What the hell was Ben up to?*

When Greg returned to the table with their drinks, he could not say anything to Ben in front of Stephie. He looked at him warily. *Would he possibly dare to? Could anyone be so crass as this? Maybe he and Stephie knew someone from the office was on the same trip. For now just clam up.* He did shoot a quick glance back at the woman. *It certainly looked like her. Had to be. Damned attractive. Oh, yeah, I remember her name, Ann.*

Greg's suspicious musings were cut off. Tall Overbite and the Disreputable Toupee were standing at their table.

The woman said, "Hi, we've seen you around. I'm Kim Simpson and this is my husband Doug. Knowing the way *Global Quest* seems to have booked its complete passenger list into this hotel, are you going to be on the cruise?"

Ben and Stephie assented.

Kim continued, "We saw you and said, 'Thank God someone from our generation will be aboard.' We know we're older than you young kids, but I hope we can at least touch base. We've met Fred and Ginger, over there, the Rilleaus. They're wonderful people, lots of fun, but they seem lost in their old world, kind of in an Arthur Murray time warp."

After some chitchat, Ben invited them to join them. The Simpsons assented willingly, and everyone joined in comparing their initial impressions of Buenos Aires. Kim seemed eager to ingratiate herself with Stephie. Doug was easy to get along with, unassuming, genial, a gentleman. After completing a dance set, the Rilleaus stopped by to say hello.

Ann and the couple were leaving the lounge. Ben saw them as they departed. Stephie was unaware of them. Just as they got to the lounge entrance, Greg happened to see Ann leaving.

After a few minutes more of conversation among the five, Stephie excused herself to go to the ladies' room. Kim said she had to go too. When Doug was at the bar getting refills, Greg turned to Ben, testing him.

"Listen, old buddy. Wow, have I got something to tell you. You remember that last winter when we were working together in D.C.?"

"Of course."

"Well, there was a fantastic looking sexpot working there. Ann . . . now I remember, Ann Glidden. You'll never believe this, but I just saw her sitting in the corner. I was building up my courage to go over, but she and an old couple left before I got a chance. Cripes, what tits. She is a . . ."

Ben was quick responding, "Oh, I saw who you mean. Yeah, she does look like that girl from the office, but she's definitely not the gal you're talking about. Believe me, it wasn't that girl from our office. They look alike, but no way, José, uh, uh. The poor Ann you're remembering has turned kind of tubby. She's lost it. No, that girl is someone else entirely."

"Well, you'd know. You've seen her more recently than I have. You plunked your share back then. But I still think the girl looks an awful lot like her."

"Not the same woman at all."

Later that night, Greg was saying his good nights. Ben and Stephie were at the lounge door with him.

"The tour you're taking tomorrow? Up the Parana River. If you wouldn't mind, I'd like to tag along. I love that area."

Ben and Stephie were enthusiastic about Greg joining them. For Stephie, Greg provided a buffer during difficult times.

Ben said, "Great. We'll see you tomorrow."

"I'll come by the hotel around one, okay?"

Stephie affirmed, "Super."

13

Tuesday morning, Stephie took her morning walk. Ben was with Ann in her room where they had just finished an episode of lovemaking. He was more tender and loving than ever, trying to make amends, and his tenderness assuaged some of her fears. Afterward, they lay spent on top of the covers.

Ben said, "Greg Pearce recognized you last night."

Ann sat up. "I thought so. I avoided looking at him, but I had the feeling he recognized me. I always thought he was a hunk. What are we going to do? Will he tell Stephie, do you think?"

"No. If worst came to worst, I could always head him off at the pass. He's a buddy. He'd stick by me."

"Yeah, you guys love to stick up for each other when you're fooling around. Bastards!"

"I think he's a fag anyway. No skin off his nose. I convinced him you were nobody he knew."

"Was it much of an effort on your part to convince him I was a nobody?"

"Hey, Ann, I'm only trying to protect us."

At quarter to one that afternoon, Greg Pearce was waiting outside the hotel. He glanced up the street and saw Ann Glidden and the silver-haired couple approaching. He moved over to a pillar so he could get a good look at her without her seeing him. As she passed, Ann was talking to the couple.

"It's a lovely part of town. Really fascinating."

Greg thought, *I'm sure. That's her voice. Ben knows. He's a fucking liar, up to his old tricks. Poor Stephie.*

Ann spotted Greg, avoided his eyes. He stared at her, was about to speak but held himself back. The couple and Ann entered the hotel.

While Ann and the couple waited for the elevator, Greg

watched them from outside. Ann turned slightly so she could observe Greg. Joey, the bartender, was walking by, said something to her, smiled and headed for the lounge. The couple and Ann entered the elevator.

Greg walked into the lobby, then into the lounge where Joey was doing his computer acrobatics.

He asked, "Joey, who was that lady you just spoke to at the elevator?"

"That is Señorita Glidden. She is very beautiful, isn't she?" With his hands he indicated a fulsome bosom.

"Yes, very. May I use your house phone?"

"Certainly. To make a date, I bet."

Greg used the house phone at the bar's opposite end. He dialed Ben's room.

"Hello, Ben?"

"Yeah. Hiya, Greg."

"Ben, could I see you in the lounge right away? Without Stephie?"

"What's up, buddy?"

"I'll explain down here."

"All right."

A few minutes later, Ben, looking concerned, walked into the lounge. He saw Greg sitting at a table. He joined him.

"What's up, Bro?"

"Ann Glidden is staying in this hotel."

"No, that's not Ann Glidden. I told you before. She just looks an awful lot like her."

"Don't hand me that shit. I know who I saw. I know her voice. It's Ann Glidden. Joey told me her name. What the fuck are you up to now?"

"No, it can't be. I . . ."

"I always knew you were promiscuous, basically a pig, but I can't believe what's going on here."

"What's going on?"

"You tell me. Is she going on the cruise too? Stephie obviously doesn't know. Screwing a girl on the side? I thought you gave up your old tricks. Bringing a broad with you on a

cruise behind your wife's back? Only a real shit would have
the balls to do that. Only a real bastard would even think of
doing it."

"C'mon. Let's have a drink. I'll tell you . . ."

"No, I'll be going. Tell Steph I was called away on assignment. I really don't want to be part of the crap you're pulling
on her. In God's name what did she ever do to you that she
deserves treatment like this? You're the worst shit I've ever
known. You bastard! I can't believe your lack of morals. And
don't worry. I'm not going to tell her. I know in my heart
you're going to get your just rewards. If you were a human
being, you'd tell Stephie now and end this farce."

Greg got up and hurried out of the hotel without a look
back.

Ben yelled after him. "Greg, let me explain . . ."

A few minutes later, Ben was pounding on Ann's door. She
opened it. He rushed in.

"Greg saw you again. He knows. He had it out with me."

"He'll tell Stephie. Shit."

"No he won't. He took off—for good. He's covered for me
before, and he'll do it again. He's not the kind to spill the
beans."

"What am I—the beans he'd spill? This whole thing is
beginning to turn sour. I'm becoming the villain in this."

"No, I'll fix it all. We knew something like this might happen. Everything is still go."

"Have you told Stephie you guys won't see Greg again?"

"No, not yet. I had to tell you first."

"Why did I already know that?"

"I'm not a bastard."

"Thanks for reassuring me, but I feel like a real bitch."

14

That afternoon, Stephie and Ben were in the lobby where he told her Greg had been called away for a special assignment. She knew the vagaries of journalism; reporters were apt to be sent to cover stories on short notice, and she thought nothing of it.

They went outside to wait for their tour van. Stephie was surprised by a voice behind her. It was Kim Simpson.

"Hi, guys, Doug and I heard you talking about that river trip last night so we signed up for it. Hope you don't mind having a little company?"

Stephie answered, "No, not at all. We'll enjoy your company. Our friend Greg got called away."

Stephie relished the idea of buffers on the trip. She'd have someone to talk to. She hadn't realized how tall Kim was. Stephie was tall, but Kim seemed to tower over her. And had Doug changed his hairpiece? This one looked just as disreputable and askew but seemed a different shade. Maybe it was the bright sunlight.

While the four waited, Kim chatted with Stephie, and Ben and Doug were talking about President Clinton's dilemma. Kim had a tendency to touch Stephie's arm while she talked, but Stephie got used to her friendly gestures.

The van pulled up. Maria was the guide again, and she announced the four constituted the full complement of tourers.

"Today we're going south of the city to the town of Tigre in the suburbs, a weekend getaway at the mouth of the Parana River. We'll be traveling by van, train, and boat."

They drove by the River Plate, brown in color with waves jogging the surface. Along the route were a series of seaside restaurants, a small domestic airport, and the River Plate soccer stadium.

Soon they were in the wealthy bedroom community of

Olivos. The van driver left the sightseers and Maria off at a
train station. They climbed some steps and stood on the
platform. The modern electric train, the Tren de la Costa,
was made up of four cars that ran on an elevated track along
the coastline and above the rooftops of upscale elegant
houses with gleaming tile roofs.

It was a modern smooth-riding train built for the prosperous suburbs. Well-dressed teenagers were aboard, apparently on their way home from school.

Kim said, "There's a Tyrolean look to some of the houses.
It's almost like being on a toy train traveling through some
Swiss or Bavarian province."

Maria herded her flock off the train at the San Isidro
depot, a Disneyesque village that had been turned into a
mall with restaurants and shops. Some of the teens got off
at the stop to do what American kids did, hang around the
mall. The local kids went into ice cream shops for treats.
Maria's group wandered around the clean sanitized mall,
and after forty-five minutes, reboarded the train.

While Kim zeroed in on Stephie, Ben enjoyed Doug's company, but he kept thinking of what a close call he had had.
And what a brick Greg was not to let the cat out of the bag.
Greg had been an enabler for him in the past. This was going
to be some trip if he had close calls like that one.

A middle-aged woman sitting across from Kim and Stephie
began a conversation with them. "I'm from New Zealand. I'm
here in Buenos Aires for a special reason. Tomorrow, I'm
going to take a ferry boat across the River Plate to Montevideo
in Uruguay. My grandfather was on a New Zealand naval
ship, the *Achilles*, that had a run-in with the German battleship *Graf Spee* in Montevideo harbor in World War II.

"Over the years, Gramps talked about the pursuit of the
German ship constantly. It was the high point of his life. He
died last year. I'm going to visit the site where the *Graf Spee*
was scuttled. This trip is sort of a memorial to him, God
bless him."

Stephie said, "The four of us are going on a cruise ship

that will be going to Montevideo this weekend. We'll think of you when we see the site of the sunken ship."

More stops, then the group was led off the train at San Fernando where the van met them. They were driven to a small harbor on the Tigres River where they boarded a sailless catamaran, a large excursion boat.

On the sunny deck of the boat at the mouth of the Parana River, Maria announced, "We'll be traveling up the river. You'll see where people have vacation homes, weekend getaways along the river."

Cottages, bungalows, and more substantial homes lined the shore. Many have wooden docks built out over the water with gazebos at the end of the docks. Canals branched off from the main waterway. Restaurants, yacht clubs, and rowing clubs were identified, and large water-taxis transported people up and down the busy waterway.

Doug, his toupee as usual at an angle, was talking to Ben. Kim was seated next to Stephie. Kim pointed to the two husbands.

"Ben and Doug seem to be hitting it off."

Stephie grinned. "Doug can feel himself honored. Ben is much more apt to connect with a woman than a man. He's a ladies' man. A nice set of boobs, and he's off and running."

Kim stared at Stephie admiringly. "I really enjoy your company." She reached over and patted Stephie's hand. "I love the way you do your hair."

Some distance from Stephie, a working class couple kept their eyes on her. Occasionally, when she was unaware, the man sneaked a quick picture of her though he seemed to be photographing shore sights.

After their river cruise, opposite what looked like a new railroad station in Tigre, they reboarded the van and headed back into the city. Kim suggested the four get together for dinner, but Stephie made excuses, saying she and Ben had a dinner date already. She found Kim pleasant, but she didn't want to be smothered by her constant attention. At times, she could be too attentive.

That night, Stephie and Ben had a steak dinner at Nazarenas, one of the city's best known posadas. It was a leisurely dinner. Ben was cautious in his drinking. Little was said of Greg. Ben suggested his assignment might take him out of the country.

They decided they wanted an earlier night, so they taxied back. As usual, Stephie's minders followed the cab back to the hotel.

When they returned to the hotel, they hurried by the lounge to the elevator. They caught a quick view of the Rilleaus engrossed in a tango.

As they stood by the elevator, a familiar voice shot out. "Are you kids coming in for a night cap?" It was Kim. She must have been on the lookout for them.

Stephie replied, "No, we've had a tough day of it. We'll see you tomorrow."

Kim looked disappointed.

"Well, you two kids get your beauty sleep. Good night y'all."

15

Very early, Kim and Doug were having a leisurely breakfast in the hotel. Doug was engrossed in his copy of the
International Herald Tribune, while Kim was watching Ann
Glidden as she ate alone, munching on a croissant and reading a Ludlam book. Kim didn't know her name, but she had
heard her talking and knew she was going to be on the cruise.
She was a knockout, very beautiful, poised, sure of herself.
Kim wondered why she was traveling alone. She sensed she
wasn't traveling with the silver-haired couple she was often
with. They were recent acquaintances, Kim thought.

Ann passed Kim's table on her way back to the buffet
table and gave Kim a smile that said merely a polite *hi.* To
Kim, she was a puzzle, an attractive puzzle.

Later, after Kim, her husband, and Ann had cleared out,
the Ably-Raniers were in the dining room for the buffet
breakfast. After light breakfasts, Stephie was out on one of
her morning walking tours. She was getting to know the
geography of the downtown.

Ben went for a short brisk workout in the gym and was
soon in Ann's room for a sexual workout. How many men
would have the audacity to keep a wife for social occasions
and a mistress for boffing—both staying in the same hotel?
It was a reckless, dangerous, exciting, mad thing to do, but
if he pulled it off, just think of the memories he'd have when
he was an old geezer. The stories he could tell, if he ever
dared reveal them.

He was somewhat deflated when he came out of her bathroom that morning by what Ann said, "You know, you really
are a self-centered bastard."

Stephie, out walking, her baseball cap pulled down to
mid-forehead, wearing her dark glasses, attired in jeans, a
sweatshirt, and trainers hadn't even drawn a whistle, a

stare, or a second look from the machos she passed. They were making love to their cell phones, pulling at their genitals, and looking in store windows to make sure they were still irresistible.

Stephie was more aware of her environment that morning, but she hadn't discerned anyone following her. Not yet anyway. The dwarfish man stayed so far back that she was unaware of his presence.

The afternoon was rainy, so Ben and Stephie decided to do indoor places. They chose the Museum of Fine Arts in an old neo-classical building that had once been the Waterworks. The building itself was not imposing or at all impressive.

Some older men strolling through the museum were very courtly gentlemen dressed very stylishly. One man wore spats. *It's almost as if we're inhabiting pre-World War II London*, thought Stephie.

After the museum visit, they crossed over to the Design Center. The lower floor had upscale home design stores for the well-off. Upstairs were long arcades of indoor-outdoor restaurants, including French and German places. The building housed branches of the Hard Rock and Planet Hollywood. They sat at one café and again had Macedonian con helado.

Stylish women around them were having lunches, talking, laughing, enjoying themselves, probably filling one another in on the latest gossip.

By the time Stephie and Ben left the center, the rain had let up. The cab that took them back to their hotel had a strong smell of urine. Perhaps some drunk or incontinent tango dancer had let go, joked Ben when they got out.

Wednesday night, they had dinner in the Broccolino on Esmeralda, an Italian restaurant, a few blocks from the hotel. It was popular with American tourists and American residents. They had Milanese cutlets, a good pasta and salad. The owner, a pleasant Italian woman in her mid fifties, told them she had lived on Long Island and later sent over complimentary Amaretto.

After dinner, they walked to Memorablia. Kim and Doug Simpson were seated at a table near the front. Stephie and Ben joined them for drinks.

Kim said, "Steph, you were right about this place. Lots of young people. It's a fun place."

On Stephie's recommendation, Kim had her fortune told by the tarot reader. When she returned to the table, Doug asked her, "What did the fortune teller say?"

"She said I have a prize husband, and that I'd met a great couple, new friends, here in Buenos Aires."

Later, the foursome stopped in the Claridge lounge for night caps. An old man was playing tango melodies on the piano. It was hard to get away from tango in Buenos Aires, especially in places where tourists gathered. The Rilleaus were seated at a table near the piano. At their urging, Stephie and Ben did a short tango together

On cue, the Rilleaus got themselves up, somewhat creakingly, maneuvered soldierly into position, and danced around the floor. He was humming. She was moving her lips, counting out the steps. Ben, Stephie, Kim and Doug applauded.

When the piano player let go with another spirited tango number, all three couples danced. Afterward, the six were seated at a table. Ben was talking with Doug, Marge, and Terry.

Kim turned to Stephie and asked, "Your friend from the other night, Greg, have you heard anything from him?"

"He got called away on assignment . . . or whatever."

By answering Kim's question, Stephie realized there might be some doubt in the back of her mind. *He was on assignment. A natural thing for a reporter. Yet . . .*

Kim reached over and touched her. "Stephie, you look so much like my kid sister. You're just as pretty as she is."

"Thank you. You and Doug are great dancers."

"It's like a hobby for us. We love the tango, but we're not dance fanatics like the Rilleaus. They live to dance. You and Ben are quite good though."

"We fake it—like we do a lot of things in our lives."

Ben overheard, was hurt by her comment, but said nothing.

Kim wondered if Stephie was ready for a heart-to-heart, woman-to-woman talk.

The Rilleaus, even seated, were swaying to the music.

Terry said, "Dancing is a vital function in our lives. Our lifeblood."

Doug said, "Ginger Rogers and Fred Astaire, Gene Kelly and Leslie Caron, Marge and Gower Champion."

Marge insisted, "Dancing keeps us fit, and alive, and in love with each other."

Terry walked around behind Marge's chair, leaned over, encircled her shoulders, showing his love for her.

Marge reached up to meet his hands. "He's the best dance partner I've ever had. When I saw him do the tango, I knew I'd found my match."

The six people started talking more expansively, drinking, laughing, and bonding, all enjoying themselves.

Kim suggested, "Folks, I've got an idea. Since we all seem to be getting along, how 'bout I fax the ship and get us a table together?"

There was general agreement and assent.

Kim added, "How 'bout late sitting? A big table for eight or ten so we can meet other folks?"

Again there was general agreement. Kim was a take-charge person.

After another tango started, the three couples changed partners and danced. Ben had a hard time leading Marge, Doug was a smooth dancer with Stephie, and Kim and Terry were like a couple of pros.

When the party broke up, everyone was exhausted, all danced out.

16

At 9:30 on Thursday morning, Ben was knocking on Ann's door. She was dressed, pocketbook in hand, ready to go out.

"Ann, hon, what's up?"

"We're going out together."

"I can't. We can't be seen together . . ."

"No, you meet me."

"Where?"

"I'll be waiting two blocks away at the corner of Tucaman and Reconquista."

"But if Steph sees us . . ."

"That's your problem, Buster."

"What's this *Buster* shit?"

"It's something my mother called my father when she was getting sick of his crap."

"Where are we going?"

"A quick trip to Evita's grave."

"But I'm going there with Steph this afternoon."

"So you'll see it twice. By the time you see it with the little woman, it'll be firmly imprinted in your mind. Fooling around the way you are now, maybe *you* should be out shopping for a tomb and a grave site anyway. You might need one sooner rather than later. I'll go first. Meet you in ten minutes at that corner. Keep your eyes peeled for the missus."

Ten minutes later, they met at the corner of Tucaman and Reconquista. When they got in the cab and asked for the Recoleta Cemetery and Evita's tomb, the taxi driver went there on auto pilot. It was a frequent tourist request.

An hour later, after their trip to the cemetery, Ben alighted from a cab at Reconquista and hurried to the Claridge. Ann stayed in the cab because she wanted to see Puerto Madera.

At two o'clock that afternoon, Stephie and Ben were let

71

out of a cab in front of the iron gates of the walled Recoleta Cemetery. Ben let his wife lead the way. She approached a sly-looking watchman in a faded green uniform. "Sir, we'd like to see Evita Peron's resting place."

The guard looked behind her at Ben, and his eyebrows raised, forehead furrowed as he stared at him. He recognized Ben from a few hours before. Then he was with that gorgeous sexpot, but true to the Latin code of the machismo brotherhood, he gave no sign of recognition. He pointed to some people about a block away within the cemetery.

"Follow those two men. They are going there. The name on the tomb is Duarte."

Ben folded a generous tip in the man's hand for which the guard nodded his gratitude, winked, proud to be in league with a fellow philanderer.

They were in a miniature city with blocks, streets, a labyrinth of miniature stone houses of various sizes brimming with statuary. It was all stone, marble, and alabaster with angels hovering, sad and pious carved faces, melancholy ornamentation. It was a cold hard-textured place, a city of the dead resting in their mausoleums, some with glass doors so mourners and strangers could look in at photographs of the deceased.

Stephie said, "Juan Peron's tomb is in the middle class Chacarita Cemetery while Eva is here among the upper classes, the oligarchs she railed against."

Ben said, "Don't forget Juan remarried an Evita look-alike who herself became president."

The two men ahead led them down a street where they stopped in front of the small modest sepulcher of the Duartes with a brass plaque commemorating Eva. Fresh red and white roses had been placed on the step. A vase sconce on the wall held some faded lilies.

Ben, quoting what Ann had told him earlier, said, "After Eva's death, her body was stolen, hidden in an attic in this city for a time, then it disappeared for eighteen years, and ended up in Rome. Juan Peron got the body back, returned it to Argentina. He was reelected president, and when he died, his new wife, Isabelita, became president. Evita's body finally made its way back here to rest among the wealthy upper class she despised."

Stephie said, "Or secretly envied. But such a small tomb for such an idol."

"The Argentine people had a long love affair with the Perons. Still do, some of them."

Stephie happened to glance down the end of the lane where she saw the dwarfish man near the corner. He quickly looked away and passed out of sight behind a monument.

She cried out to Ben, "Ben, over there. Near the corner. A man was staring at us at the end of the lane. He's been following me. Stalking me. A short man like a dwarf."

Ben hurried to the end of the row of tombs. He looked up and down the intersecting lane. Halfway down the lane he saw a man and woman devoutly kneeling in front of a tomb. He returned to Stephie.

"No stalker there."

"I definitely saw him. I've been meaning to tell you the past few days I'm sure someone has been following me."

"Like someone with the hots for you?"

"No, not that at all. People keeping an eye on me."

"Are you sure it's not your job that's making you see these guys? They're always drumming into you to be security-conscious, watchful?"

"All I know is I've seen one particular man, sort of dwarfish, humpbacked, and maybe others keeping an eye on me."

"Wouldn't it be kind of far-fetched to pick a Quasimodo to tail someone. Kind of stand out, wouldn't he?"

"I'm just telling you I've seen people. My boss told me to be on the look-out on this trip."

"Well if your boss told you to be cautious, then I guess that's what you should do, but let's not go seeing bogeymen everywhere we go."

Stephie wanted to get off the subject. "You know Sunday

when we were in San Telmo, I saw a lot of little courtyards and stores around that square I'd like to investigate. Would you mind if we went back there this afternoon?"

"No, sounds good to me."

Anything for the little woman at this stage of the game.

On the way out, the guard gave Ben a sly look, a look tinged with admiration. Perhaps saying to himself that maybe the gringos were even better at fooling around than the Latinos.

Later, as they roamed around the area near Plaza Dorrego, they made some pleasant finds. Beautiful, shaded, cool courtyards with interesting little stores, colorful, flowering plants in terra cotta pots, climbing vines, ornate wrought iron railings on inviting balconies, a place to make serendipitous discoveries.

Several stores sold old musical instruments; one was crammed with old wooden phonographs, Victrolas (some with horns), huge console radios, and old juke boxes. One store was a treasure trove of tango memorabilia.

At one corner, Stephie, pointing out a fat man, said, "He's the concertina player from the Café Tortoni. We saw him the other night when we went with Greg."

"You've got a sharp eye."

"That's why you should listen to me when I tell you I'm being stalked. By the way, any word from Greg?"

"Oh, yeah, he called and said he'd be away until after we board ship."

"I miss him."

"Me too, but in our business you never know when an assignment will pull you away."

They picked out a busy restaurant on the square for lunch, the Glorieta de San Telmo, and had pizza.

Stephie commented, "Most of the people in Argentina are of Italian stock, so they do a good job with pizzas and pastas."

They lingered over their late lunch and watched the activity in the square. Their time in Buenos Aires was beginning to run out.

17

Thursday evening, the Simpsons and the Raniers went to a full-blown tango show at El Viejo Almacen, which advertised "pure tango" and an open bar for forty dollars. The famous doorway of the Almacen club had been memorialized in thousands of wall plaques with the green doors and awning and the picture of the tango idol Gardel outside.

In the club, the two couples, among the early arrivals, had a table to the right facing the stage. The club was a two-story affair with a U-shaped balcony that hovered over the downstairs seating. From upstairs, patrons either had a head-on view of the stage or from the sides an angled view of the performance.

Taped tango selections entertained the audience as the large room filled up. The balcony had yet to be occupied with the bus groups that were such a staple of the tourist business.

Stephie remarked, "It's too bad the Rilleaus aren't here to see the show."

Kim replied, "They're at one of the tango clubs for locals where they can actually dance. They consider themselves performers, not spectators. As far as they're concerned, they *are* the show."

Doug said, "Did you notice, it's always the Rilleaus, two people joined at the hip? A team."

The four friends sat enjoying their drinks, chatting. Large bus groups kept coming in. One bus group of Japanese tourists loaded down with camera and video equipment entered. A final bus group came in. As they filed in, Ben noticed the Lewises and Ann were in the group. He had no idea she was planning to be there. They hadn't told each other of their plans.

As she passed the table, Ann and Ben exchanged glances, but neither showed any sign of recognition. The only other person who noticed Ann was Kim, who recognized her from the hotel. Ann didn't acknowledge Kim. The two had never talked, had only a nodding acquaintanceship.

Ann and her party were led up the stairs to the balcony where they were seated at a table opposite and above Stephie and the others. After they were seated, Ann glanced down quickly at Ben and his party.

Kim, ever watchful, basically nosy, casually looked around the club and spotted Ann upstairs. Stephie was pre-occupied, listening to Doug, someone else who had studied up on tango. Ben became aware of Ann's location in the balcony.

The band took the stage. It consisted of two bandeleon players, two guitarists, a violinist and a pianist. They began with a fiery tango. Then a couple in the troupe came on stage and danced a tango with great fervor. The Japanese were madly taking photos and video. Other tango duos and tango singers followed. The older of the bandeleon players was introduced as a quite famous master of the instrument. He played two solo virtuoso sets. All of the cast were professional, very talented.

While a white-haired man with precise phrasing was singing a tango ballad, Kim glanced up at Ann who was looking down at their table. Kim then happened to get a quick glimpse at Ben who was looking up at Ann. When Ben saw Kim looking in his direction, he became engrossed in the singer on stage. Kim found it interesting these two people were exchanging eye contact. It was understandable; Ben couldn't help but find her attractive. And hadn't Stephie told her he was a boob man?

After the show, the two couples entered a cab outside the club. Ben sat in the front next to the driver. As they drove along the streets, they paid little attention to their surroundings. Ahead of them in the street was a police car, with insistent flashing lights, parked so that it partially blocked traffic.

Two policemen with big flashlights signaled the cab over and instructed the driver where to stop. The cab pulled up.

The driver and passengers tightened with a sense of dread. This was Argentina after all.

A policeman, one hand holding a flashlight, the other hand on his holster, approached the car. He stood at the driver's window, and his partner took up a position at the passenger side.

The cab driver said to his passengers, "Policia. Check Punto. IDs, papers."

Both policemen leaned in the windows, shining their lights on the three in the back seat and on Ben in the front. They were studying their faces, taking their time about it. The four Americans were very apprehensive. After all, the country had a bad history of repression. The police here could be intimidating. The four were narrowing their eyes from the bright lights.

The policeman on Ben's side leaned in and said in a gruff voice, "Identification."

He thrust a large hand in the window. The driver told the three in the back seat to roll down the cab's back windows. The other policeman had moved to the back seat window behind the driver where the Simpsons were seated.

Ben said, "Our passports are kept by the hotel. Here's my *Newsweek* press pass with my picture."

Ben showed his pass. The policeman insisted on seeing his driver's license as well. He carefully compared photos with the face, shifting the bright beam back and forth to do so.

Steph and the Simpsons had their driver's licenses out. The Simpsons showed their licenses. The policemen continued to shine their lights in at the passengers. Nervous moments passed.

The policeman had finished with Ben and was shining his light in Stephie's eyes. He did this for some moments. He was very brusque.

He said, "Señorita, you, your papers."

Stephie was annoyed, but calmly she said, "Here's my driver's license. Here's my voter's registration card."

He studied the cards, shone the light again into her face. He hadn't returned the voter's card.

"Your press pass," he demanded.

"I am not a reporter. I have no press pass."

"Your work papers."

"I have no work papers."

Stephie did not carry any identification with her that showed her government employment.

The two policemen walked in back of the taxi to confer. The cab's occupants were stressful and anxious. Stephie's interrogator returned, and flipped the card back to her. He again shone his light in her face. The two policemen returned to the front of the cab. Again they conferred. Finally, they stood back and motioned the driver to move on.

As he drove back into the traffic stream, the driver was cursing wildly. Stephie was shaking; she felt she had been singled out.

Doug said, "Phew! That was a scary experience. No politeness. No 'Enjoy your stay in our city.' Just intimidation, nastiness. That has really soured my whole experience here."

Ben said, "Ignorant bastards!"

Kim, her voice shaking, whispered, "That was scary. I didn't know Argentina was still a police state."

Ben said, "There's been an increase in crime lately according to our friend Greg who's stationed down here."

Doug replied, "I almost crapped in my pants."

The four stopped in the lounge for drinks to steady their nerves. Stephie had the feeling she had been a particular target during the police stop. What if they had asked her to step outside the cab or had taken only *her* in for interrogation? Did they know something she didn't?

18

It was Friday, their last full day in the Argentine capital before they took sail on their two-week cruise. Ben and Stephie were at breakfast.

Ben said, "Steph, not much time left here in Buenos Aires. What would you like to do today?"

"I'll take my walk this morning and be back after noon time. You do your thing, then we'll decide. We'll look at the guidebook and see what we missed."

After breakfast, Stephie exited the hotel entrance. As she stepped outside, she was surprised to see Kim in a jogging suit, stretching at the door.

Kim greeted her. "Hi, Steph, out for your morning walk?"

"Yes, looks like a nice day."

"Mind if I join you?"

Steph was caught off guard. "No, I'd love to have you along."

The two set off, making a right turn at Calle Florida. They headed to the end of Florida, then turned left onto Sante Fe where they walked for some distance, then they headed through a large park. They had already dissected their run-in with the local police and were laughing about Latino machismo.

Back at the hotel, Ann and Ben were sitting on her bed. He was caressing her, trying to get her going.

She said, "I saw you and the little woman at the tango club last night. That woman with you . . ."

"Kim Simpson."

"I think she saw us looking at each other."

"She's a nosy one. We'll have to watch ourselves."

"I'm getting tired of this bullshit. You see me for an hour or so in the morning. You get your piece of ass and take off. Stephie gets all the good parts, the companionship, having a

79

guy with her. You tour together, you eat together, you even sleep overnight together. What kind of a slut am I anyway?"

"Ann, please. This will all be over when we get back to Washington."

"You bet it will. You're a lucky guy, Buster. When we get on the cruise ship, I want more of your time."

"I'm going to let her go on some of the land tours on her own. I promise we'll have more time together."

"We better."

Ann slowly responded to Ben's entreaties, and they were soon pounding away, *making love*, well, having sex.

On Sante Fe, Stephie and Kim had stopped in front of a sidewalk café where a number of fashionable women were having coffee. The dwarfish man was watching them from more than a block away.

Stephie said, "Hey, we've walked at least three miles. I'm winded. How about some café con leche?"

"Great."

They sat at a table surrounded by tables of women who were fashionably dressed.

Kim said, "I feel like a slob next to these fashion plates. They must think we're a couple of bag ladies, you in your jeans, me in my sweats."

A young, early-twenties, raven-haired, handsome waiter, the kind of male animal that Argentina seemed to specialize in, came up, smiled winningly at them and took their orders.

Kim and Stephie talked, told jokes, laughed, and began connecting. After a time, Stephie looked off into space, wistfully, sadly.

Kim asked, "So how's everything going so far?"

"I feel spooked. I've told you about my uneasiness—the feeling I'm being watched. Several times I've seen the same people behind me. One's quite short, dwarfish."

"Could it be related to your job in Washington?"

"Kim, I can't talk about that. Sorry, but no, I don't see how my job is involved in any way."

"What does Ben say?"

"He pooh-poohs it. And besides, I'm kind of uneasy about him too."

"How so?"

"He's edgier. Withdrawn at times. At other times, too attentive. Polite, but distant, distracted as if his mind is somewhere else, falling asleep at odd moments."

Kim reached over and held Stephie's hand, patted it sympathetically, tenderly.

"Sounds like Doug. He drifts off sometimes."

"If we were back in Washington, I'd swear he was up to something."

"Another horny bull rooting around in the meadow like our prez, Bill Clinton?"

"Sometimes you can tell a new friend more than you could an old friend. With you and me there's no checked baggage to worry about. Kim, I know sexually I haven't been any good for him lately. It takes two to tango, and I can't get in step when I should. There's too much finagling in his past. I should be more responsive, but I can't anymore. Maybe I'm being selfish, but there's been a lot of erosion. Stuff that the two of us can never take back."

Kim took and held Stephie's hand again.

"Jeez, I know that feeling. Thank God Doug's libido doesn't click in very often, but he's always been faithful, thank the Lord. Faithful to a fault, I guess."

"Early in our relationship, I learned Ben could be cold toward other people at certain times, not with me. He can freeze people out when it suits him. Mr. Impersonal. He runs hot and cold. He can also be quite devious when it suits him.

"Since we've been married, Ben has had two affairs I know of. Plus some brief flings. I've stayed with him, more from habit and convenience rather than anything else, but our relationship has gotten worse. Each time I've found out, I've cared for him less. It's like a glacier calving, losing part of itself as it reaches the open water. Chunks keep falling off— my love eroding. I'm sorry to burden you . . ."

"Hey, I'm a good listener."

"Ben and I travel well together, but there isn't much else. I know I'll never be as absorbed by sex as he is. His motto is gotta have it, gotta have it."

Kim said, "We know what most women know: men are basically pigs, and they want everyone to join them in their piggery. If they see a woman they want, they'll do everything to get her, usually just a quickie to say they had her. They are never satisfied with one woman, and when they get a woman through their piggish desires, they go and act like what? Why, of course, like the pigs they are. All men are pigs, plain and simple. I see you smiling, but you know I'm right."

Stephie said, "I'm not a roll-over-and-die sort of person, a doormat. Believe me, when it's called for, I can be as gutsy, as strong, as determined, and as assertive as I have to be. I taught myself that, and I will never be a sit-back-and-take-it person. I call that type a sap, a sucker. Weakness to me is not something I lean toward.

"If I feel I'm being crossed, if I get my dander up, watch out. I take a stand. I put up with a lot, but I do so because I choose to; it suits me to put up with certain things because it is a matter of convenience.

"I can be tough to deal with at certain times. Ben can be too, more often than I. We are two of a kind really. He pushes, I push, and sometimes neither of us back down, and as a consequence, we go our separate ways on certain issues.

"I found I could live with him, go on with my life, but after each episode, it left scar tissue. I don't know when the actual breaking point will come, but eventually it will come. It will be when it is more convenient for me to live without him than with him. It's as simple as that."

Soon they resumed their walk and covered a great deal of territory. Stephie was walking off her discontent and Kim was happy to be with her.

Later, Ben and Stephie were in their room planning their day. Stephie told Ben she and Kim had taken a long walk, but she didn't tell about their long intimate talk.

Ben said, "You and Kim seem to get on well."

"Yes, I like her. She's someone I can talk to. I trust her."

"What do you two talk about?"

"Mostly you."

"Me? Why me?"

"Can you think of anyone more intriguing to talk about? Your life is always so full of surprises."

Their day was spent visiting stores and wandering around a big shopping mall. Their new friends were in the lounge that night, the Rilleaus along with Kim and Doug.

Ann had told Ben ahead of time she was going to be in her room early. He wished he could sneak off there and have a brief sexual encounter, but he knew that would be skating on thin ice.

The atmosphere was festive. The Rilleaus were warming up for the start of the cruise the next day. They had improvised a tricky new dance step that they were proud to demonstrate.

19

Saturday morning, sailing day, Stephie, making sure her formal wear for the cruise would be as unwrinkled as possible, had done all her packing. Ben, too, was all packed. They were ready for the transfer to the ship that afternoon.

Soon out for her morning walk, she noticed from the English language papers that Clinton was in more trouble. One headline predicted something unpleasant was about to hit the fan.

The city was quieter. Offices and banks were closed. She wandered around the dead financial district below Calle Florida. She was about to head down deserted Calle Peron when a beat-up van with two grim-faced men in the front passed her, driving very slowly. It parked about halfway down the block.

Something about this seemingly innocuous event made her cautious, apprehensive. She turned around and headed back into an area where she saw people, where there was activity. She was probably being foolish, but she had nothing to gain by pushing her luck.

She sat in a confiteria on Florida, and she felt edgy, unexplainably squirrely. She also felt alone, isolated, thousands of miles from home, insecure about Ben, anxious, worried without anything specific she could put her finger on. She had felt as if she had been watched, shadowed while in the city.

She had been getting some really strange vibes, a feeling something was seriously wrong. She felt as though there were people out there who meant to do her real harm.

She was with Ben yet with a shadow Ben, not quite the real person. And the way Ben was acting polite but distant, distracted as if his mind was somewhere else, as if something was preying on his mind, falling asleep at odd moments. He

84

couldn't still be exhausted from the flight.

Their marriage was really no different than it had been before; it was falling apart. Sexually it hadn't been any good for a long time. They would never get to the second honeymoon phase again. They had been through that.

They had worked out an unspoken agreement. She thought he probably had an odd fling once in a while. As long as she didn't know about it and didn't know his partner, things could go on as before. Knowing him, it would be someone younger, more sexually active than she. She knew having children wouldn't help. It would do more harm than good. They both loved their careers and their private space too much. Motherhood had not been one of Stephie's burning goals.

Stephie felt that their week's stay in Buenos Aires had been a good idea. She felt they had gotten a good overview of the city. She liked the people. Many of the men were very handsome and the women beautiful. European genes. People in general seemed considerate and pleasant. They hadn't made any friends among the locals, but that was natural in a hectic week of sightseeing.

The city was a male bastion seemingly chauvinistic with a lot of male attitude, steak houses, some heavy Germanic decor, lots of wood paneling, bars and pubs with clubby men's atmospheres, a macho smell of leather.

But let the men have their boy games; so many women were chic, glamorous and independent. It was nonsense to call this and London male cities and claim Paris as a woman's city. Argentina had had two female presidents and the most powerful first lady ever, a woman who had won the hearts of the working people.

Everyone seemed to have a cell phone. She had seen businessmen in well-tailored, bespoke suits, lots of double-breasted blue blazers with crests, platoons of brass buttons. She had seen well-dressed, well-off women in groups, in trendy places, laughing, enjoying their pastries and tea. The city has gravitas and class. It was a first-rate city, she decided.

Buenos Aires was a city she could spend time in easily and comfortably. She would like to return and spend more time, but how do you capture your fondness for a place when you also have a sense of unease and even menace there, the feeling all is not quite right. It wasn't the fault of the city—it seemed to be something she had brought with her, something was due to her, a feeling the same thing could be happening to her elsewhere.

From her Uncle Lee, Stephie had garnered the habit of taking extensive notes and writing down impressions when she traveled. Later, at home, she would transfer all of the notes from her little notebooks into files on her computer. She had brought along four notebooks and would probably fill them on this trip. She thought ahead to how she was going to write the three important things on her mind: her apprehension about being shadowed, Ben's behavior, and her overall impressions of Buenos Aires.

Outside on the street again, everything was normal, and no one seemed to pay the slightest attention to her. People were oblivious to her; her nervousness didn't show, or she hid it very well.

At a store called Keyy's she bought an angora wool sweater with a beautiful Colombian Indian pattern for two-hundred dollars. She knew she wouldn't have to justify the expense to Ben; it was *her* money after all.

While his wife was out taking her final walk in the capital, Ben was with Ann. Her packed bags were lined up at the foot of the bed. Ann was sleeping deeply, breathing evenly, her body satiated and satisfied.

Gently, he woke her up. She awakened with a start. After a few moments, they were talking, conspiring.

Ann said, "I'm only doing all this because I love you. If I didn't think it would all be over soon, I would never have agreed to this."

"Ann, I promise. It will be a new start after this trip. We'll soon be free to marry. I just have to give Stephie this last trip, then she and I are finished, I swear. Stephie hounded me about this trip. I had to do it. She's still trying to get over her uncle's murder in London."

"Buster, it'll have to be over soon. I have to get my life together one way or another. Now let's get ready to see those glaciers, penguins, and go round that Cape."

When Stephie returned from her walk, she decided to say nothing to Ben about the suspicious van. He wasn't back in the room yet anyway. He always seemed to find a lot to keep him busy.

She did write her thoughts in her journal, but what was there to tell? She had thought some van looked menacing. Had it really? As Ben sometimes accused her, perhaps she was being paranoid, imagining things when there was nothing there. But then, she decided, it might have developed into a dangerous encounter of some kind.

Close to one o'clock, Ben and Stephie were standing outside the Claridge with their luggage. Maria showed up in the van to transport them to the dock. Seated in the front, she was again juggling her clipboard and cell phone. She turned to them.

"How was your week in Buenos Aires. A beautiful city? Yes?"

Stephie said, "It is a beautiful city. We enjoyed it."

Ben added, "We had a ball. Great town."

The van had one other stop at the Liberator Hotel where a mother and daughter got on with a set of matched Louis Vuitton luggage. Stephie thought she and Ben had overpacked, but laughed to herself as she counted seven pieces. The mother was a bosomy martinet ordering her meek daughter around. The mother and daughter had beaks for noses, and shared widow's peaks.

At the ship terminal, they could see the *Global Quest* beyond the stacks of freight containers. Closer to the terminal there was much bustling, with luggage being manhandled, the ship being provisioned, and a passel of senior citizens eagerly anticipating a long sea voyage as they waited for passport and ticket processing.

20

The embarkation formalities were dispensed with quickly, and they were given clearance to board. As she headed for the gangway, Stephie, as always on such embarkations, was charged up thinking of the adventure ahead of her. She likened it to settling in with a new, highly recommended book, or the feeling of anticipation she got when a theater darkened and a play or movie began.

She was a born traveler, who like her Uncle Lee, would have been content to spend large portions of her life journeying around the world, taking notes, photographing, and perhaps writing about her experiences. She would have loved to be a travel writer. Traveling in solitude might well have suited her—perhaps better, she thought, than traveling with Ben, but he made an adequate enough traveling companion for her even with his bouts of moodiness.

She and Ben walked up to the gangway entrance; the obligatory bon voyage photo was taken. It showed them both with mechanical smiles; they certainly were not a beaming honeymoon couple. Their frozen images were captured, to become part of the documentary evidence for the investigators of an ill-fated cruise.

Once aboard, a smartly uniformed cabin steward ushered them to their cabin. Ben and Stephie went out on the small verandah and viewed several other cruise ships across the pier, also boarding passengers for similar itineraries. The high masts of *The Sea Cloud* towered over the stacks of containers, and Holland America's *Nieuw Amsterdam* was readying for departure as it took on passengers.

Inside the cabin, they began reading the multitude of notices spread over every free surface: dining arrangements, a note about gifts of wine from their travel agent, the ship's newspaper, brochures for the hair salon, the spa, and specials in the casino as well as bargains in the ship's boutique. According to customary practice, the boutiques and casino would be closed until they sailed. Since they were frequent cruisers, all was familiar to them.

They had booked second sitting, and they were duly notified by a small notice. Ann, by prior arrangement, also had second sitting. At first Ben thought it might be a good idea for them to have different sittings, but Ann insisted on late dining. They would make time, be creative in arranging assignations.

Back in Washington Ben and Ann thought of an intriguing scenario. Some night he could feign illness in the early evening, insisting his wife go to cocktails and dinner without him. At 7:30, he would sneak off to Ann's cabin. Then he and Ann could be alone until just before ten when Stephie would return from her dinner. They might skip dinner or order food service in her cabin.

If somehow Stephie returned to their cabin while he was gone and found him missing, he could say he went out on deck to get some fresh air, saying the cabin had become stuffy.

Stephie read the ship's newspaper, *The Global Gazette*, dated Saturday, January 24th, with a cover photograph of the ship's captain, Christopher Marchland, and a brief bio of him.

Dress that night was casual, the usual practice for the first night at sea. The port and tour talk for Montevideo was to be given at 4:00 in the Excelsior Showroom by Sue Swanson, the land tour director. It was de rigueur for Stephie to attend all of the port talks and lectures about the areas they were visiting. At 5:15 the passenger emergency drill with lifejackets was to take place at assigned muster stations. Sailing was at 6:00.

Their baggage had not yet arrived, and since there was little to organize in the small cabin, Ben and Steph decided to make their first tour of the ship. They began their inspection on the topmost sun deck where they found the spa, gym, sauna and whirlpools. The deck below, the Lido, had a pool and indoor and outdoor dining tables for morning and lunch buffets. On the Promenade Deck, they both made a complete circuit of the outside deck, and Stephie pronounced it fine tor her compulsory walks. The bow portion was under cover, so she wouldn't have to worry about those fierce sea winds that almost knocked you over as you circled the bow on other ships.

Ann was booked on Caribe Deck, which had no verandahs. Ben had deliberately kept her away from the Promenade Deck where Stephie would do her ceaseless walking. It would be embarrassing and disconcerting, downright deflating to be shagging Ann and every few minutes see a determined conscientious Stephie briskly marching by. It could put a crimp in his style, produce a limpness, induce a certain guilty flaccidity to his penetration and concentration.

Later, when Stephie entered the Excelsior Showroom for the port talk, she looked around the crowded room for a seat and was offered one of the last seats, a single seat up front next to a rugged-looking blond man who proffered her a big smile and nod.

Two people stood on the stage, which was on a level with the audience tables and chairs. Sue Swanson, rangy and ungainly, had the wireless mike in her hand and stood next to a short solidly built man in a polo shirt. She outlined the details of the various tours being offered for Montevideo and then turned to her partner.

"Let me introduce our tour problem counselor, Tony. Gals, he can tell you about all those shopping bargains."

She handed the mike to Tony who winked at her and pretended to measure her up with his eyes, the professional flirt motif. He was a good-natured guy with a big smile and seemed to enjoy his job.

"My name is Tony Tantera, Mr. T 'n T, the ship's port coordinator, actually your translator and troubleshooter. When your guide doesn't understand you or some hustler is trying to roust you, I'm there to be your protector and your watchdog. I fill in background for Sue here. I give you some insider dope. I'm the head land tour stress-solving honcho on this tub.

"I've lived in a dozen countries; I speak six languages, including, of course, Spanish which I'll need for this trip. Because of the number of Spanish speaking countries in the world there are at least seventeen ways to speak Spanish. A Spaniard and a Puerto Rican, just as one example, find hundreds of variations in their so-called common language.

"Wherever you go, language and pronunciation can get you into trouble. When I'm not on the ship, I live in São Paulo where I am married to a wonderful Brazilian woman. We get along great because I'm at sea most of the year. I can speak Portuguese, but I haven't let her know that yet. We get along a lot better that way.

"I go on a lot of the tours, and aboard ship, I'm at the tour desk to answer your questions. There is no such thing as a dumb question, only a dumb guy like me there to answer them. I try to give you the street smarts for the places we go.

"On this cruise we are going to three countries— Argentina, Uruguay, Chile—and one British crown colony, the Falklands. You'll see how the people live, get a feel for the traditions of the people and places, and have an opportunity to see a lot of animal life, big colonies of marine animals and birds.

"The scenery will be spectacular. You'll even see glaciers. It's the chance of a lifetime to see wildlife. Charles Darwin saw many things here in South America, in some of the places where you're going, and nature taught him a great deal about evolutionary development.

"If you've been looking forward to seeing big pigeon rookeries, you're going to be amazed. If you like pigeons, you're going to love this trip."

Good-naturedly, part of their shtick, Sue poked him hard on the shoulder. "You did it again, Tony." Sue had in her hands a stuffed toy penguin wearing a *Global Quest* tee shirt.

"Oh, excuse me, Sue, honey. Oh, yeah. I keep getting them birds mixed up. Penguins, not pigeons. Penguin rookeries. We offer you the opportunity to see the huge penguin colony in Punta Tombo. If you aren't overpigeoned—sorry overpenguined—after you see Punta Tombo, you can see other colonies in the Falklands and in Punta Arenas. You'll see so many penguins before we get off this cruise, you'll start to waddle like them. And on formal nights, some of the men will even dress like them.

"And, incidentally, folks, we have on this ship a naturalist, a lecturer who gives a talk about penguins that is the highlight of this whole trip. Doctor Mike Lambert will be giving his talk Monday morning, our first full day at sea. Mike, baby, stand up, and flap your wings for the folks."

Stephie's neighbor stood and took a bow. He was a built six-footer. She had to admit he was a hunk. He acknowledged the crowd and gave her another big grin. Was he trying to hit on her? She almost hoped so.

Tony continued, "For God's sake, don't miss his talk. He becomes a penguin before your very eyes. He acts out penguin behavior, and he's a superb showman. In another life, he had to be a penguin. And gals, he's as sexy as he looks. I just hope he doesn't make penguin doo doo on the stage. That stuff really stinks. I think somewhere way back in his family tree, some family member had an affair with a penguin.

"Try to get to Punta Tombo to see the biggest rookery of Magellanic penguins in the world. Hundreds of thousands of them. It's a long bus trip, but well worth it. You'll be going along, won't you Mike?"

Mike nodded emphatically and waved his arms.

"Mike lives in the Falklands, does penguin research there, so he'll be leaving us there, eh, Mike?"

Again, another nod.

Sue then gave more information. "Before the Panana Canal was built, this trip around Cape Horn was a necessity to get to the western Americas or to Asia. Most people heading where you're going dreaded the journey. Many perished, but you're aboard a luxury liner with all the finest navigational gear and on a ship that has made this trip many times in the past.

"It's going to be a pleasant experience. You'll find we often take inland passages that make the trip smoother and calmer and give you a chance to see some breathtaking scenery. We have a schedule of land tours that will really increase your awareness of animal and marine life.

"Well, we are about to leave Buenos Aires, and we are headed across the River Plate, the silver river, supposedly the widest river in the world on our way to to Montevideo, the capital of Uruguay, across the river. This brown muddy river is an estuary where the river meets the ocean, and it's affected by the tidal conditions of the Atlantic Ocean. Tony, how did Montevideo get its name?"

Tony took over again. "Legend has it that a sailor lookout way up in the crow's nest aboard a galleon approaching the shore yelled out in his native Spanish language, 'Montevideo,' which means, *I see a mountain*. Actually, it was a hill only about five-hundred meters tall. The Portuguese ran the place for awhile. It's a great city where people with mucho dinero come from the rest of South America and Europe for seaside vacations.

"We will be docking in Uruguay tomorrow morning. At dockside, you'll see the anchor of the *Admiral Graf Spee*, a reminder of the German pocket battleship that was scuttled outside the harbor during World War II. We'll be getting to Montevideo on a Sunday, tying up amid busy commercial docks, but you'll find a sleepy kind of place without the hustle and bustle of a business day.

"This is what I call an Esso town—E-S-S-O—every Saturday and Sunday off. Offices, banks, most stores, and post offices will be closed. It will be almost impossible to get stamps. Leave your postcards at the purser's desk, and they'll be stamped and mailed. In other towns that we'll visit on weekdays, many people take siesta, and stores are closed from one to four, so plan your shopping accordingly. Don't change money; you won't need much money anyway because you won't be in Uruguay for more than a short time. Most places take American dollars and credit cards.

"Walking around town, pay attention, be aware of pick-pockets as you would in any large city. Don't wander around alone in deserted places where there are no other tourists. It's not a dangerous city, but still, use your noodle. Some cabs may offer to take you to the beach resort at Punta del Este. Don't go. It is too far away. If you do go, have your camera ready, because you may get a good picture of the ship as it leaves port without you.

"Some people are going to point out the remains of a ship sticking up in the harbor a few hundred meters from shore and say it's the *Admiral Graf Spee*. It isn't. It's the hulk of some abandoned freighter. The *Graf Spee* is four miles out, and the captain will explain that to you when we're leaving Montevideo.

"A wise man, not me, said on a cruise like this, remember you are a traveler, not a tourist. Everything won't be the same as it is at home. If everything were the same, why travel at all?

"A tourist is superficial; he's just there, and he wants everything to wash over him like at Disneyland. You're in an exotic place because you have chosen to be here, to learn, to experience. You are traveling. It will be an adventure. A traveler is more broad-minded than a tourist."

Stephie liked hearing the distinction between being a tourist and a traveler. She had, like her Uncle Lee, always considered herself a traveler rather than a tourist. A traveler researched and studied, but most important of all, a traveler recorded his travel experiences once he returned home. A tourist was in a place for the sheer entertainment value; a traveler was there to broaden his outlook on life.

Tony said, "This is summer in this hemisphere. Summer runs from December to March. Before and after those months, the weather is too cold and windy for pleasant touring. The wind whipping up from the Antarctic can be nasty at times. Patagonian winds are famous—no infamous for their nastiness.

"After we leave Montevideo, I'll tell you about our stop in Puerto Madryn and two trips to animal preserves, one of them to see hundreds of thousands of pelicans, puffins— oops, I mean penguins. Well, good luck. See you tomorrow morning in Montevideo."

After the talk, Stephie returned to the cabin. She and Ben went to the safety drill on Promenade Deck. Everyone was wearing lifejackets, learning to adjust the straps. A ship's officer in starched whites was calling off names.

Next to them, the Rilleaus were swaying back and forth, dancing in place, humming. They talked briefly with Ben and Stephie and started to introduce themselves to other passengers.

Terry sang, "We're the Rilleaus. One-two-three—kick."

The officer taking the roll called out, "Ranier? Two persons?"

Ben shouted, "Here."

"Rilleaus. Two persons?"

Terry bellowed, "One couple, present!"

After returning their lifejackets, the two couples went up to the Sun Deck to watch the ship's departure from Buenos Aires.

It was their last view of Buenos Aires where a stone breakwater extended far out into the harbor. People were fishing from it, some leaning over bait buckets, baiting hooks. Some were silently smoking and staring out to sea with their poles positioned over the harbor waters. Each person seemed separate and alone. It was an eerie feeling as the ship slowly and silently passed this long jetty in a sort of half-light, slipping out to open sea in slow-motion as the lone figures on the jetty went about their business, unaware and uncaring of the luxury liner embarking on its journey.

No one waved. What did it have to do with them? What did their lives have to do with the lives of these transients? The cruise passengers and the fishermen were on different planets. A few men leaning on the rail of the ship envied the leisure and carefree spirit provided by a day of fishing; the men on the breakwater didn't give a thought to the alien ship or its passengers.

As the ship pulled out of the harbor with the long breakwater reaching into the great River Plate, a ghostly voice, an imperfect cracking sound from an old recording of the famous Carlos Gardel, came over the ship's loudspeaker, singing "Mi Buenos Aires Querido," bringing misty eyes to a few of the elderly Argentinean passengers.

"My beloved Buenos Aires
When I see you again
There will be neither sorrow nor forgetfulness."

21

After Buenos Aires was barely discernable on the horizon, Ben and his wife returned to their cabin to start unpacking.

After hurriedly unpacking, Ben said, "Steph, excuse me for a few minutes. I'll get out of your way while you're organizing your stuff. I'm going to run down to the Purser's Desk and see about foreign currency, maybe look in the boutiques if they're open now that we're at sea. I'll be right back."

The considerate husband scurried down the nearest stairwell like a squirrel in heat, his tail twitching wildly, looking for a mate. Aft of their cabin, two decks down to Caribe, he looked up and down the port passageway, saw only a few passengers way down toward the bow, and knocked on the door of C508.

Ann opened the door. The room was strewn with clothing and toiletries; she was in the middle of unpacking. They hugged and kissed; their tongues met. He probed her breasts, and his ever-ready sexual member swelled. They pressed as closely together as they could.

"I saw the Missus at the port lecture. Are you both going on the city tour of Montevideo?"

"Yes. It's not too long."

"Me too. I'll avoid your bus, naturally."

Ann, referring to the naturalist sitting next to Stephie at the lecture, asked, "Has the little woman found a shipboard stud already?"

Ben didn't have any idea what she was talking about and ignored her.

"Ann, I'm going to leave the table immediately after dinner tonight. I'm going to tell Steph I'll be in the casino. Will you be here?"

"Unless some geezer invites me to go discoing with him."

"Okay, I'll meet you here as soon as I can break away after dinner. Shortly before ten."

"Fine, Tarzan, and remember the acronyms KISS and PISS in your maneuvering. Keep It Simple, Stupid, and Play It Safe, Sexy."

Ben asked, "How's everything going?"

"So far, so good. The ship is beautiful. The Lewises wangled seats for us at the captain's table. How's that for a coup?"

"A great piece of beginner's luck."

"I want to see more of you on this ship than I did in Buenos Aires."

"Hey, I already told Stephie I'm not going on her penguin expeditions. I'm not into penguins."

"Oh, I love penguins. They're so cute. Maybe I'll go with Stephanie."

She seemed in a playful mood; he had feared she might be annoyed with him. Apparently she had had a few bon voyage cocktails and was feeling little pain. He reminded himself of her tendency to have one too many drinks, and her ease at getting intoxicated would have to be kept in check on the trip. He dared not say anything now though.

They kissed hungrily. Afterwards, in the passageway outside Ann's cabin, he almost bumped into a disagreeable cadaverous-looking man, the Smarmy Man, who gave Ben a leering smile. His front teeth were white, but his back teeth were stainless steel which along with the leer gave him an unpleasant look.

Ben headed toward the boutique just to cover his tracks. He'd buy some toiletries as proof he'd been there.

Back in the cabin, Ben unpacked. Stephie had finished her unpacking and was seated at the small desk, writing in her journal. He shaved and showered and began dressing in casual clothes. By 7:15, they were out the door and ready to have their first drink in the Parrot Lounge.

A young amiable British couple worked the bar. Ben and Stephie, bar people, took a liking to them from first sight. The barmaid, Julie, a charming personable blonde waited on them. She introduced her co-worker, her husband Peter, a rosy-cheeked smiling Liverpudlian.

Julie said, "You two look like real toddlers just out of your prams compared to the rest of this lot aboard ship. Last cruise, our average age was seventy-two, so we didn't have much night life in the disco. It was practically deserted most of the time. A little karaoke and that was all. Maybe this voyage will be peppier seeing we have some live wires like your lot aboard."

The husband-and-wife bar team made good martinis, were very pleasant, and were good at banter.

Both Stephie and Ben liked to schmooze with waiters and bartenders, the help in general. Some passengers weren't friendly with the crew, felt they were above that; they preferred being impersonal, wanting to maintain the old master-servant mentality, but Stephie and Ben liked to get to know the staff. They often found the young and outgoing help more interesting than their fellow passengers.

Many waiters and bartenders on ships tended to be adventurous, and they were usually full of ship gossip. If you got friendly with a bartender, you found out old Mrs. Green had died last night in the balcony of the show lounge and her remains were being kept in the meat locker for the balance of the trip, or your busboy was sleeping with your cabin stewardess, or old Mr. Harley was going to be put ashore at the next port for going down to the crew bar in an attempt to seduce a young Filipino deckhand, or the captain just barely missed hitting a whale on the last trip—all sorts of tidbits the other passengers were not privy to. A ship was a goldmine of gossip and intrigue.

Stephie and Ben were egalitarians with the staff, but they did have limits. They didn't like the waiters at dinner to get overly chummy. They found they got better service if they were slightly more formal, although they often had fun with comical waiters and busboys. Sometimes a waiter or busboy was infectiously funny, and they joined in. After all, you were on a ship to have a good time.

They struck up a conversation with a cocktail waiter named Sandy who stood next to them at the bar. He was a Brit, a charmer, the personality kid. He enjoyed badinage with the passengers, schmoozing with them. He seemed to enjoy talking with everyone. He joked with casino workers who walked by, as well as with Julie and Peter. If you asked him a question about the ship or crew, he answered it in all candor.

In Sandy's case, he didn't have to be circumspect; he was leaving the ship for good at the end of the cruise. He had signed on for a six-month contract, and this was his last cruise; he would be leaving the same day they did from Santiago. He had his eye on the main chance. He was ambitious, on the make, looking for opportunities. He said he had finished college.

He was strikingly handsome, six feet tall with pitch-black hair, nice teeth, and an infectious smile. He didn't have an ounce of fat, and yet he was not thin either. His was a well-proportioned, natural body. He was probably too lazy to work out and exuded a sexual emanation and aura. He was a sexy twenty-six-year-old.

One of his tricks was to spin his drinks tray in the palm of his hand, keeping it in play as he directed his sly sexy grin at females, ever the charmer who gave you the feeling he could also be a con artist. Of course he worked for tips.

He said he had a girlfriend in Leeds. No date had been set, but it turned out her family had money, and there was a chance he might enter the family business. Two couples came in and settled at tables across from the bar, so Sandy drifted off to wait on them.

After a time, Ben and Stephie became aware of a loud and profane voice coming from further down the bar. They glanced down three stools and saw a fat, bearded, heavy smoker and beer-swilling boor. He downed his beers at quite a clip. They could hear his foghorn voice echoing around the room. He was sloppily dressed, wearing shorts that were too tight for him. Like most obese persons, he looked ridiculous in shorts, his big bloated thighs, bulbous calves, and huge buttocks overflowing the shorts and the bar stool.

His loud voice was seldom still as he bellowed at the husband-and-wife bar team. From where they were seated, Stephie and Ben could hear him say he had a son who was a purser on the same cruise line. He shared some shop talk, company details with the bartenders. He seemed like an insider with all sorts of knowledge of the cruise company, company policies, and eccentricities.

He was the owner of a pub in Exeter, and they learned his name was Budgy Brooker.

"Just call me Budgy 'cause I raise the little winged fuckers."

Normally, they might have been drawn into a conversation with the fat bearded one but were put off by his boorishness, brashness and his general demeanor.

They listened to Budgy trying to advise Julie and Peter on buying a pub in England. His loud voice chanted, "It's a good living, it is, believe me. I run a free house, not a brewery pub. And my place is a little goldmine. I have a pub that caters to chimney pots, whatcha call a permanent group of residents, rather than fuckin' tourists."

Ben and Stephie were dressed for dinner in neat casual clothes, and they were hoping Budgy would soon be changing for dinner also. They had heard him mention he had late seating. Shorts weren't permitted in the dining room. At ten minutes past eight, the wife of the loud bearded boor showed up, a large woman, very plain looking, heavy but not overly fat, taller than he. She wore a frumpy, dowdy, unbecoming floral-printed dress Stephie thought could easily have been worn anywhere from 1920 onward.

She had a broad simple face, a country farmer's wife look, a woman who didn't seem to care much about her appearance or making an impression. Did she serve behind the bar at the pub? Did she make the salads, bake the steak and kidney pie, cook the lasagna, fry the fish and chips?

The wife reminded Budgy about dressing for dinner. Surely he wasn't going in those shorts? Budgy, the boor, ignored his spouse for a time, and heaved himself up off his fat haunches for a trip back to the cabin. The wife said something about his new Marks and Spenser leisure suit waiting for him on the bed.

Ben had some choice remarks to mutter after he left. "Enormous ego matches his fat ass. Budgy the bore. If you're not careful on a cruise, you can get stuck with and tarred and brushed by association with such an ass. The fat English fuck with the beard who never shuts up and his dowdy wife. Who but a mousy woman would ever marry an a-hole like that?"

Stephie defended her. "She seemed kinda sad, quiet but nice."

"She'd have to be nice to marry and stay with a clod like him."

Stephie gained her knowledge of people slowly by accretion, layer by layer the way a pearl is formed in an oyster shell, while Ben acquired his understanding of people full-blast; they came into his consciousness fully developed and whole, all at once in a sudden burst of understanding and knowledge. From the first meeting, he had them pegged, figured out, measured.

That was the way with Budgy, the fat souse at the bar. It was a sudden burst of insight for Ben. To Ben, Budgy was a boorish waste of time, a blowhard, someone in love with the sound of his own voice who lived in and for the world of the pub. In the first few minutes, Ben had him summed up, had drawn and quartered him.

Stephie was more hesitant. It took her several incidents, several instances, moments of discovery. She was fairer, more judicial in her assessment, but the end result was the same. To Ben, Budgy was an asshole, plain and simple. It took her a couple of days of new discoveries, new little insights, new experiences to formally bring charges and indict him, but she finally came to the same conclusion: guilty as charged; a jerk, a shit, a waste of time.

22

As they were finishing their second martinis, Stephie turned to Ben, "This first dinner aboard ship is always kind of a scary apprehensive time. Other than the Rilleaus and Kim and Doug, what if we get stuck with some freaks or bores, eccentrics or out-and-out nuts? Or Budgy?

"On one cruise with Uncle Lee, we had a weird woman who brought a big doll named Agnes to dinner with her every night. She sat the doll in a vacant chair next to her, and during the meal, she would make comments to it. 'The soup is rather good, isn't it, Agnes?' or 'Would you like me to cut your meat, Aggie?' Thank God the waiter hadn't set food in front of the doll. I think I would've gone insane if he had. How did that nutty woman get that vacant seat? Had she ordered it, or was it just free by chance?

"And, of course, Uncle Lee, always the jokester, started addressing the doll as if it were a real person. The woman loved it. Lee was lecturing on board the ship. Here she was sharing her fantasies with the ship's lecturer, and Lee led her on. Lee would say in his put-on British accent, 'Aggie, how was your day? Did you play bridge today? And, by the way, did you attend my lecture on Ceylon tea?'

"He kept it up the whole cruise. After a while, another couple at our table thought he was as batty as the doll-owner. Lee lapped it up and grinned like a big Cheshire cat.

"And this is a two-week cruise. What if we get someone who drools and has horrid table manners? Some old incontinent man or woman who smells vaguely of pee or who does number two in his trousers, or farts at odd moments?

"Now I'm sorry I rehashed that memory about the doll lady, because that's the cruise I took with Lee from Singapore to Bombay, identical to his last fatal cruise. It was in London after that cruise he was so savagely murdered, slaughtered."

"Now, Stephie, let's not go through all that again, please. Let's go down to dinner. And, please, at the table, don't bring up what happened to your Uncle Lee."

The round table was set for ten with only two newbies. Ben and Stephie smiled at their six tablemates who were already seated. They briefly joked with the Simpsons and the Rilleaus, then met their new tablemates, two elderly women. Stephie and Ben were introduced to the Kaufeld sisters, Ruthie and Katie. They were two spry and alert women in their mid-seventies.

The Kaufeld sisters enjoyed telling about themselves, alternating the narrative back and forth.

Katie began, "This is our thirty-fourth cruise. We live in Boca Raton, Florida. I'm the knitter . . ."

Ruthie continued, ". . . and I'm the walker. I bet I can walk the pants off any of you here. I love going to the gym . . ."

Ruthie finished her sister's sentence. This was the rhythm of their conversation, one beginning a thought, the second conveniently finishing it for her sibling.

Katie resumed, " . . . and she works out. We're just a couple of old spinsters who . . ."

". . . enjoy each other's company. Most nights in Florida we eat together. We go out to a lot of early-bird specials because it's. . ."

". . . a lot cheaper than eating at home, than cooking meals for ourselves. I hope we don't have blackened dolphin, shrimp scampi, or grouper. . ."

". . . on this ship because we've had just about enough of that crap. . ."

". . . this past season. We're sharing a cabin because it's cheaper than paying those ruinous. . ."

". . . single supplements. I guess the reason neither of us. . ."

". . . married was the way Mom and Dad fought like cats and dogs every moment of their lives, and we didn't. . ."

". . . want to take a chance. Plus, Dad, though we loved him dearly, was a terrible. . ."

". . . philanderer, fooled around with every stray skirt in Eire. . ."

Stephie glanced at Ben out the corner of her eye. He

looked off into space. The philandering father had hit a raw nerve with Ben and her.

". . . Pennsylvania's where we grew up. Squabbling parents, a father with a roving eye, a succession of creepy . . ."

". . . boyfriends. Sometimes we dated the same guy, and we'd agree, 'I'd rather raise a feral cat than live with that slob.'"

They loved gossiping about fellow passengers, did a lot of people-watching, and speculated on the lives and personalities of people they observed.

Ruthie later chatted about her desire to see the penguins on the trip, and when she found out Stephie wanted to go on the Punta Tombo trip, she suggested they go together. Katie was quieter. She was a good listener, and had a good memory. She had studied up on the ports, enjoyed crossword puzzles, and was an avid reader of mysteries and thrillers.

Katie said, "I guess we're just a couple of old spinsters who enjoy each other's company most of the time. We ain't dykes, so don't get any kinky ideas. We each have our own condos side-by-side in Boca, so we can be close by, but still give each other a lot of privacy and space. I can get away from Ruthie, and she can get away from me when she wants.

"Sometimes a day will go by at home when we only talk on the phone. One's own space is important to both of us. We get along most of the time, but we do have occasional spats too.

"Being in the same cabin for two weeks is always an adventure for us. We live part of the year in Cornwall, England. We were born in America, but most of our cousins and nephews and nieces live in Cornwall. In Penzance. On our holidays, we each stay with different nieces so we have our private space there as well."

Stephie thought, *They also must have big bucks to have separate condos and travel so much.*

In the center of the dining room, not far from the Ranier's table stood the big oval captain's table. Ben glanced over. Captain Marchland was holding court with a large group. Ann, facing Ben, was seated next to the silver-haired Mrs. Lewis. Next to Ann was the Smarmy Man whom Ben had seen in the passageway. He was trying to talk to Ann, but she was rebuffing him on general principle. The Smarmy Man glanced over in Ben's direction as if saying, *Look where I am, sucker.*

Stephie noticed the favored table and observed the naturalist, Mike Lambert, at one end talking to an attractive matron. Later, Mike spotted Stephie, waved, and gave her a winning smile.

Terry Rilleau said, "Marge and me are going to take line dancing classes and add it to our dancing repertoire."

Marge put in, "Dance till you drop is our motto."

Doug Simpson said, "Hey, have any of you guys been watching CNN lately? Have you been keeping up with the scandal about our fearless leader, Bill Clinton? The peccadilloes and sexual life of our esteemed President. It sounds as if his girlfriend was only twenty-three. Robbing the cradle, I guess."

Terry added, "Yes, an intern in the White House, and he's old enough to be her father. How's he possibly going to talk his way out of this one?"

Katie said, "I don't think he's going to be able to get out of it this time. I think the public's going to drive him out of office."

Ben said, "If it's all true. We don't know anything yet. We'll have to wait and see how this all plays out. Who the hell is leaking all stuff? Isn't this supposed to be a confidential investigation until specific charges are made? It certainly isn't the White House leaking it."

Ruthie added, "But, please, when he was elected by such a huge plurality in '96 and originally in '92, didn't everyone know this guy liked to chase skirts? Is this really anything new? Didn't people already know? Didn't he say he had troubles in his marriage, and didn't Hillary discount this along with everyone else? Weren't there old girlfriends floating around everyone knew about in '92?"

Doug said, "But, Ben, don't they say in the news business some stories have legs, will hang around? It's not going to go away. It'll be with us for a long time."

Ben just nodded.

Stephie thought of Hillary and her position, and she sympathized with her. Ben thought of Clinton's position, and agonized over it. *God, if I ever get caught on this trip, I'm going to be in real deep shit. Deeper than the shit Clinton is in. God, what an asshole I am. Why did I ever do this?*

During dessert, Stephie thought, *So far, so good with the tablemates. Katie and Ruthie seem like they might be fun.*

Ben could be good with older women, could get them going, joking, win them over with his gentle kidding, if he was in the mood. You never could tell when it would strike him to be Mr. Geniality. He loved to find out about the essence of someone's personality and then trigger reminiscences or sometimes start mock arguments.

After a brief meeting with someone, he would know the right buttons to push. He had a good memory. During lulls in conversation or when he wanted to set someone off on a reverie, he would make an oblique reference to a topic that would get the other person going. It was a parlor trick he used. Occasionally someone would catch on and call him on it.

Often after dinner on cruises, Stephie and Ben would go their separate ways. She liked the shows; he like to spend time in the casino or looking in the bars or disco. Tonight, Ben said he was going to try the casino, and Kim convinced Stephie to join her and Doug for the introductory show.

The show began with the ship's orchestra, and the cruise director with his wireless microphone introduced himself from backstage. He bounded onstage into the spotlight, a big smile, all bonhomie, and introduced himself.

"Most people come from humans, but very appropriately for this particular voyage I come from Wales. Is there anybody on board from New York tonight?"

Much cheering and applause. "I just wanted to let you know your homes are being robbed as we speak. Hey, but you New Yorkers are insured, right?"

"Anyone here a retiree from Florida?"

Again much cheering and applause. "A new airline has been started in Florida called SCOFA, the Senior Citizens of Florida Airlines. Its motto is 'You've seen us drive; wait until you see how we fly.'"

He introduced his cruise staff. The ship's lead singers, Jerry and Debbie Blunt, sang a few old favorites, one of the ship's comedians told a few jokes, and he mentioned how great the ship's naturalist was going to be on the following day.

"You've got to hear and see Mike Lambert. He is absolutely fabulous. Before your very eyes he becomes a penguin, not with a costume, but with sheer acting ability. It isn't a lecture. It's a show I think would make it on Broadway. The man is incredible. He's so entertaining and informative."

Directly from dinner Ben had gone to Ann's cabin where the two soon became deeply involved in a sexual encounter. Their passionate twinings seemed to take on more excitement when they knew they were playing with fire and had a limited amount of time. There was enough time for a passionate consummation. It turned out to be more of an oral experience than either had expected.

23

On Sunday morning, a little after eight, Ben and Stephie were sitting at a window in the Parrot Lounge, watching as the ship approached the Montevideo harbor. The ship was late making landfall. They were waiting for the ship to tie up so their city tour could be called. Sandy, twirling his tray, was working in the lounge serving coffee, soft drinks, and an occasional Bloody Mary.

He leaned over their table saying, "Aha, there's the pilot boat coming alongside. Let's see if my mates made it back. Friday night when we left Montevideo, three of the lads stayed there to have a good time at the dance clubs. We do it on each cycle. They said they'd catch the pilot boat and meet up with us when the ship pulled in so they could get to their jobs aboard ship on time today."

He leaned way over for a better view. "Yeah, there they are, looking much the worse for wear after spending two nights in all of the dens of iniquity the town has to offer. I hope they'll be able to jump aboard when the pilot boat pulls alongside without falling in the drink. They look decidedly unsteady to me. Ah, good show, mates. Cheers. They made it aboard, and the pilot boat is clearing away now."

Uninhibited Sandy had let them in on a little inside crew lore they otherwise would have been unaware of. Passengers and crew lived in two separate worlds, and on this ship with the huge age difference between crew and passengers, it wasn't unusual for them to exist in different galaxies.

The Silver Cloud, a super luxury sailing ship along the lines of a mega-yacht, was just entering the harbor, following in their wake from Buenos Aires.

Later, Stephie and Ben descended the gangway and were on Uruguayan soil. Huge piles of timber were stacked up on the dock near the ship either to be shipped in or out of the country. A short distance from the gangway was a memorial, the *Admiral Graf Spee* anchor, a reminder of one of the city's most famous historical events.

The guide on the bus was a pleasant woman named Alexandra who announced, "You are to reboard at 1:30 in the afternoon. Our city tour will be over before that so you'll have some free time to wander around on your own.

"Our country has three million people, and nearly half of its inhabitants live here in the city of Montevideo. Today, the downtown will be deserted. Because of the beautiful weather, people will be out enjoying the summer sun at the beaches or at resorts like Punta del Este way out of town.

"The city was founded in 1726 by the Spanish who were vying with the Portuguese. Great Britain was instrumental in establishing Uruguay as a buffer country between Brazil and Argentina because it did not want one country, Argentina, to control both coasts of the river and put it in a position to limit international traffic. We are on the Rio Plate, named according to tradition, because it looked like a river of painted silver.

"Uruguay has had a tradition of democracy except for the early seventies to the mid-eighties when we had a military government and dictatorship."

Stephie thought, *So what else is new? Here in South America there were always these swings between military governments and democracies, back and forth. It's a fact of life, a typical condition in South America. The military down here have a mindset which enables them at certain times to seize control, supposedly for the good of the country. It has become a cultural tradition.*

Alexandra continued, "Now I must say something we cannot be proud of. It is our treatment of the Indian population. The European settlers, the European white population, exterminated the indigenous Indian population. One of the flimsy excuses given was the Indians were annihilated because they didn't know how to read or write. The real reasons were the Indians had claims to land; they posed a threat; the whites were of a different religion, a different language, and a different cultural background.

"Today, we would call it ethnic cleansing and genocide. You will see hardly anyone of Indian heritage in this country, and it is something we cannot hide or evade. Argentina has the same dark history."

Stephie believed Alexandra had more social and political consciousness than most guides, and she doubted other guides would even bring the subject up. Maybe their guide had her own agenda and a subversive streak.

This was a prelude for a tour around the deserted capitol grounds. Both Stephie and Ben agreed the building was monumentally boring.

Back on the bus, Stephie was trying to catch Alexandra's words about the city, but a familiar blatant voice behind her was making it difficult to hear the guide. She glanced around, and there was the fat bearded boorish Budgy seated next to his dowdy wife. The guide, over the bus's deficient public address system, had an accent which in the best of conditions would be rather difficult to understand, but with competition from the oaf was annoyingly difficult to hear.

The loudmouth was talking to his wife about somewhere in Spain, comparing it to the streets they were passing through. His information was neither interesting nor pertinent.

"That gray building at the corner is tilting at an angle, I wonder why they don't tear it down."

On he blathered. Stephie was a stickler for listening to tour guides, paying careful attention, taking notes, something she had garnered from her travel-writing uncle. She was sorely tempted to turn around and shush him, but her good manners and innate reticence to create scenes prevented her from doing so. Ben was in another world, looking out the window, apparently unaware of the distraction or perhaps preoccupied with his own thoughts. *Who knew with him?*

Stephie caught some of what the guide was saying, but because the boorish bearded wonder was so in love with the sound of his own voice, she missed some of what was said.

That self-important asshole. I'd love to turn around and ream him out. In a way I feel sorry for his poor wife. She learned long ago to put up with her churlish clod of a husband. She genuinely seems to enjoy being a tourist while he is bored unless there's a beer tap in front of him. She seems very contented.

The next stop was in the city's old central plaza, which in the years before automobiles had been the center of action. The zocolos or central plazas were a frequent stop for city orientation tours—easy parking and historical and cultural significance without a hint of any relevance to the life of most residents' present-day lives. Old downtowns every-where tell nothing about the life of contemporary ordinary people. Every South American city and town had its central square, its Independencia or Plaza De Armas, and every town showed it off to its tourists. The old and the poor were left to shuffle around in these downtowns.

Here they were at 9:20 AM on a Sunday morning looking at the lack of life and action. Even the usual downtown types, the bums, drunks, cranks, weirdos, and whackos hadn't had a chance to wake up, have their breakfasts, and start wandering around. Even the stray dogs and pigeons were in short supply amid the neglected, decaying, bird shit-spattered monuments.

Even so, the square overall was an attractive one with palm trees, a big poster of Gardel, a variety of architectural styles surrounding it, and a pleasant downhill view of the parliament building they had just left.

The only action around the square was provided by the busloads full of tourists who had been dumped there, and who were now taking pictures of things long forgotten.

Some tourists hurried across the street to take pictures of the Teatro Solis, a beautiful and important old opera house. The guide told them Caruso, Pavlova, Toscanini, Nijinski, and Bernhadt had appeared there.

Back aboard the bus, their guide told them the square was the dividing line between the old and new city. Before crossing over into the newer city, they drove deeper into the old part where there were a number of ornate old European-style buildings with exquisite nineteenth century architectural details, florid and flamboyant touches.

As they drove through the major avenues of the old section on that Sunday morning, everything was quiet and dead. It was like an old movie set that hadn't been used for years. Perhaps these were like Hollywood backlots, just facades held up by wooden braces from behind.

Alexandra commented on a beautiful old building, previously the home of an important shop, once headed for the wrecking ball; it had superb green tile-work and had been converted and resurrected into a McDonalds. It was situated on an important city corner. At a movie house nearby, the film *Titanic* was playing.

Alexandra said, "I know you came from Buenos Aires. Like the Argentines, we are great eaters of beef. Uruguay raises mucho sheep and cattle. Leather and wool goods are important here. When wool prices are low, the economy suffers.

"We are also great lovers of tango. You will find many similarities between the Argentines and us. We, too, like our maté, the strong herbal tea. Many Argentines take ferries over here for an outing and go to our beaches.

"If you had the time, you could visit our gaucho museum. Gauchos were very important to the life of our country, legendary like the American cowboys. Originally they were nomadic; they went where the work was. Then with the establishment of the big estancias, they settled down to work in one place. The ranches became bigger and bigger, and eventually they were owned by a few wealthy influential families who ran the country."

Stephie, the traveler, was trying to absorb the words of the guide, taking notes. Her husband was thinking of his next sexual encounter, fantasizing about oral sex and new pleasurable positions.

One of their stops was at an impressive lifelike statue grouping that almost looked like a scene out of the American

West. A stalwart ponchoed gaucho astride a rearing horse was alongside an oxcart drawn by a team of six sinewy straining oxen. His cart had become mired in the mud. It was a naturalistic scene that depicted the spirit and independence of a pioneer people.

Stephie and Ben circled the statuary. Both were taking pictures, impressed by the size and emotional feelings expressed by the piece.

The bearded loud mouth Budgy had not been getting out at the various stops, but his dowdy wife dutifully got off to snap pictures. She would take pictures of inconsequential things at strange angles. He encouraged her to do her own thing. She had few outlets traveling with a boozer like him. Often she would aim her camera at objects outside the windows of the moving bus. She was unlikely to get very telling pictures, Stephie thought.

Her bored husband kept her occupied. "Take a picture of that building. Take a picture of that man and dog. See if you can get that filthy beggar." He had no interest in taking photographs. His conversation, rather his monologue, would be about some event in his life completely unrelated to the places they passed.

The bus drove by a big soccer stadium. Through the curtain of blah-blah-blah issuing from Budgy, Stephie thought she heard the stadium held seventy-thousand fans and also thought she heard Alexandra say Uruguay had hosted the first World Cup soccer match in 1930.

The bus started to drive through a wealthier residential section. They drove along beautiful broad boulevards, tree-bordered avenues, with walled homes, estates, and golf courses.

The bus stopped at a real oddity, a building that looked like it had been designed by Barcelona's Gaudi. It was a small castle or mansion in a state of disrepair, being renovated to turn it into a museum. The people on the tour bus got off and wandered through the small elegant ruin. In places, the roofs had disappeared.

Just as they stepped from their bus, Ben caught sight of

Ann who was just boarding the bus that preceded them at the castle. With Stephie looking the other way, he was able to nod to her. She smiled imperceptibly. They both got a little buzz from this intrigue, the frisson in what they were doing like a couple of adolescents fooling their parents.

A gay man named Peter who had designed the castle died in his eighties in 1966 and left his castle to his French lover who, in turn, left it to the city to become the Museo Pitanglio. Peter had been an alchemist, a strange hobby for a man of the twentieth century.

From the speculative science of alchemy had come various symbols and signs, which he had incorporated into the design and ornamentation of his house such as circle motifs representing eternity. Alchemy had searched for means of prolonging life and conquering incurable diseases. The guide brought them inside into one little atrium where she explained the exotic symbols duplicated in various parts of the house.

Built in 1911, it was not overly large, but was an individualistic house crowded between other buildings on an ordinary street. Some parts were badly in need of repair; other sections had been renovated.

Next came the highlight of their trip, the busy beach area, mile after mile packed with people out early in the day. They passed people sunning themselves, enjoying the balmy weather, lying on beach chaises, in parks, relaxing, swimming, drinking maté. It was a real revelation how active the beaches were after the deserted downtown.

Stephie commented, "It's so early and already so many people at the beaches."

Ben answered, "It's Sunday. Everybody's working on their tans, enjoying their maté."

It was Montevideo at play, a prosperous relaxed place. Alexandra reported in their summer many vacationers came from other South American countries such as Argentina, Brazil, Colombia, and Venezuela to enjoy what was the playground of South America.

The guide said, "Our country has a reputation for safety

and security. Prices are right. People come for our glorious beaches, our casinos, restaurants, discos, and clubs."

The seafront promenade and its sandy beaches were full of tanned people, many in skimpy bikinis, alive with the morning joggers, walkers, and sports enthusiasts all on the twenty kilometers of sandy beach on the River Plate.

The bus made a vista stop at the top of a hill overlooking a wide expanse of beaches. In the distance they could see row after row of high condos, hotels, and apartment buildings. It was a pretty spot in an upscale residential area.

Stephie said, "It reminds me of Estoril in Portugal."

Alexandra, at the end of the tour, said, "We will be stopping at the Casio Mario, a leather factory and store. You can walk down that hill to the port, take a shuttle back later, or you can stay with me, and we'll take you back in twenty minutes after you've had time to look around and shop."

Tony Tantera climbed onto the bus and got on the P.A. "For those who are good walkers and adventuresome, you can go back by walking downhill on Calle Rio Plate to the port. It's a fairly long walk with nothing to see, so don't say I didn't warn you."

The leather store was in the middle of a business area where everything else was closed. A series of stalls had been set up in front of the store. Even Budgy deigned to step down and examine the merchandise. Stephie heard him.

"Mostly shite," he commented to Dowdy.

Stephie needed to get in some walking; she wanted to get away from Budgy, wanted time to herself.

Outside the bus, Stephie turned to Ben. "I'm going to walk back. Want to join me?"

"You go along. I'm not into hiking right now. Hon, you can go without me. I want to get back to the port and maybe take some pictures around there."

Ben stopped to examine some leather coats. Stephie wandered around on her own. She happened to look off to the right. At the end of a row of stalls, the dwarfish man appeared for a second, then suddenly disappeared down an aisle. Stephie was disconcerted, completely unsure of what she had seen. Tony was standing at a stand piled with magazines. She approached him.

"Tony, pardon me, but I could swear I saw someone I saw on the streets of Buenos Aires."

"Oh, that wouldn't be unusual at all. Buenos Aires is right across the river from Montevideo. Ferries go back and forth all the time. People go between the two cities just for the day. Unless of course the person is on our ship, a passenger or crew member."

"I don't think so."

"A ghost maybe?"

Stephie looked for Ben, and saw him climbing on the bus. The bus pulled away before she had a chance to change her mind. She turned and started walking briskly down Calle Rio Plata in the direction of the port.

24

Once Stephie was away from the leather store, she was on a deserted street. As she headed downhill, a grimy gray van passed her. Further on, she could see the port and the ship. She noticed Calle Eduardo Lanze seemed to be a shortcut street leading to the port. She headed down the street, still in a completely deserted area.

Not a smart move, girl. Dumb!

The street had no life at all, only closed office buildings. The dusty beaten-up gray van parked about one hundred-yards ahead of her in the middle of the block on the opposite side as she headed further down the street. The rear doors of the van opened, and two men in coveralls alighted. A third man was in the back of the van. With its doors left open, Stephie could see the van was full of boxes. The driver's door opened and remained ajar.

The men were glancing back casually, but not staring at her. Stephie was very apprehensive. Should she go on or rush back? She hesitated a bit, then decided to continue on. A fourth man, wearing a black leather jacket, got out of driver's side.

The two men in coveralls headed slowly in her direction. Stephie was terrified. She looked behind her for an escape route. What would happen if she turned and ran for it? She was frozen in place momentarily, trying to decide whether to turn and run like hell. Then she looked back up the street and saw a vehicle approaching. After a few scary moments, she realized it was a very slow-moving police cruiser with two officers in the front seat.

The two coveralled men saw the cruiser approaching. They turned back, returned to the van, and started unloading boxes from the rear door. Stephie speeded up, passed the van, half running. She reached the end of the street where it intersected a main boulevard with numerous pedestrians.

The police car passed her; one officer flicked his hand to his cap in a greeting to her. She smiled and waved. She was shaking. She hurried on until she was inside the port area.

She was frightened. It had seemed like a close call although she couldn't be sure what the men in the van had been up to. Stephie entered a roofed market within the port boundary next to the ship. Passengers from the ship and crew members were roaming around.

After buying an international phone card from a stall, she was soon at a pay phone talking. "Chief, I'm sure I wasn't imagining it. That's exactly what happened. I'm sorry to be calling you at home, but I wanted to keep you informed and find out what I should do. You told me to call you if something untoward happened."

Stephie could imagine the tall burly man, the Director of the National Security Agency, sitting in the greenhouse behind his house, a trowel in one hand and a mobile phone in the other. Her boss's voice sounded soothing, reassuring, confidence-building.

"No, Stephie, you did the right thing calling me. Don't overreact. We know more than we can say on the phone. You're not out there alone. Brace yourself. Is there any possibility your husband Ben could be involved in any of this?"

Stephie gripped the phone tightly, her eyes widened. She looked horrified.

"What in God's name do you mean? How could Ben be involved? And why?"

"Steph, promise me you will not bring this up with him. Don't say anything to him about it. And listen to me carefully . . ."

"I am. But what the hell's going on?"

"If anything, anything, comes up about Ben, promise me you'll call and tell me before confronting him."

"I. . . but. . . okay. I will. But you have to explain."

"All I can say right now is watch your pretty little rear end. We're keeping an eye on you from here on out. Stay alert and focused."

"But, this Ben thing?"

"One thing may have nothing to do with the other. Just play it cool with him, and watch out for yourself. Remember, don't give anything away to him."

Stephie stepped away from the phone. She could hardly feel reassured. More questions had been raised than answered. What was this Ben stuff? All she could think of was he was somehow gathering material for a story there in South America, and she had become entangled in some intrigue. She promised herself not to let on to him what she had heard.

She wandered around the Puerto Mercado, an outdoor and indoor complex with its warren of food stalls, seafood and steak restaurants, and sidewalk cafés.

Kim and Doug were seated at a coffee place down one of the aisles. Kim called Stephie over.

Kim said, "Steph, have some of this pure caffeine espresso. Hey, you look like you've seen a ghost. Are you okay, hon?"

Ben had hurried back on board and scurried directly to Ann's cabin. She had just returned from her tour. They put out the "Do Not Disturb" sign and had a passionate session. While his wife sat considering her fate, he was engaged in his single-minded pursuit of his next orgasm.

When she left the Mercado, Stephie stayed close to Kim and Doug. It seemed to bring her a feeling of security. Doug took pictures of some half sunken hulks that lay in the harbor beyond the *Global Quest*. Then he photographed the anchor of the old *Graf Spee* with its 1939 inscription.

As they approached the *Global Quest*, he took shots of a junky old rust-bucket of a ship called *The Calypso* tied up next to their liner.

When she reunited with Ben that afternoon, Stephie gave nothing away and said nothing about her frightening run-in. It wasn't difficult playing a role with him; after all, they had both been playing parts for years. Actors who performed eight times a week in a play probably had it easy compared to them.

Actors had a set script to follow. A lot of what the Ably-Raniers had to do, like many other teetering married couples, including the Rodman-Clintons, involved innovative choreography and improvisation. You had to learn to think fast and act on your feet. Unlike real actors, you didn't have the playwright's lines to fall back on.

25

As the ship left Montevideo, many passengers, including Ben and Stephie, were up on deck to listen to Captain Marchland's account of the Graf Spee encounter over the P.A.

Captain Marchland was on the bridge of the ship, looking out over the sea, speaking into a microphone while a helmsman tended the wheel. Two officers peered through binoculars.

The captain said, "We are now four miles out from Montevideo. To our port side, you can see a buoy that marks the remains of the scuttled ship, the *Graf Spee* in its watery grave under not too many fathoms of the briny deep. You cannot see any of the wreck above water. It was one of the most remarkable stories of World War II. I beg your indulgence as I narrate the story of that epic event."

The ship slowly circled the gravesite as he gave his commentary.

"One of our next stops on our great recreative sea odyssey will be the Falkland Islands where so recently in history, Argentina and Great Britain fought a war over the sovereignty of the islands.

"Off the Falklands in World War I, in December of 1914, Admiral Maximilian Graf von Spee, a great German naval war hero, went down with his ship.

"In the month of December, twenty-five years later, a historic event took place at this very spot. In the early days of World War II, the Germans had a battleship named after their World War I naval hero, Admiral Graf Spee. The battleship, *Graf Spee*, a surface raider, a menace, was loose in the South Atlantic, terrorizing, preying on helpless English merchant ships it was sinking with impunity.

"If the Germans could disrupt shipping with submarines and marauding surface raiders like cruisers and battleships, they could seriously hamper the efforts of England and indeed Europe to survive. The *Graf Spee*'s captain was named Langsdorff.

"A small British fleet of three smaller British warships was sailing against the German behemoth. The British Allied commander, Commodore Harwood, was in charge. His mission was to protect British shipping from the River Plate to Rio de Janiero. A cat-and-mouse game was taking place between the German battleship and the British warships. There were parallels with 1914 when the Admiral von Spee was tricking the British. Harwood hoped the *Spee* would take his bait. He lured her toward the Rio Plate, into a route full of rich targets for the German marauder.

"On the morning of December 13, 1939, Harwood's ships, the *Exeter*, the *Ajax*, and the *Achilles*, were near the mouth of the river. The *Achilles* was a New Zealand ship."

Stephie reminded Ben of the New Zealand woman they had met on the little train in the suburbs of Buenos Aires who had talked about wanting to see the site of her grandfather's wartime experiences. Her grandfather had been stationed on the *Achilles*.

Stephie couldn't believe she could be so civil to Ben, still her husband, but a man she had been warned about by her employer. But, by instinct, she knew how to play her role. She had been well-schooled in deception and deceit as part of her job training.

The captain said, "The German Langsdorff misjudged the force before him, thinking they were one cruiser and two destroyers when actually they were three cruisers. Cruisers have more firepower than destroyers. The three ships attacked the battleship from different quarters. Langsdorff made for the *Exeter*. He should have taken off under a smoke screen. It was a battle in which the courage of both sides was sorely tested.

"The Commodore dispersed his tiny fleet of three ships against Langsdorff, who had superior range and weight by virtue of his eleven-inch guns. The *Exeter* sent eight-inch salvos, which struck the *Spee*, but the *Exeter* was hit and badly crippled. Salvos from the other two ships, however, were reaching and damaging the *Spee*.

"The German battleship was getting hit from three directions. It was too much for the *Spee,* which finally turned away under a smoke screen and headed for the River Plate. The *Exeter* was hit again and put out of action. The *Ajax* and *Achilles* were in hot pursuit. *Spee* turned its heavy guns on the *Ajax* and several of her gun turrets were knocked out.

"Fight was broken off. The *Ajax* and *Achilles* turned away from the German battleship and followed at a greater distance while the *Spee* made for Montevideo. At midnight, the *Spee* entered the Montevideo harbor. The crew started repairing damage and landing their dead and wounded.

"The *Ajax* and the *Achilles* waited outside the harbor and were soon joined by the *Cumberland,* which had sped from the Falklands. Winston Churchill, head of the British Admiralty at the time, wanted the *Spee* interned for the duration of the war and neutered as a naval threat.

"Langsdorff radioed German high command. Hitler and his admirals would not accept internment in Uruguay. They ordered, 'Fight your way through to Buenos Aires, or attempt effective scuttling and destruction of the ship.'

"On December 17 Langsdorff had seven-hundred men transferred to a German merchant ship in Montevideo harbor. Later, they were made prisoners and confined in Argentina in the province of Cordoba where many of their descendants still live.

"The *Spee* headed out of the harbor, watched by an enormous crowd on shore. She steamed seaward where she was awaited by the three British cruisers. Rather than risk capture, Langsdorff blew the ship up, scuttled her. On December 19 Captain Langsdorff committed suicide.

"It was an exhilarating great victory for Britain. It enhanced prestige and morale at a critical time in the war when British morale was at a low point. Winston Churchill called the tactics of the *Graf Spee* 'daring and imaginative,' but saw the event as a crucial turning point for naval warfare in World War II."

The engines of the *Global Quest* had restarted.

Captain Marchland said, "Here lies a famous chapter in the history of world naval history. It was twenty-five years between the time Admiral Graf Spee died on his ship off the Falklands and the time the *Admiral Graf Spee* was scuttled here outside of Montevideo. We are going through historic waters, the graveyard of many ships, the tombs of many brave men. It offers us an opportunity to reflect on the futility and the horrible waste of human lives that come from war. Amen."

Stephie decided the captain was either a good showman, a man who thrived on melodrama, or a man given to pomposity either by nature or for comic or dramatic effect.

26

The second evening, the table had been set for nine. The newcomer turned out to be Eddie Fisk, a dapper nattily dressed man in his late fifties, who was already seated. Introductions and polite conversations began. Eddie was one of the ship's compensated hosts, hired to squire female guests.

Kim tried to get Eddie into the conversation, and it turned out to be a breeze, because he was used to polite social conversation as part of his job.

"So you're one of the ship's escorts?"

"Yes, I'm engaged by the ship to dance with the ladies, make myself useful when needed, mostly schmooze with the old broads."

Katie, in jest, exclaimed, "Shame on you. My sister and I are not to be considered old broads."

"With knockouts like you and Ruthie, I'd be glad to dance the night away. You're not broads, you're dolls. I love this job. The only way I can afford to take cruises is as a subsidized host."

Terry commented, "Well, you're a good dancer, aren't you?"

The Rilleaus began swaying back and forth rhythmically as if they were dancing while they were seated.

Eddie said, "I love dancing. It's a good way to get a free cruise, but it's tough on your feet. I'm either dancing with the gals or going on the land tours, chaperoning, pushing wheelchairs, maneuvering walkers, finding lost canes and crutches. My feet are killing me at the end of the day."

Marge said, "But think of the free cruises."

"Yeah, dancing with all those gals for about three hours a day. Listening to them whine at meals. Constantly having to make small talk."

Kim asked, "Any chance for romances, flirtations, aboard ship?"

"That's frowned on. A host joke told on many ships is about a woman who warned a host, saying, 'I don't play doctor and nurse, so don't get any weird ideas. I've seen it all, done it all, and had it all, so just make small talk and dance.'"

Katie said, "You must meet some younger women on the cruises."

"Last cruise, there were two women at my table, a very attractive younger one, a real knockout, and a not-so-attractive older one."

Kim noted, "Like a mother and daughter?"

"Uh-huh. I met the attractive one by paying lots of attention to the older one. You have to throw a bone to the old dog in order to pet the puppy."

Everyone laughed at Eddie's frankness and the humor he brought to his job.

Ben glanced over at the captain's table where Ann was listening to the captain. The Smarmy Man always seemed to be leering in Ben's direction.

At his table, the captain was talking about some of the passengers giving him advice or looking important while the ship was docking or setting sail. He called them passenger bridge assistants. They would often motion to stevedores ashore as if they were giving disembarkation or embarkation instructions.

"They're harmless. Just a little bit dotty. When they have whistles and blow them as if they are deck officers assisting in landings and embarkations, then we have to chastise them and take their whistles away from them. No offense meant, ladies and gentlemen, but on a long cruise, you do get your share of nutters. Maybe they empty out the loony bins to fill up our cabins, eh?"

27

Monday was a blessed full day at sea. Stephie was looking forward to the widely anticipated talk by the ship's naturalist. That morning in the Lido, Stephie and Ben were having breakfast.

Stephie said, "This morning the penguin man, Doctor Mike Lambert, the ship's naturalist, is giving his talk. Everyone says he's one of the highlights of the trip. You're going to be there, aren't you?"

"Do I have to? I know all you gals have been creaming over him, but he's not my type. Do you think I really have to listen to someone talk about dull strutting penguins?"

"Yes, you should! I'll meet you in the showroom after I do my laps around the Promenade Deck."

Stephie got to the showroom early and took a front row seat. She saved a seat for Ben. Eventually, she had to give it to Ruthie Kaufeld who wanted to go on the penguin trip with her.

The theater darkened for about twenty seconds, then loud miked donkey-like braying filled the room. The stage area was suddenly lit. Mike Lambert, dressed head to toe in a black outfit, hopped onto the stage on his knees, wearing penguin-like feet attached to his knees. He waddled across the stage with the gait of a penguin. He wore a close-fitting cap that made his head resemble a penguin's.

He hopped around with his knees together as if they were hobbled. He spoke, almost in a squawk.

"I am a male Magellanic penguin. I cannot fly, but boy can I swim. I am one of many thousands of us penguins at Punta Tombo along the beaches, in the dunes and hillocks.

"I am looking for the exact burrow I used last year. By some instinctual biological magic, I find my former home, a hole in the ground, out of all the thousands of burrows. I kick around some dirt and prepare my burrow.

128

"It is late September. I give my squawking male call like the braying of a donkey, just like this: hee haw, hee haw, ee, aw. That's why some of you dumb unthinking human beings call me the jackass penguin.

"I am here four or five days ahead of my mate. I get some presents ready, rocks, twigs, bright objects, just stuff. Oh, here come the broads now. Instinct is a wonderful thing. Hey, one of you show some interest in me."

Mike popped a shiny smooth red stone out from between his joined knees, pushed it in front of him.

"Here is a present. Look at that; how's that for a pretty stone? My present, my trophy. I'm looking for a good-looking bird to mate with. I will hear her braying. I'll listen for strong resonant braying, which means she is a good breeder. The bray that is solid betokens health and fecundity and all that is maternal and, of course, sexy. Being well-fed, fatter, plumper, is a good sign too. Pick a good mate, and I'll get better offspring. We'll get better chicks, me and her. Hey, I ain't no dummy, you know."

Mike kicked the stone with his penguin feet, really his knees, over to Stephie who was seated in the first row. Stephie thought he had picked her deliberately. He looked intently at her. With his head, he motioned toward the stone. He kept gesturing. She smiled, reddened and picked it up.

"Wow, babe, doll, now you're in for it. That's my gift to you, baby. We penguins are monogamous birds. I'm still braying. Hee, haw, ee, aw. Here I am. Look at me. Come to me. You look like a partner who is great for breeding, even though you're not quite plump enough. Hey, I'm also a politician. Oh, wow, but are you in trouble, babe. You have accepted my gift. We have just mated for life. Now we do some mutual preening of each other.

"You took my rock, sweetie; now you better be prepared to get your rocks off with me. We'll make beautiful music, have chicks together. After we prepare our burrow, we'll have twenty whole seconds of bliss for the actual breeding, so don't blink, mon cheri. It may be the best twenty seconds of euphoria you ever have."

Stephie blushed deeply. Lambert let out a series of ungodly brays. The theater was full, and the audience, roaring with laughter, applauded, loved every minute of it. This man had become a penguin and was imparting essential information in the most dynamic of ways.

"It is breeding time. Listen to me. You look like you have been to midnight buffet and would make me a fine mate. How about it? Look at the gifts I am proffering. We touch bills. After we preen each other, it's time. Now we have about twenty seconds of exquisite breeding. Real quality time. And afterward we light up Kool cigarettes and breathe in deeply, contentedly, and we are richly satisfied."

Mike waddled around the stage, braying, then returned to Stephie.

"You, the female, stay ashore for about fifteen days in mid-October. The first egg comes after four days."

Mike took out a red Delicious apple and deposited it on the stage.

"Four days later, another egg is laid."

Mike laid another Delicious apple on the stage.

"For sixteen days, you cover and heat the eggs while I go grocery shopping in the ocean. I return and settle in for seventeen days while you do your chores. Thirty-two days after the first egg is laid, it hatches. A baby chick is born. Our chick."

Mike produced a furry downy little stuffed gray creature, a baby bird. "Folks, they sell these in the ship's boutique for eleven bucks and change. They make great souvenirs. I know a Magellanic penguin shouldn't be shilling for the ship's store, but what the heck, we all gotta make a buck. Our eggs, Stephie, are hatched several days apart."

Stephie was surprised he used her name.

"Four days later, a second chick is born."

He produced another furry stuffed chick.

"The births are staggered in this way so that there is more of a chance of survival. If one dies, there is a second. Now competition for food begins.

"We, the mom and dad, have exactly the same markings, though being the male, I'm slightly heavier. We have to feed our chicks enormous amounts of food.

"Scientists studying us penguins call it insulative biparental rearing. Safety of the chicks is critical. If we go away from the burrow, the chicks will follow us, so we shoo them back.

"For thirty days, we two parents gather food for the chicks, food like krill, little shrimp, and squid. Off Punta Tombo, there's a great food supply. We forage for food, an amazing amount of food."

Lambert became a real actor as he reenacted the feeding rituals, moving his neck and head over the stuffed chick.

"It's a straight regurgitation pipe from us to the chicks. In five days, our chicks double their weight, then triple in the next five, and within thirty days, they weigh about two pounds. As we feed, we shake our heads like this in the feeding ritual.

"By January, our chicks weigh about four pounds. During the day, we make many trips going and coming, to and from the sea. You will see us penguins making our trips, shopping, going to the ocean supermarket. We are daytime birds. One of us usually stays at the nest with the kids, but sometimes if food is in short supply, both of us parents will leave for two or three days for food-gathering expeditions."

Mike addressed Stephie again.

"Next year, I'll do the same pretty rock thing. It says, 'Here I am. Come back to me, cheri.' I'm monogamous. As long as you turn up in the breeding ground, I'll find you and stay with you for life. Each year, I'll come back to the burrow, seek you out, we'll rebuild our burrow together, and we'll mate again. I'll never desert you as long as you appear each year. You are mine for life. And you're a good-looking bird too. You're on second seating too. I know because I've admired you from afar."

Stephie turned red again while Mike laughed, again waddled around the stage, braying. He was also milking the applause. He returned to a spot in front of Stephie.

"When you see us awkward clumsy ungainly birds on land, you can't imagine how transformed we are in the water. We are graceful ballet stars in the sea. Our bodies are like sleek fish as we dive to great depths and shoot gracefully and speedily through the water. We scare and chase our prey toward the surface and attack them from underneath. The ocean is our natural environment, swimming is our metier. With our pin wings, we are an ideal bird for swimming.

"The name *penguin* comes from the Welsh *pen gwyn* or white head. In the water, you'll see only our black-and-white head exposed. We dive and exhale. Often we will dive sixty meters.

"Are you going to be able to see us close up if you go to Punta Tombo? We're going to be in the parking lots waiting for the buses to come in. We'll be waiting to see you. Please, whatever you do, don't feed us people food. It can change our feeding behaviors, making us seriously dependent on handouts.

"We can be very dangerous if we think we're being provoked. If you ever get bitten by one of us, you'll know it and carry the scar forever. We have strong beaks. And remember, don't put any trinkets for gifts in front of us. That means you are ready, willing, and able, and the last thing you want to do is have a penguin chasing you for sex.

"We live in burrows. One or two of us will peer at you from the burrows. Be careful not to step in a burrow by mistake. You'll get a serious bite. If you stare at us in our burrows or look at us for quite a while, remember we are very curious, nosey.

"And we have no fear of humans. You can explore near the burrow, but remember, don't proffer a present. That means you choose one of us as your breeding partner. You may end up smoking a Kool cigarette next to my burrow after twenty seconds of absolute bliss.

"We are also great follow-the-leader animals. We just naturally follow each other, thinking whoever is in front of us has discovered something worth seeing and knows where he's going. Our chicks wander off. They follow because we are all great followers. One walks off, and thirty or sixty will follow. Often a line of us will go off a cliff into the water not because we jumped, but because we got pushed from behind.

"We have many predators. El Niño has created a shortage of food. More than half of us die of starvation. Sea lions feed on us. Orca whales, you know, killer whales, eat us, and foxes along the beach savage the eggs, the chicks, and our weaker buddies.

"The wise ones among us stay near the burrow. In February and March, our chicks lose their downy coat. They go to sea and head north to Brazilian waters where they are seen surfing along the coastline in the winter months.

"If you wish to study our Magellanic behavior and make contact, sit about six feet away and get down at our height. Sit and watch us. Patience will pay off. Our head waving shows our curiosity. We will rotate our heads to get a good look at you.

"Mimicking our behavior can cause you trouble. To us, if you are wearing black tennis shoes, you are another penguin. If we start to extend our beak, extend our wings, vibrate our bills, lunge and hiss with our wings extended, watch out. This is our hostile behavior. Get out of range— fast. If we lock bills, we can open a can of tuna with our bills.

"Have patience when you observe us. We do not like cameras. We don't like a large lens. It can annoy us. We may lunge and hiss. We're myopic, so don't use a flash.

"You people are funny. You get to the parking lot at Tombo and rush to the beach overlook to get photos. A lot of us will be right there in the parking lot awaiting your arrival. We wonder where everyone is rushing off to."

Mike Lambert stood up, took off his penguin feet and shouted, "See You at Punta Tombo."

The room erupted into deafening applause, and he received a standing ovation. He reached over and kissed Stephie's hand, whispering, "Thanks for being such a great sport."

Stephie pocketed the smooth red stone Mike had proffered, and from that moment on she kept the token with her wherever she was.

After Lambert's lecture Tony and Sue Swanson took over the stage.

Tony said, "Today will be a nice relaxing day at sea, and tomorrow we'll be back in Argentina in Port Madryn. For you penguin lovers, this is where you get to make the long bus trip to the largest penguin rookerey for Magellanic penguins in the world at Punta Tombo.

"For those not going to see the pigeons, there is a chance to visit one of the original Welsh settlements in Gaiman and have a real Welsh tea with all kinds of little sandwiches and cakes. The Welsh settled in that part of Patagonia in the mid 1800s. Before going to Gaiman, you'll be stopping at Punta Loma, a national park where you will get a good overlook view of a big sea lion colony. Sea lions are huge and, boy, are they ugly suckers."

28

Stephie came back in the cabin to face Ben after the lecture. She was pissed, and she wanted to vent partly because of what her chief had told her and partly because of the attempted rape in Buenos Aires that had been bugging her.

"You bastard! You missed probably the best thing on the whole cruise. The guy was fantastic. I ask very little of you, expect very little, and you can't even do that. I can't understand you. You missed a real treat. The guy is a natural actor. He became a penguin. Your sense of priorities is unbelievable."

"Hey, Steph, I'm sorry I missed it, but I didn't know Laurence Olivier would be playing a penguin. What the hell are you getting so excited about? It was only a lecture. I missed it. So I didn't see the star performer, the hunk. The important thing is you saw it, not that I didn't see it."

"You can be so infuriating. The man was fantastic. You said you'd be there."

"Well I wasn't. I was busy in the gym. I spent so much time waiting for equipment, I wasted so much time, I couldn't help it. I'm sorry, but I don't know exactly why I have to be sorry, Steph. I can't get that hepped up about penguins. I'm sorry over and over again, and I apologize. I don't share your penguin fixation. To me, it's just another big bird that can't even fly for Christ's sake. To you it's a fucking idol. An icon."

"That talk was prepping for our trip to the penguin colony."

"No, not my trip. Your trip. I'm not spending nine hours to see a bunch of penguins for forty-five minutes. Life will just have to go on without me knowing much about penguins. I've said right along I want to go on the other tour, the Welsh town. I can't spend long hours on a bus just to see a penguin rookery. You can go with Kim and be happier without me."

This gave Ben an opening. Now he could force a deal he

135

might have had difficulty with before she pulled out all the stops. Stephie had overreached.

"You really are a prick."

"No, I want to do my thing. I want to see more of Puerto Madryn and that Welsh settlement. I'll still see a lot of animal life. I don't know what the hell you're getting so upset about? You've gone on many trips by yourself before. You can enjoy yourself. It's not as if I have to be there for your security. Hell, you'll be better off without me. I'd be in such a pissed-off mood, I'd be lousy company. You'll have to go by your lonesome. Go with that dyke, Kim."

"Dyke?"

"I calls 'em as I sees 'em."

"We're on different wavelengths, and we're growing further apart. We're going off a cliff!"

"No, I'm going off the cliff, and you're the one doing the pushing!"

Stephie turned, opened the door, stormed out, slamming the door. She had pushed one too many buttons on Ben's keyboard; he was genuinely, probably rightly, teed off at her. He enjoyed being the aggrieved one for a change. She felt like a harridan, a bitch.

Once out in the hall, Stephie realized she had vented, had her initial burst of anger, and she knew she'd have to pull back. There was a threshold she dare not cross until the cruise was over. She could tap into his anger, but then she had to be careful not to overreact and tap into his huge mass of boiling rage that lived not too far below the surface. Her boss had cautioned her to play it cool. Why, she didn't know. Better to be safe than sorry.

His rage was there, and it could easily be breached. It was an uncontrollable rage that could and had become physically threatening, an all-consuming rage. She did know it sprang from and was a holdover from a childhood filled with family fights. The anger could quickly shift to extreme rage at times, dangerous, overwrought, and overreaching. It was a line Stephie had learned not to cross, that crossing it would be at her peril.

She was genuinely angry, but she'd have to deal with it. And where had that stuff about Kim being a dyke come from? Simply verbal warfare, sparring, or had Ben tapped into something she missed? For years, she and Ben had been on two different planets on the subject of sexual proclivities.

Ben had a sixth sense about spotting lesbians. It would take her forever to see it, but to the rutting cock of the walk male Ben, spotting a lesbian was often an easy call for him to make, but it was an intuitive leap she was seldom able to make. It mattered far less to her who was a lesbian than to him. The reason wasn't too difficult to figure out.

On deck, walking off her distress, she thought back to her encounter with Ben. *God, I really am a bitch. I overreacted. I'm losing it. I was picking on him for one thing when I'm really pissed off at him for a whole lot of other things. He pisses me off in general, and I pick on him for a lecture, for God's sake. Welcome to the world of bitches!*

Her boss's warning came back to her, and she realized she had to pull back and cool it.

That afternoon, to let off steam, Stephie went on deck and brought three books with her. She sat in a deckchair, skimming and skipping around among the books. Gradually, she got her mind off Ben and into a different realm altogether. From a deckchair further down the row, Ann glanced at her occasionally, wondering what made her tick.

One of Stephie's books was called *In Patagonia* by Bruce Chatwin, one was *With Chatwin*, a book by Chatwin's editor who had worked with him on *In Patagonia*, and the third was Paul Theroux's *The Old Patagonian Express*. Ben always chided her on the number of books she brought with her on a trip, but since he brought none of his own, he would often read hers. He was a faster reader and seemed to remember more details than she did.

He was better at making parallels and comparisons among books than she was—as if he tapped into some unifying themes she was unaware of. She thought he had a better Gestalt mechanism than she did.

She took Mike's stone out of her pocket and rolled it around in the palm of her hand as she read. It might become the equivalent of worry beads for her.

That night aboard the *Global Quest* was the captain's gala, his welcome aboard ship cocktail party, the night when he introduced the officers, chef, hotel manager, and cruise staff to the passengers. It was the night when you had your picture taken with the captain, had a portrait taken by a photographer and got blotto on the free cocktails served at the captain's shindig.

Passengers on formal nights had their real revelry in puffery, became peacocks, strutting in their finery. These were their nights of glory, the formal nights when men and women could act proud of themselves, preening and showing off. The men were often worse than the women. Some Scots wore their kilts. This ship was very formal; almost every man was in a tux for second sitting.

At the captain's reception, the Rilleaus were dancing their hearts out to the ship's orchestra. Perhaps they would even wear out a pair of dancing shoes on this long cruise. And Ben and Stephie did what most couples do. They declared an unspoken truce. It was an unspoken but necessary part of living in a civilized society. You had to fake it at times, and by now they were both experts at faking it. Even close observers would be hard-pressed to detect any friction between them, because it was in the best interest of both of them to make this whole thing click—at least for the duration of the cruise.

During the day, some passengers in their cabins had watched *The Full Monty*, which was shown on the ship's cable television system. Most had attended Lambert's talk; it was the hit of their day. Some had gone to line-dancing classes, and Ann and Ben had been able to manage a bout of sex.

The ship's two comedians had spent the afternoon telling each other the raunchiest, vilest, most scatological and extreme forms of the old insider comics' joke "The Aristocrats." If they had dared tell variations on the joke on the stage of a cruise ship, they would have been thrown over the side for shark meat.

29

The next morning at seven, six buses were lined up on the pier near the ship. It was overcast with the cloud cover low and moving in. There were gray clouds, black clouds, brownish clouds, swirling clouds, everywhere clouds. It looked like it was sure to rain later in the day, although the passengers had been told there hadn't been significant rains in the region for months.

Stephie and Ruthie Kaufeld were dressed warmly, both in jeans, sweatshirts, and windbreakers. Ruthie was elderly, but she was in good health and was a spry tough old bird, a no-nonsense person. Both were venturesome types. Neither was expecting quite the ordeal that lay ahead of them. They boarded the third bus in line and were lucky enough to get seats in the first row behind the driver.

Mike Lambert got on, carrying a lot of camera equipment. He winked at Stephie, greeted her warmly, and headed to the back of the bus where he spread out his gear on half the rear seat. The tour guide for the day announced his name was Geraldo, "But call me Jerry." He sat in the first row across from them.

Before they were about to pull out, Tony Tantera hauled himself aboard, gave a big hello to everyone, and took a seat next to Jerry. He, too, greeted Stephie like an old friend. Stephie felt relieved to have him along. The bus was full before they pulled out. They had a good view out the front windshield and side windows.

Tony was on the horn. "Well folks, we're headed for Punta Tombo. It'll be a long ride, but when you see the pigeons—sorry, Mike in the back—penguins, you'll be amazed. It hasn't rained here in many months, but today they're predicting rain. Let's hope we don't get too much because it could slow us down."

In the grayish morning light, the buses stole through Puerto Madryn, almost like a ghostly funeral procession through a dreary town. The streets were deserted as they headed for the highway beyond town.

Jerry announced, "Punta Tombo is about a hundred miles away. The trip down to the penguin reserve will take about three hours if we're lucky and everything goes hunky dory, okay? Puerto Madryn is about midway between Buenos Aires and the Straits of Magellan. The sky right now is overcast, but although it may be cool and windy, it *never* rains here this time of year. I am a native of this town, and I'm descended from Welsh settlers. You noticed my light reddish-brown hair? That ain't no bottle job, okay? I got good English most of the time, no?"

Tony took over some of the narration. "We're going through desolate countryside with few places to pee. We'll be stopping in a small town about forty miles away from here for a toilet visit. This will be our only stop until we arrive at the penguin preserve, and since the countryside along our route is quite barren, there will only be a few bushes offering shelter for those of you who don't avail yourselves of the facilities at our toilet place."

Stephie and Ruthie were talking quietly. They noticed a few rain drops on the windshield. The wipers made one sweep, and a few more drops appeared. Nothing too much yet.

Stephie said, "I have a feeling this is not going to be a trip we'll remember with great fondness."

"Yes, your husband Ben must have been prescient. It might have been a wise decision on his part to pass this one up."

"Let's hope when we get to the penguins, it'll clear up and we'll be able to get some good views and some good shots of them. I have my own camera with me. It's an aim and shoot. Ben's has so many damn settings it takes forever to take a shot, and for the most part my pictures seem to me to be just as good as his. Sometimes he'll get a really memorable shot with his elaborate camera, one I could never get, but for the most part, it's a lot of time and effort for the same results."

Ruthie said, "Don't belittle the poor guy. He's very handsome. A real catch, I think."

Stephie smiled politely, but didn't answer.

The precipitation had changed to a light drizzle, and the driver was using his wipers intermittently. As the bus approached the stop-off village, the drizzle had become more of a steady rain, and the wipers were working overtime. The village seemed to be no more than a way station.

Their bus and the other buses pulled into the terminal. Inside a stand offered newspapers, soft drinks, snacks, and candy bars. Several locals were waiting for buses to God knows where. The people there were more Indian-looking than Stephie had encountered before in Argentina. The toilets were typical bus stop variety, dreary and dirty, with several booths, some with toilet paper, some without. People had been warned in advance to carry a supply of Kleenex for emergencies.

After twenty minutes, they reboarded their coach to continue the journey. More rain was coming down. Then the drops got larger, and gradually the rain outside intensified. The bus's windshield wipers worked sporadically, not by design but because of some malfunction. When they did work, apparently the rubber on them was not quite adequate because it never seemed to leave the glass unstreaked. In addition, there was a certain amount of fogging up. The driver had a dirty rag he continually ran over the window to clear it.

The word drizzle was no longer operative. It had been a light rain at first, then real rain, and finally it began to come down heavier in sheets.

Jerry remarked about the rain being needed in this generally parched region. Tourists, getting one shot at a place, look askance at and often don't appreciate it when they are told the rain on their particular touring day is blessedly needed.

Along the way, they passed farms or estancias, raising cattle and some grains. Tufts of grass and small ground-hugging bushes were the feed for animals. Sometimes they saw ranch buildings and farm equipment, but basically the land seemed deserted. Rarely did they see people, except for a few in cars passing the coaches and probably headed for the penguin preserve just as they were.

The road was becoming rougher but was still paved until, at one point, they got on a road that was bumpy and poorly maintained. They were heading south on a route that ran not too far from the coast, but not in view of it either.

The terrain soon became monotonous arid desert land. Stephie recalled something she had read the day before. She pulled out the book and read it to Ruthie,

"If you see a little of the landscape of Patagonia, you've seen a lot of it because it is much of the same, a boring monotonous sameness, a forbidding land not beckoning or picturesque."

Jerry said, "We're getting more rain in one day than we've had on any day in the last two years."

They could see the road was primitive. When they turned off the black-topped road onto the gravel and dirt road, the surface was more affected by the downpour of water. After a time the line of buses headed more toward the coast. On a map, the road paralleled the coast, but rarely could they make out the ocean or a shoreline.

They passed an industrial site producing cement, cinder blocks, and some other building materials. Soon a large fenced area proclaimed itself a military base.

Jerry announced the unpaved road would lead to the penguin preserve still some forty miles ahead. The road bed was saturated because of the rain, which continued unabated. The wind blowing in from the ocean was very strong with frequent whining gusts.

Stephie, sitting behind the driver, watched the wind pelting down on the windshield, the wipers working erratically, and saw Tony talking anxiously on his cell phone.

The further they went along the road, the more primitive it became, bumpy with huge potholes. The road was only dirty red mud and muck. Ahead, they saw a line of halted traffic: cars, buses, farm tractors, and trucks. The bus was forced to stop. Their driver and Tony, both wearing ponchos to shelter them from the heavy rain, got out of the coach and conferred with the drivers of the other buses.

Tony returned to inform them the rain had caused heavy mud in the low-lying sections of the road ahead, and several vehicles were stuck in the mud. Bulldozers and tractors were attempting to pull them through. As the traffic inched forward, they could see vehicles trying to plow through the mud. Small cars were able to skirt around the mud pool, but the larger trucks and buses invariably reached the mud and got stuck. A bulldozer or tractor would attach a cable and pull the vehicle through. All of this, of course, was delaying their arrival at Punta Tombo.

Tony announced, "We are on a very tight schedule since we are now nearly one hundred miles from the ship. But we'll get there, and you'll get to see the pelicans, uh, puffins, the whatever, the boids. Don't worry."

Finally, it was their bus's turn to try to breach the mud pits. The driver gunned the engine, hoping to force his way through. They reached the middle of the pit and the rear wheels began to slip. The rear of the coach swiveled to the right. The driver tried to compensate by turning the wheel and down-shifting. The slide to the right continued, and the wheels lost all traction.

A bulldozer operator approached with his chain, wrapped it around the front end, boarded his vehicle and hauled them through. They were soon on their bumpy way again, and for a time the rain seemed to let up a bit.

30

That Tuesday morning, the Gaiman tea trip operated at a much more leisurely pace than did the penguin trip, which was a full field-pack expedition. The tea tour was a genteel outing for the less adventurous passengers who wanted to get a whiff of the Welsh connection in Argentina, see a bit of the country, get in a little slice of nature with a sea lion preserve and rookery, but mostly have a relaxing afternoon with a pleasant cuppa—part of a traditional British tea.

At the more civilized hour of ten in the morning, four buses assembled on the Puerto Madryn pier for the tea tour. Ben got on Bus Number Three, and it was like old home week. In one row from the back, he sat with Katie Kaufeld who had brought along her knitting bag. In front of him were Doug and Kim Simpson sitting opposite the dancing Rilleaus. Further ahead in the bus, partly by design, was Ann and Mrs. Lewis. Mr. Lewis was staying aboard with a touch of the gout. Across from Ben and Katie were Budgy and Dowdy with her camera.

After the bus took off, the group got to see Puerto Madryn in sunlight under more favorable conditions than the penguin-seekers. Their tour guide for the day was a girl in her late teens who seemed bright and had a good knowledge of English. She said laughingly she was called Evita. She was clever and kind in dealing with older people, which certainly was an asset with a group like the ship's passengers.

Near the land end of the pier in the harbor were the rusted rotting hulks of eight ships lying on their sides, half-submerged in water. It was a ship graveyard.

Evita explained, "Those junked ships you see are Russian vessels, abandoned because they couldn't pay port taxes. They were confiscated, and have been left there to rust."

The passengers found such rotting hulks to be frequent sights in some of the South American ports they visited.

Evita began her spiel, "Our seasons are the opposite of yours. We have a very short tourist season. When those wicked winds start coming up from Patagonia, believe me, you know it. Today is a little overcast, and we may get a little rain.

"Because of our short season, buses have to be brought from a long way for the tours, drivers have to stay overnight, and it makes your tours expensive. Even porta-potties have to be trucked in. Puerto Madryn is the gateway to Patagonia, a place with a reputation for being windswept and desolate.

"Welsh nationalists settled in Patagonia in 1863. They left Wales for freedom to worship as they pleased. They planned to be farmers in a land basically hostile to farming with a lot of arid land and desert, land in need of irrigation. The Welsh settled in Puerto Madryn, Rawson, Trelew. and Gaiman where they irrigated the land with canals.

"Our first stop this morning is going to be a nature stop, Punta Loma, a sea lion colony."

After driving through town, they headed south along a beach road passing houses with big picture windows facing the sea, homes in all styles of architecture, some two-story and some three.

They left the blacktop road and drove along an unpaved dirt-packed road where the bus kicked up dust, then headed along the coast through an area of flat dunes and moors that reminded Ben of Cape Cod. The harsh winters played a part in the shaping of the environment. At one spot was a camp of RVs and trailers.

They passed an area where a local rugby club was practicing. Then it was open country with moors that were yellow or brown with no greenery. The road was basic, roughly graded, hardened but bumpy. The sky was full of clouds, but it didn't yet look as if a storm was brewing.

Clumps of bushes by the side of the road were frosted with a silvery gray dust reminiscent of a morning northern frost.

The powdery dust sugar-coated the roadside plants. Tumbleweed rolled by the side of the road. There was a stark uncompromising beauty to the terrain; in the sky, clouds hugged the horizon.

Soon they arrived at the marine life overlook, a sea lion viewing area under national park control. A steep path led down to a wooden platform overlook. With the help of the bus driver and his caregiver, a heavy man in a wheelchair was able to make it over rough terrain to get to the overlook.

With Ann, Mrs. Lewis, Kim, and Doug ahead of him, Ben carefully and theatrically shepherded Katie Kaufeld down the slope to the viewing area. He made it seem like a task, so he could avoid contact with the others.

The overlook platform was high on a cliff that gave a view of a rock-strewn beach a hundred feet below. In a cove on the shore were hundreds of sea lions of different sizes, some huge flabby males, some sprawled on rocks, and some wallowing in the water. A few massive males towered over the rest, dominating the herd.

Occasionally, a young male would challenge one of the massive patriarchs. The big lord would roar and bluster, and the young one would cower away, perhaps regrouping for a successful challenge in the future. The big males were fighting and protecting territory with loud snorts, guffaws, and plaintive trumpeting calls. The social structure didn't take long to figure out: docile submissive females and aggressive willful males. It was an impressive sight, a treat to see the animals in their natural habitat.

Around the sea lions and on the cliffs above them were flocks of cormorants. The cliff faces were streaked and stained with guano. Around the cliffs was a fenced area, and the tourists were well away from the colony below. In the distance to the north was the skyline of Puerto Madryn.

After their brief stop at the nature preserve, the buses soon got back on the paved road and headed toward Gaiman.

Evita was back on the loudspeaker. "The names of the towns we're going through have Welsh origins. Farther south is the town of Rawson. From there inland to the west is Trelew. Head farther west and you get to the town of Gaiman, famous for its Welsh tea places.

"Now if we got to Rawson and headed south instead of west, we would eventually come to Punta Tombo, the reserve for the largest colony of Magellanic or jackass penguins."

From across the aisle Ben could here the beer-sodden croak of Budgy, complaining and bitching as usual. "When are we going to get to the fuckin' penguins?"

He could hear the ever-patient Dowdy saying, "I told you we were going for tea, not to see the birds."

Still later, he squawked, "Why are we bothering with those bloody penguins?"

"We're not, love. We're going for tea."

"Shite. We could have had tea on that old tub we're on."

The road to Gaiman was a good paved road. Some of the terrain looked like the American West, with clumps of bushes like sagebrush. Trelew, a town of some sixty-thousand souls, was not an impressive place; it had the look of a hub, an agricultural center with an airport and high-rises. On the outskirts was a slummy area near the road with what looked like public housing and some shanties here and there. All in all not an attractive town, thought Ben.

After a time, the buses pulled into the town of Gaiman, not looking particularly noteworthy or charming; it looked like a dull place. It could have been in the middle of anywhere. It was not, to Ben, particularly Welsh-looking— although it was difficult for him to determine, since he had never been in Wales.

They stopped at the town's oldest house, a museum. It was made of stone and had been built in 1874. It was plain with tiny rooms and low ceilings. Nothing was very impressive as they circled through the Welsh settlement. Nice houses were mixed in with nondescript houses; some had pretty gardens. There were tiny farms amid a system of canals that had been constructed to irrigate the arid land.

The bus drove over a small wooden bridge across a canal

with fast clear rushing water. Near a car park was a charming chalet-like building. They were at Ty Gwynn with the greenest of greenery and a pleasant garden. It had quaint Alpine kitschiness. Someone from the Disney organization must have been consulted about its design. A drizzle had set in, making the place misty and gauzy, like a place out of a fairy tale.

Evita was on the loudspeaker. "At tea, you will be served twenty-five varieties of cakes and sandwiches, and music will be provided by a Welsh choir."

On the house outside, a sign read, "This house was visited by Lady Diana, Princess of Wales, November 25, 1995."

Inside, a small table was maintained, fully set, in memory of the Princess's visit, her portrait prominently displayed on the wall above the table. They were informed later the tea house was one of several in the town; a local cottage industry had been built up of such businesses providing teas for tourists.

Inside, it was spotless, smelling like a wonderful bakery. Tables were set with white tablecloths, sparkling china, and plate after plate of sandwiches, cakes, scones, pastries, breads, pots of butter, jars of jams and jellies, and Olive's special walnut cake.

The young waitresses were pretty, perky, cheery, eager, and kindly—as if they had been assembled by central casting. They wore peasant-type dirndls and bright aprons. It was hard to tell the provenance of the costumes. Were they Welsh, Bavarian, Patagonian, or had they been supplied by some Hollywood costumer offering a sort of generic home-made peasant outfit?

Budgy said in a gruff voice, "It's like Emerald City in the *Wizard of Oz*. All that's missing is Judy Garland, the aluminum man, and the seven munchkins."

Ben and Katie sat with Kim and Doug, the Gnarled Old Lady and the Bowed Old Man. Ben noticed Ann was seated with Mrs. Lewis, the Rilleaus, the Smarmy Man, and the ship's doctor.

Ben usually was not too good with older people; he disliked things that seemed old-maidish like tea cozies and tiny tea sandwiches. Was it unmanly of him to be having a genteel tea when his wife was off on a rough and tough expedition? This was a tame exercise with real old-timers, the halt, the lame, and superannuated. What bucked him up was seeing his lover across the room making civilized conversation and going through the tea rituals.

And here he was stuck with an old biddy—Katie Kaufeld. Men ought to be playing handball, biking, jogging, shagging, not sipping tea and making small talk. *I think I made a mistake. I should have done the real man's thing, seeing the penguins, a real campaign, a real adventure. . . but yeah, there'd be no Ann for now and later in the afternoon back in her cabin. This is the price I pay for being a lecher.*

If Ben had a feminine side, it was deeply buried under a load of macho shale. Here was a man used to gonzo gotcha journalism imbibing tea. Katie interrupted Ben's reverie and declared it a quaint little touristy place, very British in character.

As tea progressed, the tea house's mistress announced, quite distressed, that the Welsh choir, usually in attendance was absent, had been decimated because several of its members had been stricken with the flu.

On board the ship, there were several passengers who were coming down with flu-like symptoms. The Bowed Old Man was saying to his wife, the Gnarled Old Lady, "First I have to pee, then I have gas, then I need to take a shit, then my nose gets stopped up, then it's heartburn, a cold sore on my lip. My goddamn body seems to be giving out. It's a bitch to be ninety-one. Mother, do I like this kind of bread? Do I like jam on my bread? Do I like this yellow cake?"

"Of course you do. Eat it and hush up. Chill out!"

"After this, are we going to see the penguins?"

"No, Dumbo, that's the other tour."

After the tea, with everyone groaning from the food and sugar intake, people were lined up to buy homemade tea cozies, aprons, and cassettes of a choir singing Welsh melodies.

Outside, some tourists clambered aboard a wagon pulled by a draft horse for a brief tour of the grounds.

In the drizzle, Ben was wandering outside on the lush lawn in the garden with its waterwheel, its bird-feeders, gnomes, and fountains. He approached the canal with the torrent rushing by, crossed a small footbridge, and stopped at a garden plot next to Ann who was standing by herself admiring the flowers. They stood side by side, staring at the garden display. Their hands brushed together. They turned and smiled at each other. It looked as if they were about to kiss.

He said, "How did you enjoy the tea?"

"Scrumptious. Only about five-thousand calories. The nut cake was great. Shouldn't you be taking care of your little old ladies?"

"You look so beautiful out here."

"And you look so horny."

Some distance away, they were noticed by Kim who wrinkled her brow, had a quizzical look. *Ah, I thought they knew each other ever since Buenos Aires. Something's going on there Stephie really ought to know about.*

Unseen by Ben, Ann, or Kim, the Smarmy Man crouched behind an evergreen in the mist, taking in the whole show. He smiled his creepy gloating grimace. He seemed almost to drool with satisfaction.

Ann said, "I've got to get back. See you later aboard ship?"

"Oh, you can bet on that."

Ann drifted away, walked over toward her bus. Ben continued to walk around the elaborate garden as other people started to explore the grounds. A light rain began falling.

Back on the bus, Budgy, across the aisle, was in full throat. "That was a rip-off if I ever saw one. That tarted-up teahouse looked like it had been built yesterday. Phony little waterwheel and everything phony. They promised a live choir. All we got was a cassette playing some crap that could have been singing from anywhere. They were as Welsh as our Filipino cabin steward. Except for sea lions we saw at too great a distance, this was a real nothing trip. I kept telling you we should have gone for the penguins."

Katie leaned over and said in a loud voice, "Shut up, you old blowhard. No one wants to hear your stupid opinions on anything."

Ben gloated at Katie's words.

Budgy thought, *The old twat.* But he was completely silenced for the rest of the trip. Budgy's wife with a big, grateful smile, gave Ben and Katie a great nod and a wink.

On the way back, they started to hit heavy rain and fog. Ben knew it didn't bode well for Stephie's penguin trek.

Behind Ben, a man kept up a steady stream of humming in a very quiet voice. He would sing a few lines in a pleasant melodious voice. It wasn't intrusive; no one was bothered by it. He seemed to be a happy man, content with his lot in life. His family all smiled indulgently at him. They talked quite a bit, sometimes in Spanish, bantering back and forth without inhibitions. It was an amiable happy group.

One of the older women in the group directed a comment to Ben. "I'm sorry your wife couldn't come. I hope she's not ill."

"Oh no, she went on the long penguin trip. Too much for me."

"Yes, we thought the trip was too long ourselves. We agreed we'd all have a nice tea instead."

She patted Ben on the shoulder and said laughingly, "You must think we are all pests?"

"No, I'm fine. No one bothering me. Glad to see everyone enjoying themselves."

"We're from Ponce in Puerto Rico. On our first long cruise."

The group all spoke very good English, but from time to time would speak in snatches of Spanish, probably unaware of it since they were all so casually bilingual.

31

The penguin-seekers on their odyssey were finally approaching the preserve. As the bus drove slowly over the curving and hilly dirt road, the scenery became more coastal. The rain let up for a time, changing to a light misty drizzle. It was bleak terrain with low bushes hugging the hardscrabble landscape.

They could see winding pathways over the dunes ahead and below, and in the distance, the ocean looked gray and forbidding with many whitecaps.

As they crested the final hill and reached the parking lot, they saw hundreds of Magellanic penguins going about their business, some huddling under the bushes to avoid the still falling drizzle. The buses lined up in the parking area. They had to be careful to weave around and away from the waiting penguins.

The coach stopped. Tony announced since they were so late in arriving, they would only have about forty minutes to visit the rookery. With much complaining, the now grumpy and crabby passengers stumbled off the coach, pulled on their hoods and hats, and headed down toward the beach against the wind-blown rain. The penguins in the parking lot watched the passengers rushing toward the beach to see the penguins.

Some penguins stood very close to the buses. Right there in the parking lot were hundreds of them. Anyone wanting a close-up view had only to stop and peer a few feet away and get a good look at a penguin. Penguins were at their feet examining these raincoat and windbreaker-clad creatures. Were the birds able to talk, they might have said, "Where you going, folks? What are we, chopped liver?"

Tourists had been warned not to take flash pictures because the birds were myopic, but still they insisted on their right to be more important than the animals whose environment they were invading. One woman was trying to feed a morning buffet unskinned banana to a penguin who probably thought she was nuts. The woman's husband was sure of it.

Because of the strong wind, umbrellas were useless. As the passengers headed down toward the sea, everywhere they looked were small tufts and mounds where penguins gathered. Some burrows had penguin heads peering out. Trails had been roped off, and lines of penguins were marching back and forth toward the beach and the sea. The people studied the penguins, and the penguins returned the favor by studying the people. Stephie was surprised by how small they were, two or three feet at most.

Mike Lambert, after a quick hi for Stephie, dashed far off to the right with his equipment to get more fodder for his vocation and avocation. It was a lousy day for photographs. Stephie and Ruthie followed the crowd toward the beach and the wooden viewing platforms. Stephie had a hard time keeping up with Ruthie who took off in third gear. She was not about to miss any precious viewing time.

The people headed down the coastal trail. Stephie stopped to peer at a creche of four penguins gathered around a burrow. Other birds waddled purposefully, but in an ungainly gait along a path, some slipping in the mud when they came to a small gully.

Along the way, the penguins continued their business aware of, but unafraid of these strange creatures invading their habitat. People paths were roped off from the penguin nesting areas and paths, but at some points, penguins and people were on the same paths making a beeline for the sea—the people to the viewing platforms, the penguins waddling singlemindedly down to the water for food gathering.

The people path led over rocks to the edge of the cliff. Wooden viewing platforms had been erected. Looking down at the beach below, the tourists could see thousands of penguins walking, strutting, diving into the waves and doing what penguins do. Several visitors climbed part way down the cliff to get a closer view.

Flash bulbs flashed, shutters clicked, camcorders whirred, capturing forever the sight of hundreds of tourists and hundreds of thousands of penguins coexisting on a rainy rocky coast in Argentina.

Stephie caught up with Ruthie at one of the penguin blinds. Ruthie pointed out several foxes that were preying on penguins separated from the main body or who were lame or weak. The foxes seemed ruthless as they dashed among the penguin colony. In the ocean itself lurked the sea lions and killer whales who also preyed on the penguins. One killer whale flopped onto the beach and grabbed a penguin in its jaws. The predators seemed frenzied and frantic even though the slow-moving penguins were easy targets.

The tourists' viewing time expired. The damp but cheerful, fulfilled tourists reboarded the coaches to begin the long return trip.

Tony asked, "Well, Stephie, did you see enough penguins in Penguin City?"

"Except for the long drive and the rain, it was one of the most fulfilling sights of my life. It makes me feel great to know so much of nature is still intact."

Jerry informed everyone their lunch stop would be at a local farm only a few miles back on the road they had come in on.

The rain had let up. This time there was little traffic, and the mud pits had dissipated, so with some slipping and sliding, the buses made their way back over the road. After thirty minutes of retracing their route, the buses turned off the road onto a seemingly private lane.

Jerry announced, "This is our lunch stop, okay?"

They joined the already arrived tourists in a big barn, which was a shearing shed for sheep. The farmer had brought in porta-potties from hundreds of miles away for the tourists.

In the barn, long picnic tables had been set out for their arrival. They had a spread of chicken, beef, fish, rolls, salads, cold meats, desserts, and drinks.

Tony yelled out, warning them, "Do not linger too long. We're late, and we must be on our way shortly. Outhouses are to the right of the barn, but do not linger. The pee lines are long."

Lunch over and duty done, Stephie and Ruthie reboarded the bus for the return journey; just then the sun came out. On the way back, Mike Lambert stood in the bus aisle above Stephie for part of the trip to report on some good video he was able to get. He seemed especially interested in her, and for that she was grateful. After all, Ben had been treating her as a doormat, but perhaps it was because she had been treating him as an old shoe.

She thought, *Mike is a hunk. God, he's good-looking, and he has that great smile. But the guy does go on about penguins.*

In her hand she held Mike's gift stone, but she didn't show it to him. Maybe sometime later—something to laugh about?

32

Like many piers in South American harbor cities, the long pier in Puerto Madryn had not been built for cruise ships, especially in a part of the world where cruise ships were a relatively rare sight because of the short season, the weather window of opportunity. Puerto Madryn's was a working pier for loading and unloading cargo. Next to the *Global Quest*, stood massive loading equipment for handling bauxite. The machinery dwarfed the ship. As she was berthed, the *Quest* was receiving a pervasive dusting of bauxite powder.

That afternoon, after the tea tour and a steamy sexual encounter with Ann, Ben decided to take the shuttle bus into town. It drove down the long pier past the half-submerged wrecks. The bus held mostly crew members, young people going downtown to shop and unwind. Everyone was dressed warmly for the cool weather; the wind was kicking up. A light chilling rain was falling.

Once off the pier, the bus drove down the long town beach promenade. Puerto Madryn was, at certain times of the year, a beach place for vacationers, and it had a pleasing beach-front. The town seemed fairly prosperous. The houses were modest, but most were well cared for with flower-gardens in the front yards. The few trees were stunted and cruelly hunched over, bowed by the wind and harsh weather.

As Ben walked around, he noticed the town drew its share of backpackers. It was an entry point for the vast Patagonian plateau region. The crew members had taken over various bars and restaurants and seemed to like the town. They were enjoying themselves, getting something other than the ship's food. A lot of beer bottles were raised.

Ben liked to shop for tee shirts, and he found some shops open even though it was siesta time. He bought some good

156

quality tees with nature themes: penguins, sea lions, save the whales, seagulls. He also went into a farmacia for two dozen condoms. *Be prepared* was his motto.

Ben headed into a café where the tables around him were loaded with relaxing crew members. An off-duty Sandy gave him a wave. Ben had a beer at the small bar and watched the crew members become more raucous.

Later, when he stepped out of the café, a strong wind and sheets of driving rain met him. For a time, he stayed under an overhang, but the wind picked up, the air got very cold, and the rain pelted down furiously.

He decided it wasn't going to let up so he ran for the bus. Sandy climbed aboard shortly after he got on. Knowing the way cruise ships worked their crews, he knew Sandy would soon be on duty. As the bus headed back to the harbor, the wind and rain intensified. On a building wall he saw a crudely painted sign that read "The Malvinas are Argentina's."

Back on the pier as he headed toward the gangway, he saw the sea around the ship loaded with jelly fish. He walked past a neighboring vessel, *The Odysseus*, a small tinny rinky-dink ship used by students for oceanic observation trips. He realized he had left his cap, a Baltimore Orioles one, a gift from Ann, aboard the bus, but it was too nasty to go back for it.

Aboard ship, he went to the bar for a beer. Budgy was ensconced on his regular stool, and Sandy, who was already on duty, told him the Punta Tombo trip had run into difficulties: heavy downpours, flooding, roads out, buses mired in mud, buses having to be towed out of flooded roads, and the passengers would be delayed returning. He heard people had to walk in mud up to their ankles when they got to the penguin place.

Sandy said, "Tony Tantera is keeping in touch with the ship. The penguin expedition was not like that bloody Gaiman tea party tour for pissarsed punters. But you'll never see me taking a thankless trek to see a bunch of shuffling penguins who don't know enough to migrate to

Florida where it's nice and toasty. Those dumb penguin bastards don't know when they're bad off. Stupid farts. I bet a
penguin fart would knock your skivvies off."

Sandy commiserated about Stephie and said she'd be well
cared for as long as Tony was around. Ben started to worry.
If they had faced the heavy driving rain Ben had just experi-
enced, they were in for trouble, he thought.

He really should have gone along just to be near her if she
needed help, felt guilty about letting his gonads interfere
with his other obligations, although it hadn't bothered him
up to this point, had it?

All afternoon, Ben waited anxiously for Stephie to return.
He had a hangover from too many beers. Bored, he went to
see Ann. When he got to Ann's cabin, she was in a sour
mood so he had to get away from her. He went back to hang
around the bar and listen to more of Budgy's rantings. Then,
as darkness came on, the call could be heard.

"The penguin people are coming back."

Ben watched from Promenade Deck as the first few buses
pulled in on the pier. No sign of Stephie. They had said six
buses. Finally he saw a sixth bus pull in and saw Tony
Tantera running through a wall of rain for the gangway. At
last, he saw Stephie getting off with Ruthie and the ship's
naturalist who was loaded down with all his gear. Ben
watched as his exhausted wife trudged up the gangway,
really dragging.

He greeted her in the passageway, and all she said was,
"I really need to get to the toilet, and I have to take a long
hot shower. Catch up with you later. Wow, you smell like a
brewery."

33

The day after the Puerto Madryn stop was a day at sea as the ship sailed toward the Falklands. The captain spoke on the loudspeaker in the morning.

"I must apologize to you, and indeed share my concerns about some blustery conditions we may encounter tomorrow. At times, as we near the Falklands, we meet up with southerly gale force winds bringing cold air from Antarctica. On Thursday, when we are in the Islands, the weather is expected to be unpredictable, starting off with clear weather and tapering off to more iffy stuff. As it is prudent to enter the Port Stanley harbor in daylight, we anchor, as expeditiously as possible.

"Given our present latitude, one would expect weather one might have to apologize for, so I would like to thank you for the rather benign weather we have enjoyed thus far on our journey whether you brought it with you or not. We crossed the continental shelf earlier.

"Wherever your perambulations take you Thursday, we wish you Godspeed. As you may know, I conduct the Sunday worship ceremonies, a tradition I uphold, yes, indeed. If you have time, please share worship with me. Dolphins are cavorting alongside the ship, and albatrosses are slipstreaming in the stern at the moment. Thank you for your time."

Stephie and those around her walking the Promenade Deck smiled, rather puzzled by the captain's remarks. Later, she went to the land tour talk in the lounge.

Tony said, "After Madryn, we need this day at sea. Some of us, me included, won't soon forget that trip to see the puffins, uh, the penguins. Tomorrow, Thursday, we'll be in the Falkland Islands, where you can visit British pubs and get a real British beer or ale.

"You'll see a little English island, a miniature version of Great Britain. You'll see sheep, heaths, peat bogs and horses in small backyards. If you wish, you can eat bangers and mash and mooshy peas and fish and chips. Also, for the penguin fanciers, there is a penguin rookery not far from the town at Gypsy Cove.

"The people there are naturally very sensitive about their war with Argentina. The Argentines call the Falklands the Malvinas. The islands are still loaded with mine fields. You'll see and hear lots of reminders of the 1982 war.

"There is a monument to the war over there. On one trip, an English lady asked me to help her over to the monument where the names of the war victims are inscribed. She fainted in my arms when she got there. She saw her son's name. It turned out that's why she had come on the cruise in the first place, to visit the place where her son had given his life for his country.

"I was working on the big P&O cruise ship, the *Canberra*, when we delivered three-thousand Argentinean prisoners from the Falklands War to Puerto Madryn. I met one of the Argentine prisoners on the dock years later. We talked about the ship I was working on then, the *Royal Princess*. He recognized the P&O sign he had seen on the *Canberra*. I invited him on board, and brought him to the Lido for lunch. Afterwards, the man thanked me, said the food was wonderful, but said one thing hadn't changed on a P&O ship; they still had the same lousy coffee.

"The weather can often get nasty at Port Stanley, so wear layers of clothing. It can be very changeable weather. Dress for the four seasons. You may get sunshine, drizzle, hail, sleet, snow, rain, and gale force winds, all within an hour. Just be prepared.

"We're going to be tendering off Port Stanley, the main town at the extreme eastern tip of East Falkland Island, located about as far away as it can get from Argentina. They only have three tour buses on the island, so trips are staggered and rationed, but if you're not booked for a bus tour, it's a small walkable town with an interesting museum and the West Store, which is good for reasonably priced souvenirs. These people are proud British people; they'll make you feel right at home. So, cheers, folks."

34

Thursday morning, the *Global Quest* anchored out in the Stanley harbor. Stephie and Ben clambered down the shaky stairway that hugged the hull of the ship. With the help of crewmen on the seaside platform and the swaying tender, they boarded the small boat with its distinctive orange roof. Some of the older passengers were having trouble maneuvering. Stephie and Ben rode the tender into shore, about a two-mile ride. The sea that morning had a slight chop and wasn't bad, though word had it the seas would get choppier as the day progressed.

The town hugged the sides of a gentle rise with successive streets running parallel to the harbor road. They watched the buildings of the little town grow larger as they came into the dock. The town had a quaint inviting aspect with brightly colored roofs. It seemed to be built in three layers, like a tiered cake, rows of houses on each tier with the slopes between the layers gradual rather than steep. Most of the houses and buildings appeared to be basic; it didn't look as if anyone had struck it rich and felt inclined to erect a mansion for ostentatious display.

Near the dock, they boarded their tour bus. Both the driver, young tow-headed Clayton, and the young woman guide, pretty blonde June, were friendly and welcoming. It was probably a treat to see new faces and get a change in daily routine in this end-of-the-world place. The town reminded Stephie of the way Provincetown on Cape Cod used to look out of season anywhere between November and April.

The bus started its drive slowly along Rose Road, the road parallel to the harbor. June pointed out the Christ Church Cathedral, too modest a little church to be called a cathedral.

June said, "Yeah, this is the southernmost cathedral in the world. That gateway, looking like a gazebo, is made of the jawbones of whales."

Stephie noted June said "yeah" often; it was a yes, a punctuation mark, and also an interjection that sounded slangy, but might be a feature of the local dialect.

Along the harbor road, they got off the bus to examine the memorial to the two-hundred-fifty-five soldiers and three civilians who had lost their lives in the 1982 Falklands War.

Back aboard the bus, farther along, they passed the main general store, West Store, which June said sold all the essentials: "Food, groceries, souvenirs, clothes, cassettes, CDs, with a video rental section. It's like a supermarket and department store combined, yeah."

June said, "Yeah, these islands are a place where you have to make do with what you have. If you forget your Marmite or Heinz beans on one trip to the store, you might have to wait months for the store to be restocked. A supply ship comes every two months with fresh goods from England.

"Things here are so dear because everything has to be brought such long distances. Since we raise lots of sheep, mutton is a real staple here. Ladies, we have one hairdresser, and she only works part-time; she does very well and shears sheep as well, yeah.

"Big oil reserves have been discovered off our coast, and this place may be drastically changed when the big oil rigs begin operating offshore. People have mixed feelings about the future. Money will come in; there may be progress, but everyone can also see problems. Here we've always had a safe simple way of life. Dull, yes, but secure and tranquil, and most of us are quite content here with the way things are, yeah.

"There is a waiting list for new people who want to come to the Falklands to live. We have a housing shortage so we use prefab houses, which I'll point out at the top of the town. We have no unemployment."

June knew everyone in Stanley by name and past history. She knew all the relatives. It wasn't just anyone's house they were passing; it was Mrs. Allen's or Mrs. Webster's. They stopped to see and photograph Mrs. Smith's yard with all the flowers, decorations, and a dozen or so gnomes. If one gnome was good, a dozen could be awesome. Mrs. Smith did have gorgeous roses. Probably the sea air.

They stopped to look at the yard of Mr. Charters, a metal worker who was an anti-whaling fanatic. He had made metallic sculptures, had whale bones, and a whale gun in his yard. A homemade sign proclaimed his opposition to whaling: "No more killing of Whales!"

June said, "Yeah, I think you get Mr. Charter's message. The whaling industry was once big around here, and whalers from around the world used to pull into Stanley."

A large pile of peat was in his backyard; similar big piles of peat graced other backyards.

June said, "Peat absorbs water like moss. There are peat fields around here where you can dig it up. We use the stuff for heating and for cooking."

The houses looked very English because of their gardens, hedges, and fences, and a certain busyness to the yards. The little houses had different-colored metal roofs with some houses having neat tidy orderly lots and gardens while a few looked run-down with disreputable yards.

In answer to why one house looked quite dumpy, June answered, "Mr. Sweeney likes a wee drop a little too often, yeah, and he gets a little too far gone to tidy up his yard, yeah, but he's a wonderful snooker player, and very generous to boot."

Stephie saw geraniums everywhere, and pots of house plants in lace-curtained windows where sometimes a person would peer out and wave. The town had a cozy look with mostly modest wooden houses, not terribly attractive homes, a lower-middle-class look to the place. The houses had to be sturdy to stand up to gales that pestered the South Atlantic and suddenly came up out of Antarctica to remind folks of where they were living—on the edge of the world.

June pointed out a shipwreck sitting in the harbor. "We used to have wreckers and scuttlers who would deliberately beach ships, then pick the ships clean of their cargoes. Over two centuries, many ships, damaged going around Cape Horn, limped to the Falklands. Others, seeking safe haven in the Falklands have foundered and sank in the treacherous waters of the islands. Some broke up in the narrows."

They drove by the governor's house, an official appointed by the Queen and sent from England. The house was more imposing than others and had a broad drive and lawn down to the road.

"The current governor is very nice, very pleasant; he does a lot for us."

June said, "The guns on our army base give a twenty-one gun salute on the Queen's birthday. We are still very English here. We learned our British connection came in handy. They came to our side when we really needed them. Maggie Thatcher proved to be a battle-ax like Churchill. They recommissioned the *QE2* and sent it over as part of an armada. Since then, the *QE2* has stopped here as a passenger cruise ship.

"We have four hotels here in Stanley. The nicest one is the Upland Goose Hotel. We have a sixteen-man police force, and a major crime wave is when Jetty Sawyers and Belinda, our fearless cab driver, have one of their three-day boozing bouts. Both of them get drunk and start stalking each other all over town, yeah. When she catches up with him in the Globe, she decks him; he gets up and gives her a karate chop, yeah.

"Crime over here is petty, and the tiny criminal element can and sometimes are found in or under one small dory. Occasionally, people will have a bit of drink and have a driving problem.

"Yeah, yesterday the weather was absolutely foul. Awful weather. Today is not too bad, a five or a six. The weatherman must have known you were coming, but if you don't like the weather here at the moment, blink, yeah, and it will change.

"It's a bit of a wriggle for the buses to get through some of these narrow streets, but we're making it nicely thanks to Clayton here, Falklands' best bus driver.

"Our school over there has an indoor pool. The kiddies need something to do in a small town. When kids grow up in a tiny place like this and get of age, a lot of 'em want out. They want to see the world. Some of them come back disillusioned, but most of them make a go of it and come back only for holidays."

Several yards had sheep and horses. "Some people keep those animals as pets so they don't have to buy lawn mowers."

They stopped at Stanley's little museum. It wasn't a fussy museum full of dull exhibits. It had something for everyone. It was a homey place with items that traced a history of pop culture in the Falklands for the last one-hundred-and-fifty years. It was a combination of an antique store and a junk shop with marine and naturalist exhibits.

The curator was delighted to be able to show off his stuff. He activated the mechanical zither as the busload entered. It had a war room with an Argentinean flag. Replica store shelves from the old days had a can label for Malvinas brand boiled mutton. The museum contained items salvaged from ships blown into the Falklands, and whaling paraphernalia, including harpoons.

Stephie was interested by the chart that showed pictures of the five kinds of Falkland Island penguins: Gentoos, Kings, Magellans, Macaronis, and Rockhoppers.

Back aboard the bus, June said, "We're going to take you on a little ride outside of town over the bridge to Gypsy Cove where the penguin rookery is. Some of you may want to come back to this area on your own later to see the penguins."

They crossed a rickety bridge and were in an area with moors that looked like Scotland with peat bogs, some windy desolate spots, and highlands overlooking pretty inlets.

"We have a time in winter of about two weeks when we are likely to get significant snow. Flights go to and from the Antarctic from here. The ocean here is too cold for swimming. We have only one beach without mines where we are allowed to swim in warm weather."

When they returned to the town, Stephie saw Mike Lambert loading duffel bags into the back of a Land Rover, and she regretted she'd never see him again. His stone gift was nestled in her jeans pocket.

35

Stephie and Ben got off at the Falklands Knitting Store. Sheep farming was one of the Island's primary occupations, so wool was readily available. Stephie found the hand-knitted wool sweaters attractive but pricey. She saw a wool jumper she liked, but it was 160 pounds.

"They're rather dear, but I think they're very beautiful," she told Ben.

They decided a coffee would go well, and Ben had to use the facilities, so they headed for the Kit Kat Kafé, a tiny place built in what looked like an enclosed porch with only a few tables. Everything in town was on a smaller scale with small stores, small businesses, the feel of a small town.

The menu was simple, with meat pies, fish and chips, and a few basic items. Ben went up to the counter and ordered coffee and toast.

After their coffee, Ben went to the toilet in a weather-beaten outbuilding where wallpaper rolls stood in one corner of the unfinished toilet.

As they strolled around the town, the wind picked up suddenly; it became cloudier, got very chilly, blustery, and they felt a few sprinkles. They even encountered a brief snow shower.

Stephie said, "God, they were right. I think in the short time we've been here, we've quickly gone through the four seasons. Have you heard that frequent refrain on the ship? 'Will it be cool in Chile?' People answer, 'It will be chilly in Chile.'"

Ben laughed. At least she was loosening up. Maybe their civility would get them through this trip.

He replied, "Remember there are often rough seas around Cape Horn."

Ben said he was feeling cold and thirsty, so they went into

the Burridge Hotel Bar. It had an inviting old British pub
look to it, cozy and full of pub knickknacks like Toby mugs.
They sat at the bar, the only customers; it was, after all,
barely eleven-thirty. A short woman in her fifties greeted
them from behind the bar.

Ben asked, "Do you have any draft beer or ale?" He had
planned to order a half-pint for Stephie and himself.

"No, I'm afraid not. You won't find any draft anywhere in
Stanley. We're a little off the beaten path here, and I don't
think we'd be able to keep fresh draught on hand. A few
years ago, a man started a mini-brewery in town, made a
draft and called it Penguin Ale, but it never went over.

"With only a little over two-thousand people, and what
with everyone having his own beer preferences, there weren't
enough people in town to start a trend. That's the way with
a lot of things here. Somebody will say, 'Why don't we have
a such and such?' They'll try it and find there aren't enough
customers to buy such and such."

They agreed on bottles of Foster's. They asked the woman
if she had ever been off the Islands.

"Of late, I've been visiting a sister in Southampton every
other year. I go to Scotland, and I like it there because it
reminds me of the Falklands, with its heather, heaths, and
moors. I've seen a little of London and a few other places in
England. It's nice to walk around the big department stores
and just look, especially the food courts.

"Planes take eighteen hours to get to England from here.
We fly to the Ascension Islands enroute. Some people have
never been off these Islands, but to me it gets a bit much
having to stay here all the time. I think I'll make it to Florida
and Disney World before too long."

They asked her about the war. She became sadder and
more wistful as she spoke.

"It was a dicey time what with the invasion. We had no
idea what would happen with all those Argentine lads here.
The people here have very strong feelings about the 1982
war. We still won't have anything to do with Argentina. We

were invaded. The Argentine servicemen became a real presence and a threat. The soldiers used to come into town from
the hills. A lot of them were no more than kids, fifteen, sixteen or so.

"We had safe-houses we went to when there were bom-
bardments or when the fighting started. I can still remember
how scared I was.

"Three civilians died in the war. One of them, unfortunately, was my own sister. She was killed by what they call
friendly fire; a British mortar round went astray and killed
her and two other women. Friendly fire, a strange name if
you ask me. Friendly to who? Unfriendly fire if it kills your
own. But that's war, isn't it? I bear no grudges against the
English army. When it's a war, you have all sorts of terrible
things that go wrong. So there you are, you see. Imagine
what could have happened to this town if the war had actually been fought right here in town.

"We still don't have any airplane flights to Argentina. We
have flights to and from Chile. No contacts with Argentina."

Ben said, "I noticed we passed the Malvina House Hotel.
Do the people here object to that name? The Argentines call
these islands the Malvinas."

"No, I never heard anybody say anything about the name.
That was the name long before the war. I think the owner
named it that for no particular reason. The name doesn't
bother anyone. I never even think about it. That's been the
name for years, and I guess changing it now would be like
saying they control everything we do. A name is just a
name."

They told her they liked the look of the town on their tour
and about their coffee stop at the Kit Kat Kafé. Ben asked
her about the place.

"I've never been in there. Of course I know where it is, but
I never got around to going in there. Never had a need to."

To Ben and Stephie, two curious cutting-edge pioneers,
every place was fair game. To them, it seemed odd in such a
small place, she hadn't ever been in. It might be a competi-

tor, or perhaps it was a place for a different age group, or were certain places disreputable? Perhaps it had to do with some family feud or enmity. Stephie thought, *But what insularity even in this insular place. Envelopes within envelopes.*

Neither of them could ever imagine existing in one of these end-of-the-world places. When she was single, Stephie had once spent almost a year in Provincetown, another small end-of-the-world place where the weather could turn nasty during its six-month untouristy period. She had gone there to get her head together and ended up with severe cabin fever and a severe case of the blues that could only be cured by moving back to the big city with a Starbucks on every corner.

Stanley, quaint, cozy, but no thanks. She had found the greatest thrill of places like Stanley was being able to see them for a short time and get out of town.

The woman recommended the Globe. Stephie knew the Globe would be jumping, because bar life and tying one on was one of the chief crew distractions in such towns. Sandy had clued her in on the place.

A local came into the bar, said hello to them, and started a conversation with the woman. Soon after they said good-bye and left.

Outside, Stephie said, "Ben, I really would like to go to Gypsy Cove and see the penguins. Maybe hire a cab."

"Uh-uh. I'm chilly enough now without trudging around those hills looking at penguins. Why don't we wander around town a bit, look in some stores, then go back to the pier? You can arrange for a ride to see your penguins, and I'll head back to the ship.

"Okay, I'll go out to see the penguin colony, then maybe I'll drop in the Globe for a couple of quick ones after I get back from the penguins."

They looked in a small backyard where the owner had a horse grazing. It seemed a tiny space to keep a horse, but such was the temper of this place where they had seen several Dickensian outbreaks of eccentricity; only the British could carry off these little oddities: gnomes, horses in tiny yards, and piles of peat. The smell of burning peat fires was in the air at times, but in general the air was exceptionally clean and clear.

They stopped in the West Store where the souvenir department was filled with ship passengers. The town was inundated by many of the ship's twelve-hundred passengers and crew of five-hundred. Of course not all of them had come ashore to this tendering port, but there were probably at least eight or nine-hundred ashore. Stephie picked out some tee shirts, one with a sheep design, another with penguins. Ben greeted some of the Puerto Rican contingent who were looking at a large selection of stuffed seals, sea lions, sheep, and penguins.

Stephie and Ben looked in the Upland Goose Hotel because they had seen a large group of their fellow passengers entering or leaving. It seemed like the nicest and most upscale place they had seen thus far. The hotel's restaurant was crowded with passengers who were having substantial-looking lunches.

The bar-lounge was crowded as well. Doug and Kim were there having drinks with others. They waved and called out greetings. In front of the cathedral, they met the Kaufield sisters who were bundled up for winter. They compared notes about their tours.

Near the pier, the wind again had started acting up. The water in the harbor was choppier than when they had come over. It was full of skipping white caps.

Ben fastened the strip around the collar of his anorak and said, "You go ahead and do your penguins. I'm heading back to the ship. I've got a chill, and I've seen as much of Stanley as I need for the moment. Put it in the refrigerator, and I'll eat it later."

It was one of his favorite expressions, an inside joke between the two of them when he was putting something off.

Stephie watched as Ben hurried toward the tender. He was going like a bat out of hell with the wind shaking out his anorak. Her face couldn't help registering her annoyance at being abandoned, but she knew she could get along well without him.

She shook her head ruefully. She headed up the hill to the taxi office. It had a serving window facing out on the street. The dispatcher leaned out of the window. His ruddy face looked as if he'd seen too many windblown days.

Stephie asked, "I'd like to get a cab out to the penguin colony at Gypsy Cove."

The dispatcher smiled and said, "So would I. No, but sorry, Ma'am. We're all booked up right now. The first cab won't be free for an hour or more. Your fellow passengers have us swamped."

Just as she turned away from the office, Mike Lambert approached her and said, "Stephie, did I hear you say you wanted to go to Gypsy Cove?"

"Hi, Mike. Yes, I do. Do you have a car for hire?"

"I have a Land Rover available."

"What'll the cost be?"

"I go out there a couple of days a week. I photograph the birds, draw them. If you want to accompany me, you're welcome, but I certainly wouldn't charge you."

"But I insist on paying."

"No, I insist. If you want to join me, fine. You're more than welcome, but I'm not for hire."

"Okay, if you don't mind."

"I wouldn't have asked you if I minded."

Stephie climbed into the front of the Land Rover. He took off, and in the blink of an eye, he was outside the small town on the road that circled the harbor.

Mike said, "Wow, that water is rough today. This is a harbor that can get wild and woolly at times."

The Land Rover passed over the small bridge on the far side and headed up a slope opposite the harbor and town. Along the beach, signs with skulls and crossbones, warned "Land Mines."

Stephie said, "Why land mines after all this time?"

Mike answered, "Unfortunately, so many were planted during the war by the Argentines that it's a major job getting rid of them. Once in a while, one gets uncovered by the sea. The British army has tried to sweep everywhere and get rid of them, but they can never get them all. Most are plastic, so a metal detector is useless."

Stephie was looking out the driver side of the vehicle. She looked at Mike in profile. *God, he was good looking. Strong face. Nice chin, cute nose, nice body, no paunch . . . Calm down, girl.*

He drove the Rover off the road and parked on the shoulder. They took off trudging up the bluffs, heading for Gypsy Cove. The wind was strong, cold and relentless. Stephie pulled her anorak tighter around her and shoved her hands into the jacket's pockets. A few stray snowflakes hit her face as she trudged along the ascending path.

She said, "It's a rugged place. The wind keeps whipping through here. And snow this time of year?"

Mike replied, "Yeah, we can get these snow bursts at any time."

"Do you like your life here?"

"It's lonely, but it's what I love. I received a generous grant to do penguin research here and on Great Georgia Island where there's a huge penguin colony, so this is where I'll be for some time. I'm going to monitor the oil drilling that starts soon—too soon for comfort."

"Will the drilling threaten the wildlife here?"

"We hope not. We're doing everything we can to avoid it. That's going to be part of my job—to make sure the oil rigs don't interfere with the environment."

Stephie, following Mike, heaved herself over a low fence, off on an expedition to see the flightless birds again. As she headed up the sandy path, to her right was the barbed wire fence with signs that read, "Danger! Land Mines" with a skull and crossbones. Mike said, "Imagine the jerks who steal these signs for souvenirs. The danger they pose to others."

Inside the precincts of the mine fields were what looked

like small geese foraging for food. They and the penguins were too lightweight to set off the mines, Mike told her.

They headed up the hill to the cliffs above the beach. At certain points, the path verged off, heading down to the pristine sandy beaches, but the beaches were encircled by the mine warning signs. Around her were the moors so reminiscent of the tail of Cape Cod, with stands of sea grass, bushes, and hummocks. She had her small knapsack hoisted over her shoulder.

They reached the other side of the bluff with the sea below them. It was a beautiful cove. Mike and Stephie threaded their way through the cliffside nesting grounds with burrows everywhere.

Mike said, "Magellanic penguins are true burrowers. It's a trait of theirs."

Curious penguins stared out at them, two heads to a burrow. Stephie started to take photographs.

Mike warned, "They're myopic. Please don't use flash. Their eyes are very sensitive to light, and flashes harm them."

They reached a high spot overlooking the cove below. Stephie stood there, her face glowing with pleasure.

Mike said, "It's a beautiful spot, isn't it?"

"Glorious. Picture perfect. Completely unspoiled. You're a lucky guy to have all this beauty to see whenever you want."

"At last I've found someone who shares my love of this place."

Mike looked at her admiringly. He said, "If you'll pardon me for a few minutes, I have to go over to that bluff and check on a few burrows."

He took off. Stephie looked around her. The sky was a vivid blue where it wasn't covered by fast moving clouds in all shapes and sizes. The headland gave breathtaking views of the beaches and the choppy ocean. The hills and green-tufted sandy soil, perfect for a painter, the beauty of it all. She felt gloriously alive amid the natural surroundings and was inspired by her adventure.

Stephie began laughing at herself and this bizarre expedition of hers. Here she was being whipped by strong gusts of wind and occasional spritzing of drizzle in her black trainers, jeans, a heavy blouse, a sweater, and a thick windbreaker and cap, trudging up and down hills and dunes, over headlands, into rills, slipping into holes that just might bite back, alongside inadequate fencing that demarked active mine fields.

Later, Stephie and Mike were in the Land Rover headed back into Port Stanley.

Stephie said, "That was fantastic. I love to observe the penguins. They have a purpose in life."

"Yes, a purpose of their own. They're not here to entertain us. I never tire of studying them, sketching them, photographing them. By the way, where's your husband gone to?"

"He had to go back to the ship. Maybe he had to take a dump. He said he might be coming down with something, a cold. Or maybe he lives on a different planet than I do."

"He won the lotto when he snagged you. Does he know that?"

Stephie blushed. "He may have won the booby prize. No, but sometimes I think the two of us inhabit different worlds."

36

Mike pulled the Rover up in front of the Globe Pub and Hotel and said, "Will you come in and have a drink with me? It'll warm you up."

"Great, but only if I pay."

"You got a deal, Steph."

The Globe was a thriving busy smoky pub full of locals, passengers, and crew members. Loud music and voices filled the place. Everyone seemed to be wound up and getting a glow on. An overturned dory hung over the bar; the upside-down dory made a good touch for the bar's nautical décor. A good-looking young guy was burning beer cartons in the blazing fireplace.

It was the island's main local, but on this day, the pub's two rooms were overflowing with passengers and crew, all getting a buzz on, keeping out of the chill air.

Young guys and girls from the crew were in full swing. Many were dancing. They had let down their hair and were buzzed. Sandy was in the middle of a snooker match. He grinned at Stephie and yelled a greeting. The pub's two rooms were full. The room to the left held mainly tables where people were talking in loud voices; some were eating lunches.

Fat Budgy was on his way out the door. In the tap room, three barmaids were trying to keep up with orders. Julie and Peter, the ship bartenders, were at one end of the bar in deep conversation with a young couple, performers from the ship.

As usual, the Rilleaus were dancing. Stephie and Mike sat at the bar. Stephie was laughing, having fun. She looked transformed, felt more relaxed and contented than she had in weeks.

Meanwhile, on the ship, Ann and Ben were on the bed in her cabin. He was ardent, erect, a bull in heat, but she was not responding.

She said, "Not now, Buster. This cabin is getting claustro-phobic, stifling. I feel as if I'm a sex slave locked away in a cell with a sex ogre. I'm going out on deck and get some air. Look at that sea out there. It's really choppy. Those waves and swells. I want to be on deck. I need air."

Ben hated it when she called him *Buster*. He looked out the cabin window at the choppy harbor.

He said, "I hope Stephie got back. If she didn't, she's going to have a rough ride on the tender coming back."

Ann said, "It's funny, ironic really, how you get so agitated when the Little Woman might be in danger. How come you don't worry about her when you're shagging me behind her back?"

Ben looked at her, his look downcast. *Jeez, these broads can stick together at the wrong times.*

Ann ignored him, put on her jacket, and left the cabin without a further word.

Ben watched television in her cabin for a time, then went to the lounge and had a drink at the bar. Budgy walked in. He had gotten from one boozer to another in record time. He saw Ben and addressed him directly. Ben knew he was doomed for the rest of the voyage.

Budgy roared, "Now that was a real town with real pubs and good British beer. That Globe was a gem if I ever saw one. Nice fire going, great atmosphere."

Ben got away when Budgy started talking to a bartender about pubs in England.

On shore at the Globe, Stephie and Mike had just finished their second gin and tonic. When he suggested they switch to beer, she agreed, and they were served frosty bottles. The fireplace was roaring. Mike and Stephie had peeled off their outer jackets. Some of the crew and passengers had left. Tony was at the bar with a good-looking girl from the ship. Mike talked Stephie into dancing with him. She was less inhibited. The dancing started to get more intimate. They were really bonding.

Mike said, "I feel so happy being with you. Like I've known you forever."

"I really enjoy your company, even though you are a penguin nerd."

He laughed. "You seem on your way to becoming one too."

Stephie and Mike continued dancing. She was happy, energized. Her hair was wild. After a time, she looked around her. All of the ship people had left.

She stopped dancing and yelled to Mike. "Oh my God, what time is it?"

"4:10."

"The last tender leaves at 4:30. I've got to get out of here."

Stephie and Mike grabbed their coats, ran outside, and rushed down the hill to the pier. The harbor was swirling, boiling with roiling water and swells. Whitecaps were everywhere.

Stephie said, "Cripes, there aren't any of the ship's tenders at the dock or in the harbor."

A young man and woman were standing near them on the dock. Stephie asked, "Where are the tenders?"

The man answered, "Hi, guys, we're singers on the ship. Jerry and Debbie Blunt. We've got to get back too. One more tender is due."

Stephie asked, "Are we going to be able to get back to the ship?"

Jerry said, "They'll get us back . . . I hope."

Mike had his arm around Stephie. He looked like her husband-protector. She felt comfortable leaning on his shoulder. Perhaps too comfortable.

Mike said, "Oh, there she is now."

He pointed to an orange-topped tender coming around from the other side of their ship, tiny like a toy boat way out in the harbor. The cruise ship was rising and falling on the huge swells, and the tender made little headway as it headed toward them.

The harbor seas had become rougher and choppier since the morning. There were high swells farther out. The little tender was bobbing and bouncing as she came into the Stanley dock. When it docked, Stephie noticed the young

British ship's officer in the bos'n's chair looked concerned. The boat's Filipino deckhands, all wearing orange life vests, were unsmiling, anxious-looking.

Mike gave Stephie a farewell kiss on the lips that was quite intense. "Steph, I hope to see you again. If anything changes in your life, anything, please get in touch. God be with you. I'm never going to forget you as long as I live."

Stephie said, "I can't remember anyone I've felt closer to in such a short time."

Mike handed her a card with his various telephone, snail mail, and e-mail addresses on it. They hugged tightly, then Stephie stepped aboard the tender and climbed down the few steps into the covered cabin where Jerry and Debbie sat huddled together. The deckhands insisted the three passengers don life-vests. They all sat below the tender officer, the helmsman, in his starched whites who was seated on a high seat above them.

The tender took off toward the ship. Heading out into the harbor, at times the young officer at the wheel would let the wheel spin by itself, then do some furious turning. It was a rough ride, the bow barely clearing the waves at times and coming down with a hard slap. They were experiencing powerful swells, huge waves for a sheltered harbor. The little boat was rising and falling precipitously, and the four deckhands had come below the deck line into the covered cabin area. One of the younger ones looked panicky.

Stephie thought, *If we ever capsized or turned over, how would we possibly get out of this covered coffin? It's like a prison.* She was huddled in a bow seat near the couple. In her hand, she tightened her grip on Mike's talisman stone, hoping it would bring her luck.

The tender eventually got near the hull of the ship with its little boarding platform and gangway clinging to the ship's side. On the first approach, the seas were so rough the tender almost smashed into the ship. It had to back off. The helmsman was trying to angle it so he could bring the tender safely alongside.

Many passengers were on deck watching anxiously, including Ben, Kim, and Doug. A distance from Ben, in another cluster of people was Ann. Ben had been told Stephie was aboard the tender.

Ben said aloud, "C'mon, Stephie, we're praying for you. C'mon, make it back, hon."

Ann said to herself, *God, this guy really knows how to live in parallel universes.*

Kim said, "Oh my God, poor Stephie."

The helmsman made another pass at the ship. They were now experiencing huge waves. The tender was bobbing and weaving, swaying and bouncing, riding up, and sliding down. The helmsman was in constant voice contact with the ship. Apparently, the captain warned him off at the last minute because he made a wide circle out beyond the ship and started another run. Stephie watched as the helmsman's wheel spun. The helmsman tried to time a big wave that would bring him alongside.

The liner itself was rocking and swaying and being maneuvered by the heavy swells while the tiny tender seemed to be making ever wider circles in her approach to the platform. It was being thrown around and tossed. It seemed to climb the huge waves and then, like a surfboarder, roar down into a trough. The helmsman's pass had been for naught. The radio voices were crackling back and forth. The helmsman was getting directions from the bridge.

It was no go. He had to back off and come around for what might have to be his last pass. As the little tender came alongside, it was again almost flung against the hull.

The helmsman turned to the three passengers and shouted, "The captain has waved me off. He's ordered me to return to the pier and make a try later when the seas calm down."

The tender had trouble making it back to the pier. Stephie and the Blunts clambered with difficulty out of the bobbing boat at the pier.

When Stephie stepped onto the dock, Mike was waiting.

He used the opportunity to give her a welcoming hug and another intense kiss.

"Stephie, I could tell they weren't going to make it. It's very dicey, very touch and go. I'm afraid they might have to give up and wait for calmer seas. They'll make a try later when the sea eases up, or they may have to leave you here and fly you to Ushuaia by way of Chile."

She looked at him, dumbfounded. He was serious.

She said, "Oh, you're a great help. You don't mean I'd be stranded over here?"

Jerry and Debbie stood shivering on the dock next to them.

Jerry said, "They could put us up in the Globe, and as long as the booze doesn't run out, we'll be comfy."

A big sea-seasoned man wearing a thick quilted jacket, approached them. "Folks, my name is Tim Andersen. I represent your cruise line and the ship. I've just been in touch with the captain. Because of weather conditions, your ship has to get out of the harbor and back on course."

"They're pulling in that tender you just returned on. They can put cables on the tender and haul it aboard with the winches with the tender crew aboard. That way they don't have to dock the boat, but the ship's insurance wouldn't cover hauling aboard passengers that way. It's a dangerous procedure in seas like this. Too many chances for accident.

"This harbor isn't going to get calmer. It's going to be a boiling cauldron very shortly. Your ship has to go at full speed on their itinerary to reach Ushuaia in Argentina by Saturday."

Steph said, "Today is Thursday."

Tim replied, "Ushuaia is a long way away. Tomorrow they'll be at sea. This is the plan for you people. The cruise company is going to put you up at the Upland Goose Hotel tonight and Friday night. All expenses for food, lodging, and any essentials you need for your stay on the island are on us. That goes for you three stranded passengers.

"But not for you, Mike. You have a place of your own, and

anyway I heard you left the ship today. Early Saturday morning, we're going to fly you three to Chile. Enjoy your room, your meals, and do all your shopping for so-called essentials—all compliments of the cruise company. You guys look like you could use some of our hand-knitted jumpers, so break the bank and enjoy yourselves."

Stephie said, "Chile? Ushuaia is in Argentina."

Tim answered, "The Falklands has no direct contacts with Argentina because of the war, so you'll go to Chile, then direct to Ushuaia. Don't fret. Because of heavy seas, we went through this drill a couple of other times when the *Global Quest* stopped here before. You're not the first ones to be stranded here for a couple of nights."

Mike led Stephie to the Upland Goose Hotel. She was quickly registered and shown a pleasant room overlooking the turbulent port. They could see the ship just starting to steam out of the harbor beyond the breakwater.

She went with Mike to the West Store where she filled a shopping basket with toiletries, a thick hand-knitted woolen sweater, blouses, a plaid skirt, a track suit, underwear, and extras. The cashier told her they had been alerted by the cruise company's agent, and there was no need for her to pay. She left the store with a large cloth tote bag bearing the logo and name of the store and loaded with her purchases.

Stephie said to Mike, "God, I'm going back tomorrow and get a couple more of those hand-knitted woolen sweaters and some other pricey goodies."

Mike said, "It sounds as if you're taking advantage of your situation."

"You bet your tush I am. Oh, I'm sorry. I didn't mean to be crude."

"Hey, Steph, you can bet my tush any day of the week."

And a gorgeous tush it is. Does he realize how luscious his buns are? Stop this stuff! I'm acting like a teenager chasing after the high school's top stud.

In the hotel lobby after her shopping trip, Mike said, "Now, Stephie, don't worry. It's going to be all right. If you don't mind, I'm going to have drinks and dinner with you tonight here in the hotel. Afterwards I'll bring you on a pub crawl if you want. We have six pubs. I'll be here at 7:30, okay?"

Stephie said, "Yes, thank you, Mike. Thank God you're here to look after me."

Mike said, "It'll give us a chance to really get to know each other."

He left. She went up to her room where she put in a ship-to-shore call to Ben to tell him about her stranding and the company's plan to return her to the ship.

Minutes later, on board ship, Ben and Ann were talking in her cabin while looking out at the fierce seas.

Ben said, "I just got off the phone with Stephie. She's going to be stranded on the Falklands until they fly her out early Saturday morning. The cruise line is arranging flights so she can pick up the ship in Ushuaia, so we've got two nights on the ship alone together."

Ann said, "It's as if you arranged all this."

"I try to arrange certain things, but I can't control Mother Nature."

"You can be a prick, you know that. I feel sorry for Stephie. She must be panicking. God, if I were in her shoes, there wouldn't be enough Xanax to calm me down."

"Hey, Ann, I feel terrible about this. That tender could have been swamped in those wild seas."

"That poor woman has had to put up with a lot. More than her share."

Ben looked at her, dumbfounded. He had read it was always dangerous when the mistress started to sympathize with the wife. Ben thought, *Might be dangerous shoals ahead. Better tighten the straps on my life-jacket. These bitches really stick together!*

37

In the hotel Stephie took a long shower and changed into some of her new loot. Being stranded wasn't so bad after all. New duds, a good-looking escort, and especially some quality time way away from Ben.

That evening, Stephie and Mike had drinks in the hotel bar, then went into the dining room where they were shown to a candlelit table. They enjoyed their dinner and had a chance to talk. Stephie was intrigued by Mike's knowledge of a myriad of subjects. The more she saw of him, the more she was attracted to him.

She sipped her wine as she looked across at him. The Blunts waved at them from another table. Jerry Blunt smiled broadly and gave them a thumbs up sign.

Stephie said, "I can't believe this. Enjoying myself while I'm trapped on an island, stranded, abandoned, as my cruise ship sails blithely on without me."

Mike said, "It's a wonderful chance for me. The more time I have with you, the better. Stop me if I'm out of line, but is yours a happy marriage?"

"I'll be honest. My marriage is over. It's at a dead end. In the last few days, actually in Buenos Aires, I made up my mind. This afternoon when we were out on those bluffs, I realized there's a big glorious beautiful world out there for me—a world without Ben."

"Has this been coming on for a long time?"

"I put up with too much for too long. I missed my ship long before this cruise even began. You know that's so true. I don't know why I'm telling you all this, but, it's no big secret Ben and I have had it. He couldn't care less."

That night aboard ship, as Kim was coming out her cabin door, she looked down the hall and saw Ben coming out of a cabin farther down the passageway opposite the elevator.

185

She ducked inside before Ben had a chance to see her. The Smarmy Man had his cabin door open and was peering out. He also saw Ben sneaking out of his mistress's cabin.

Later, when Kim and Doug were leaving their cabin to go to dinner, Kim saw Ann come out the same cabin door Ben had exited. Ann entered the stairwell.

Kim turned to Doug and said, "This ship has more intrigue than that old Orient Express movie. I think Ben has found a shoulder to cry on, a new port in the storm."

Doug said, "Huh? What's up?"

"I hope they put Stephie up somewhere nice in the Falklands while her hubby is catting around."

In the ship's dining room, the group, gathered at the table, were worried about Stephie, and Katie questioned Ben, who said, "Stephie and I have called back and forth. She's staying in a nice hotel. She's being well cared for, and she's with a couple from the ship's show cast who were stranded with her, so she has company."

After dinner, Ben said his good nights to the tablemates, while Ann excused herself from the captain's table. Kim saw this, as did the Smarmy Man.

On the island, Mike and Stephie, after their dinner and pub crawl, were in her room, sitting on the edge of her bed. They were kissing, eagerly, hungrily. Mike smoothed back her hair tenderly. She was breathless from his long urgent kisses. Their mouths were open, their tongues exploring.

When she broke away from him, Mike said, "Please let me spend the night with you."

"I want to so badly, but I can't just now."

"I'd love to be with you. To hold you. Just cuddle with you and be with you."

"Oh, God, Mike, I want to be with you so much it hurts, but not tonight. I have to be alone and think and step back. I need space and . . ."

"Please."

"Mike, give me a little space. Give me a chance to . . ."

"I think I understand, but I want to be with you so bad."

They kissed very tenderly, longingly, lovingly.

He left and stopped at the Globe on his way back to his rented apartment near the top of the hill.

He had two whiskies and ignored people who tried to talk to him. Even the island's intrepid cab driver, Belinda, couldn't get through to him.

38

The next morning aboard ship, as the vessel was making considerable headway toward the Argentine coast, Ben was exercising in the gym, working up a heavy sweat. He took off his shirt in front of the mirror. His pecs were firm, his abs defined, his body pumped up. Pedaling slowly on a stationary bike, the Smarmy Man, reptilian, watched him.

A short time later, Ben was lying in a chaise on the pool deck. He got up, walked to the pool, and climbed down the ladder into the water. The Smarmy Man had been watching him. He followed Ben to the pool where he slithered snake-like into the water. They were both paddling around at one end.

The Smarmy Man smiled his insincere crooked smile and said, "You're a very lucky guy."

Ben said, "Pardon me, are you speaking to me, pal?"

"Yes, indeed. Ben, isn't it?"

"Yes, how did you know my name?"

Ben didn't like the man and didn't like where he thought it was going. *The guy's a fag.*

"I happened to overhear someone using your name. I salivate when I think how lucky you are. Such gorgeous fulsome breasts your lady friend has."

"What the hell are you talking about, Buddy? I think you're asking for trouble. I don't know you. You don't me."

Ben started to swim away, saying, "I don't know what you're talking about."

He stopped swimming when he heard, "Oh, but I'm sure you do. Your wife Stephanie is attractive, but she's not a sex pot. That other woman, Ann, now there's a tasty morsel."

"Why are you insinuating such rubbish about me? You know some people are born assholes, and you're one of them."

The Smarmy Man said, "I have my ways of finding out secrets. My prurient mind is a great help, and I keep my eyes open. A vivid imagination helps me . . ."

Ben paddled away from the man toward the pool ladder. "I've heard enough. I'm getting out of here . . ."

"No, I think you'll want to hear what I have to say. You stowed your wife in one cabin, and you've got that other one hidden away on my deck. Ann, your concubine, stays out of Stephanie's way. Very conveniently for you, your wife is trapped over on the Falklands as we speak, he-he."

The Smarmy Man was salivating, drooling.

Ben said, "Hey, Fuckface, what do you want anyway, you sleazebag a-hole?"

"Nothing much. I don't intend to let the cat out of the bag. I'm just going to watch. I like that. I love this kind of duplicity. You must love the danger too, the possibility of being discovered, or you wouldn't do it. For you, the danger, the thrill of it all must be better than Viagra. Keeps you hard, doesn't it?"

"I'm outta here, asshole. You better watch your back. You're going to end up in the drink one of these dark nights."

"Enjoy yourself, Ben. Be careful. Your bride is a smart cookie. If she finds out, you'll be dead meat. I hope she's able to rejoin the ship at some point."

Ben hurried up the ladder, grabbed his towel and hurried back to his cabin. The guy knew too much and could pose a real danger to him. He decided not to tell Ann about him yet—it would only spook her.

39

On her first morning of abandonment, Stephie and Mike took a ride out to Gypsy Cove where Mike wanted to take some photos and make sketches. It was a beautiful day in the Falklands. The previous stormy day was replaced with rich sunlight, a cloudless sky, and clean air. A light breeze instead of a gale. As he pulled up to the lay-by near the cove, he pointed out a parked Land Rover with a large woman standing beside it.

He said, "Uh-oh, there's Belinda, our infamous island taxi driver. She's a real character."

Belinda was six feet tall, wore khaki cargo pants bloused over her size eleven combat boots, and although the weather was chilly, she wore a light tee shirt and was obviously bra-less. She was smoking a cheroot.

After Mike had parked, and he and Stephie alighted, Belinda said, "How's it goin', Penguin Man? I see you finally found yourself a chick. Good for you. You should see the two nut cases I brought up here. They're over the bluffs looking at your penguins. A weird couple. You'll meet them over there. I think the penguins will get a bigger charge outta them than they'll get out of the penguins."

After she was introduced, as the two islanders talked, Stephie had a chance to study the cab driver. A massive young woman, tough looking, with her spiky hair dyed an unnaturally reddish color, a rose tattoo on the right forearm, an anchor on the left, a nose stud, and items speared in her ears, she was a formidable presence.

Her face, her attitude, her speech, her stance betokened a person who had lived not wisely or in moderation, but with too much gusto. She was encrusted with the barnacles of tough life experiences and the jolts a street-smartened and street-hardened woman would encounter.

She looked like she went looking for trouble and didn't have much trouble finding it, probably because she was the one who initiated it. The salt of the earth? Perhaps, but Stephie wondered about booze and drugs, and having a good time at all costs. She probably always ended up with the wrong type of man, or did her type seek them out?

Stephie could be wrong, way off the mark on her first impressions. After all, she had fallen for and married Ben, hadn't she? Belinda might be one of those Islanders who knitted those beautiful sweaters sold in the woolens shop, though Stephie seriously doubted it. Some women had the look and attitude, the belligerence of a bull dyke, but often they turned out to be staggeringly heterosexual.

Stephie asked, "How much do you charge to go out to see the penguins here at Gypsy Cove?"

"Thirty dollars. Dollars 'cause most are tourists."

"Out and back? Round trip?"

Belinda lowered her brows and looked at Stephie as if she were addressing a cretin.

"That's right. I drive 'em out, leave them at the pathway, and come back and pick them up in about an hour-and-a-half or so. They need that long to walk up the path, get to the nesting places, look at the boids, slip into burrows, slide along penguin shit, then walk back down the path. It's almost a mile of uphill and downhill walking and rough terrain just so you'll know, dearie."

Stephie said, "I was up here yesterday."

"Oh, you're one of them gluttons for punishment. If it was me, I'd be up here, too, if I could get Mike alone in the bushes. He's one hell of a stud muffin. Loves his penguins though. Maybe he gets off on 'em."

Mike said, "Well, Belinda, Stephie and I have to get up and visit my children."

"You know, I haven't been there for years. I think I'll go up and surprise my screwball passengers. See if they're making out on the bluffs."

The three of them started up the path, Belinda taking up

the rear. The path led up and around the hill and over the moors.

Belinda yelled out to Stephie, "As you know, Missie, follow the path. Stay clear of the fuckin' minefields and watch out you don't step in a hole, or a bloody penguin will give you a bite you'll not soon forget."

At the peak of the bluff, from behind a stand of bushes, two human heads popped up over the top the way penguin couples stuck their heads out of their burrows. When they came out from behind the bushes, Stephie saw a large jovial fat man, early forties, in a black leather coat. His companion was a small woman in a flimsy black raincoat. Her hair was silvery white, though she was only in her forties.

He introduced himself. "I'm John and this is me wife, Peggy, and I see you've already met our buxom cab driver, the Amazon Belinda."

Peggy had a loud cackle of a laugh. It could pierce through a listener if the hearer wasn't prepared. Almost everything she said or anyone else said ended in that cackle.

She said, "We're visiting from Birmingham. We've relatives here on the island."

Stephie said, "I'm Stephie. From the States, Washington, D.C."

Mike introduced himself and spoke about his work on the island as a naturalist.

John, Peggy, and Belinda began a conversation. They were apparently related in some way. It was difficult for Stephie to make out what they were saying. They talked rapidly back and forth with many slangy expressions thrown in. There was Peggy's loud cackle, John's occasional high whine, and Belinda's slangy profanity and mixture of accents.

Belinda commented, "I told that fuckin' asshole of a dispatcher, Eddie, we'd be getting a lot of business yesterday what with the ship in, and what does the wanker do? Nothing. Holes up with Gloria in Deano's. That's his method of dealing with problems. Wouldn't fuckin' listen to me so I had to gas up on my own. I told him to get my Land Rover ready, and he does absolutely shite. Nothing. A lot of bloody talk. You'd think the prick would learn from the last time a ship was in, but no, he's too fuckin' stupid to learn."

Stephie smiled; she wasn't going to ask any tourist questions about local hydroponic gardens or the migratory habits of killer whales to this harridan. Better to just keep her mouth shut.

The machine gun conversation went on. There was much laughing and jollity, but they might as well have been conversing in Polish for all Stephie picked up. Dialects, slang, intonations, argot, accents, rapidity of delivery all turned their English into gibberish.

John and Peggy were highly entertaining, and Belinda was one of those big brash women perpetually pissed off about life in general.

John and Peggy had a midlands twang, and Belinda had a Falklands accent mixed with Cockney and some Welsh strains. Stephie was able to decipher that Belinda had spent a considerable time in Britain, had followed a bloke to Britain, a bum who turned out to be "a pissass shite." She was left in the lurch and had to send a daughter back to Stanley to be raised by her parents.

Belinda said, "Yesterday I brought a group over here to see these fuckin' boids, and I got a fuckin' poontcher in the right rear tire. Shite. Fuck. Eddie was supposed to check the tires in the morning. I was on Bridge Road. I got passengers, and I get the bloody poontcher. I told him to check the tires. Bastard. That asshole don't know diddly squat about car maintenance."

John was fatter than Stephie first thought. He and Peggy were in a good mood, and laughed at adversities. The hennish cackling sounds of Peggy seemed to warm John's heart.

The sun had come out strongly, and everyone but Belinda was overdressed for this sudden burst of warm weather. Stephie felt like she was baking in her layers of clothing. She took off her outer jacket.

Belinda, finishing another cheroot, announced, "I'm going to start heading back to the road."

Mike had to go to a nearby cliffside to take pictures. Stephie left Peggy and John behind as she explored the burrows. From time to time she glanced back at them, smiling, enjoying their adventure, an equable couple. Peggy waddled along at a brisk clip, and good natured Falstaffian John in his black leather coat followed.

Neither one was dressed for this kind of hiking. John had his leather jacket, which reached below his waist. He was carrying a paper shopping bag, stuff they had purchased at various stores in Stanley. Peggy wore a pair of high-heeled shoes not meant for hiking. Walking was difficult for her, but she enjoyed being with her man. Stephie thought how compatible and contented they were versus her relationship with Ben.

At times, the walking was rough, slippery, and muddy in spots. They would scramble up a bluff, then partially slide down an incline into a little gully. It was a path with occasional holes to climb over.

Stephie thought to what end was all this? To find penguins—again. Searching for penguins in the middle of nowhere after encountering a frowzy, brawling, profane giantess named Belinda who could probably deck any male in the Falklands, and had probably bedded most of them, quite a sight for sore eyes with her tattoos, studs, and pierced body parts, those showing anyway. Stephie wished a camera could catch the irony, the insanity, and the absurdity of her penguin expeditions.

After about an hour of exploring and photographing the penguin lairs, she had seen probably about three dozen widely separated penguins in or near their burrows. There had been no penguin highway leading to the ocean below.

Along the sides of the hills and in amongst the greenery, the bushes, and high grass, Stephie could make out burrows. At one point, the path ended, and she had to go up a small hill to another path that brought her through clumps of bushes and some hidden holes. She slipped into one and thought, *God, what if a penguin bites me.*

Luckily it was an empty burrow.

She saw one penguin, standing nonchalantly about ten feet away, not paying any attention to her. She went over a rise and began looking through the maze of bushes and burrows for others. Here and there Stephie spotted some. She saw two penguin heads peeking out a hole, one head deeper inside than the other.

At another hole, two heads popped out at once, which brought on a staring match as Stephie took pictures. The penguins stared with only one eye on each side of their head. They watched intruders warily.

As she explored the little hillocks and gullies, she realized there were not a large number of penguins there. They could be off gathering food, or it could be there wasn't enough shrimp and other food to sustain a large population. Amid the penguins, other sea birds wandered around as unmindful of the people as the penguins were.

Looking down at the beaches, she didn't see signs of penguins, but she did see a lot of sea birds flying back and forth. It was a beautiful spot, the quality of the light remarkable.

Stephie was not a professional birder; she wasn't even an amateur. She'd never made a study of bird life, bird behavior, never hid in the wild with binoculars poised, ready to identify species. She knew the names of only a few birds. What did fascinate her was being in a natural habitat like this, seeing a life completely unfamiliar to her, walking, exploring, getting some fresh air, having an adventure.

Mike had crept up on her. There on the bluffs of Gypsy Cove, they walked together, looked in the burrows, happily bonding. At one point, he leaned over and kissed her. She responded and leaned into him. It was a long ardent kiss. When they broke apart, she had a fulfilled look on her face and faced out to sea so he couldn't see how radiant she felt.

Later, they were kneeling in front of a burrow above the beach and the ocean. They were studying two curious fearless penguins who were poking out of their burrow. Stephie took out Mike's gift stone and placed it in front of him. He laughed.

"You kept it?"

"You bet, Stud Muffin."

With his right knee, Mike pushed the small shiny red stone toward Stephie. He smiled at her, looked down at the stone, back at her, pointed to the stone with his head. She smiled, picked up the stone, turned it around in her hand for a considerable time, admiring it. Mike wordlessly nodded his head. Stephie pocketed the stone. He leaned over and kissed her. They kissed for a long time, then she got up and headed toward another burrow, leaving him to wonder.

Peggy and John were close by now, craning their heads here and there to get views of the penguins. John had a videocamera and was recording scenes. Peggy would cackle briefly when she sighted a burrow with the occupants at home, and he would come over to film. They called back and forth to one another, but Stephie couldn't fathom what they were saying. *They really should wear subtitles or have supertext flashing over their heads.*

Mike said he and Stephie would like to meet Peggy and John in the Globe for a drink later. And Belinda if she was available. Peggy and John readily agreed.

Mike asked, "How were your penguins then? Did you see enough of them? If you want to see millions of them, go to South Georgia Island, part of the Falklands. It's hundreds of miles from here, but the whole island is absolutely covered with penguins."

When the two couples reached the road, Belinda was her usual profane lusty self. John, Peggy, and Belinda again held a three-way conversation, carried on at top speed with regional accents, vocabulary and intonations that made their British speech unintelligible to American ears. Mike held hands with Stephie as they listened and pretended to understand. She edged closer to Mike so their bodies were touching.

40

When Mike and Stephie entered the Globe, they were greeted by the trio from the rookery. It seemed as if the three had already taken on a cargo of beer. Belinda ordered bottles of Foster's for Stephie and Mike. It was warm and cheery in the bar, but it was less crowded than when the cruise ship had been in port the previous day.

That night, the second night of Stephie's stranding in Port Stanley, Stephie and Mike and the Blunts were with a large group of people in the Globe Pub. Everyone was having a good time, bonding, drinking, enjoying themselves. Mike and Stephie had five beers, danced, took part in a singalong, and Stephie and the Blunts were sworn in as temporary citizens of the Falklands by the town's mayor.

Mike walked Stephie back to her hotel. They stood in the hallway outside her open door. Soon they were kissing tenderly, gently, very intently. As he pressed against her, she could feel in his manhood his need for her. She leaned into him. Their mouths opened to a long serious kiss.

As one, they moved slowly into her room, edged toward the bed and were soon pressed together on top of the afghan. For a long time, they cuddled and kissed as their hands probed. He whispered to her. They rose from the bed, stood clenched together, and kissed hungrily for a long time.

Clothes flew off. Quick visits were made to the bathroom, and soon two nude bodies were clinging to one another in a wordless coupling. Hands explored. The two bodies merged into one. Mike kissed and fondled Stephie's breasts. At one point, she held Mike's head in both her hands and kissed him with an earnestness even she could not fathom. Motions, movements, feet caressing legs, bodies intertwining, pressed tightly together. So much for each to learn about the other's body.

Ben's lovemaking had always been aggressive, controlling, and somewhat brutish. To him sex was a power play, had more to do with control, being satiated than making love.

Mike's gentleness and unselfishness made his lovemaking much more satisfying. He excited her more than Ben ever had. How incredible she felt—unbelievably alive and fulfilled. Stephie knew she had never had a comparable sexual experience. Mike was a marvelous lover, and she responded in kind.

That night, they both used the word *love*, and when it was uttered, they both knew they truly meant it. It wasn't used as a ploy, a cliché, or a bargaining chip. It was said as a genuine authentic response to their physical joining. Neither one got much sleep that night.

Early in the morning, they showered together and again explored each other's bodies.

Stephie packed her new acquisitions into two new carryalls emblazoned, "I Fell in Love with the Falklands." Mike drove her to the small airport where she was to board a two-engine jet prop for the flight from Port Stanley to Punta Arenas in Chile. There she would change to an Argentine plane bound for Ushuaia.

On the airport tarmac they stood embracing each other as the Blunts looked on.

Mike said, "We have to stay in touch, and we have to be together. Please don't make this the end of something. We have to make it a beginning."

Stephie said, "Yes, for sure. I'm thinking of coming back here and being with you when I get everything settled in Washington. That's if you'll have me."

"If I'll have you? I wish you'd just stay right now and forget that cruise. I make enough to support you. I love you so much. I need you so much."

"I love you, too, but I have to get back to close out that phase of my life. I'll be back to the ship by afternoon if everything goes all right, finish the cruise, get back to Washington, tie up a lot of loose ends, then we can be together."

"I love you. If you don't join me here, I'm going to follow you and join with you wherever you are. I have to be with you for good. I love you."

Stephie said, "As soon as I get things sorted out, I want to be with you too. I'll get in touch with you from the ship."

"Please come back here and be with me as soon as you can. Your penguins are already missing you."

They said their goodbyes. She walked up the stairs, waved, and entered the plane where she took a seat behind the Blunts.

When the plane took off, Stephie and Mike were both in tears. As she sat on the plane, watching the island become a speck, she knew she had made a conscious decision to have sex with Mike the night before. Before she had married Ben, her sexual experience had been limited. She had loved Ben, but had soon realized he was a womanizer. *What an awful word.*

In the last year, she knew their marriage had reached a dead end. She loved Mike. He was a beautiful lover and a kind man. He seemed altruistic, idealistic, a giving person, while Ben had become an opportunist, a taker, a user.

She had thought if she made love with Mike, she'd be what she despised in Ben, but she realized her life was ebbing away, and she needed to get on with *her* life. Ben had ceased to matter or count for her. She remembered her boss's warning about him. He was up to something that was going to put a nail in the coffin their marriage had become.

She had thought of waiting to have sex with Mike, but the reality of geography made her make her move. It was either then or never. She wanted to have said to him, "Please, let's wait, and when the time is right, it'll be right for us."

She knew he'd have been understanding, but disappointed. She'd say, "Somehow we'll get together again. I can feel it."

And then the reality of thousands of miles of separation made her realize they didn't have time to wait.

Stephie took Mike's red stone from her anorak pocket and looked at it, clutched it tightly in her palm, and said a prayer.

41

That afternoon, the *Global Quest* lay at anchor in the harbor of Ushuaia. The town sat on the side of a hill with snow-covered rugged glacial mountains behind it. A damp haze partially obscured the mountains. A ship's tender pulled alongside the ship, and Stephie climbed up a gangway to the hatch where Ben was waiting. He rushed to her, hugged her, kissed her, held her close. Her arms hung down, without reciprocating the hug, but he didn't notice.

Ben said, "Steph, oh my God, what a horrible ordeal. It must have been awful for you."

"Actually, the locals took good care of me. They went out of their way to be super-nice to me. I had a great time. Fantastic. Better than I ever imagined. I think I've made some lifelong friends there. How about you?"

Stephie loved the irony of her words.

He said, "All I could think of was you over there on that island alone."

"I hit the island pubs and met a lot of people."

She wanted to deflate his balloon. She felt like saying, "I had the best shag of my life over there. Better than any of the ones we ever had together."

But instead she said, "Oh, how's the cold? You look like you shook it off."

"Yeah, I think I'm a little better now, Steph. It was so cold and nasty over there in the Falklands, I had to hightail it back to the ship."

"I got used to the weather over there. Kinda liked it."

Stephie was smiling. She was enjoying this. Maybe she'd think of some nice put-downs as she went along.

Ben, all sympathy, said, "You'll probably want to go to the cabin and nap."

"Hell no, darling. I'm going back to the cabin and freshen

up. While I'm here, I want to see Ushuaia. I'm going to rent a cab and see all the sights."

"No, hon, we'll go together."

"Oh, Ben, you don't have to."

Ben said, "Of course I want to go with you. I just thought you might be exhausted after your adventure, after being stranded. I don't want to let you out of my sight. You might miss the ship again."

"Missing your ship isn't the worst thing in the world that can happen to you."

Later, when they got ashore, they hired a cab driver to show them the sights. The city of forty thousand had a kind of frontier look. Backpackers were on the streets. The place was humming because it was a take-off port for visits to the Antarctic, and many hikers began Tierra del Fuego treks from there.

Stephie and Ben got out of the cab in a national park and took a walk through a wooded area with high pine trees, their trunks coated in moss and lichen. The smell of pine in the air was invigorating. Everything was damp. Steam and haze rose from the wet ground. In front of them lay the Beagle Channel.

The cab driver came up to them and said, "This is the end of the Pan American Highway. Ushuaia is the southernmost city in the world. This is where the Andes fall into the sea."

After the cab tour, Stephie and Ben joined other cruisers at the dock for a catamaran trip that went up the Beagle Channel. The boat circled an island where hundreds of huge sea lions lay in mounds on the rocks while thousands of cormorants preened themselves on the cliffs above.

On the loudspeaker, the boat captain said, "This island could sink under the weight of so many animals and birds. If we don't stay downwind of this island with all that bird guano and sea lion crap, your eyes will water, and you'll beg me to change course. The stink is awful. I don't think any people are dumb enough to try and go on the island to bother these fellows. Sea lions can be very aggressive and territorial."

After Stephie and Ben got off the excursion boat, they walked up the hill to the main drag of the town. Ben went into a casino to try his luck while Stephie went into a shop to look at souvenirs. When she came out, she glanced down the street. About a block away, she saw the dwarfish man. He scurried away and disappeared around a corner.

Was she hallucinating? How could the same person stalking her in Buenos Aires and Montevideo, show up in Ushuaia at the farthest tip of Argentina, hundreds of miles away? She thought, *I have to be imagining this. It isn't possible, is it?*

Here she was in Ushuaia on a street, still in Argentina, and again she felt someone was following her. It seemed silly, insane, but she would declare herself a complete paranoid if it happened in Chile, their next stop. She had never had that feeling of being followed in the Falklands. She decided she wouldn't mention it to Ben.

Early evening, the *Global Quest* sailed from Ushuaia, land on both sides as it made its passage through the Beagle Channel.

Kim and Doug were seated on their separate beds in their cabin.

Kim announced, "I'm going to tell Stephie I think Ben has been fooling around with that blonde."

Doug said, "The operative word here is *think*. You don't know anything for sure. Why are you going to tell her anything when you really don't know? Why butt your nose in and get told to mind your own business?"

"Why not tell her? You guys stick together no matter what."

"It's none of your business, Kim. Not anyone's business but theirs. You could be destroying a marriage."

"He's doing that. In fact, from what she told me, he already destroyed it."

"We don't know what he's doing. We don't know the dynamics of their marriage any more than they would understand the subtleties and intricacies of our strange marriage."

"But . . ."

"You have no right to interfere, especially with someone

you've known for such a short time. Every marriage has its own compromises, understandings, and secrets. Their marriage is no one else's business, right?"

"You've always given me good advice."

"Pretend I still do. Don't do a thing. We'll all go about our business. In a few days, they'll be home, we'll be home, and we'll be cruise ship acquaintances who exchange Christmas cards. Forget it. Drop it, honey. Don't rock the boat. Don't go overboard. Don't walk the plank. Don't go off the deep end. Don't . . ."

"Aye, aye, captain. Okay, already."

Later, in the dining room, all the regulars were at the table. The group roared greetings to Stephie.

Eddie raised his glass and said, "A toast to Stephanie, whom we sorely missed for the last two nights. She set sail for an epic journey around South America and found herself in the middle of an adventure, stranded all by her lonesome on a desolate windswept Falkland Island. Glad to have you back, my dear. We all missed you."

Ruthie said, "I think she did it on purpose to have more time with her beloved penguins."

Katie said, "Folks, in my diary, I'm going to call this the Last Passage to Santiago, which makes it sound like a mystery voyage with . . ."

Ruthie said, " . . . lots of skullduggery and intrigue aboard ship. People getting stranded on Godforsaken islands in the South Atlantic. Maybe finding love in all the wrong places, eh?"

Everyone laughed. The people at the tables around them looked over at the festive table. Ann, at the captain's table, glanced over. She caught Ben's eye, but also Kim's. All Stephie could think about was Mike. She worried that maybe she'd get caught up in this life again, and maybe they'd forget each other. *We can't. I can't go back to the Ben crap.*

Kim looked at Stephie, studied the expression on Ben's face, and glanced over at Ann. At that moment, despite her husband's advice, she decided on her course of action. She knew it wasn't altruism making her act.

42

The next morning, a bright Sunday, the *Global Quest* was cutting through rough seas. On Promenade Deck, Kim and Stephie were having a brisk walk, doing laps around the open deck. They were getting blown around by the strong winds and bent over as they neared the bow.

When they finished their laps, Kim said, "Steph, Doug is playing bridge with the old ladies. Could you come to my cabin for a few minutes? There's something I have to tell you."

Stephie said, "You sound so mysterious. This better be good."

In Kim's cabin, the two women sat on Kim's bed.

Kim said, "Steph, I've been having a battle with myself over this—whether I should interfere and tell you something. Also an argument of sorts with Doug, who advised me to keep my big mouth shut. He's always given me good advice, but I don't always take it."

"About what?"

"I really don't know whether I should—whether I'd be butting into your life, but here goes. I think Ben has been seeing a woman aboard ship and probably in Buenos Aires. The same woman."

"You've got to be kidding. I knew he was a fast worker, but that would be beyond belief. How sure are you?"

"Fairly sure. Here you are the loyal faithful wife, and he's fooling around. God, men."

Stephie looked through the window out to sea. Kim had hit a nerve when she said *loyal faithful wife*, but something within Stephie felt a sense of relief hearing Kim's information. If it were true, this would make a lot of things easier for her.

She said, "You were right in telling me, but I don't want to know any more. I don't want to hear who she is. I don't want

204

to hear any details. I just want to finish this cruise and get back home in one piece. When Ben and I get home, believe me, this is all going to get sorted out for good. What you've told me explains an awful lot about how he's been behaving. I have to tell you this much. I was going to end this farce of a marriage when we got back home. You don't know how much I wanted out, and this even makes it easier in a way. The bastard. The shithead!"

Kim put her arm around Stephie, comforting her.

Stephie said, "The marriage is a sham anyway."

Kim started to smooth Stephie's hair, affectionately, intimately. She leaned over and kissed Stephie on the cheek. The kiss soon took on a life of its own. She was no longer comforting. She was becoming ardent, passionate. For Stephie, Kim's behavior was embarrassing, serious stuff she couldn't handle. She remembered Ben had called Kim a dyke. He was very good at sussing out a woman's sexual orientation, way before she ever did. Stephie pulled away. She got up and stood by the cabin window.

She said, "Please, Kim, I have enough on my plate right now without more emotional complications."

"I'm sorry, Steph. Ever since I met you, I've been attracted to you. You remind me so much of a close friend I lost. I know I'm out of line, but I can't help it."

"Let's forget it. I'm not that way. Let's stay friends, but promise me, you won't do this again . . ."

"It won't happen again, but I wanted you to know I care for you deeply."

After leaving Kim's cabin, Stephie went to Tony's office to ask him if she could use his phone.

After a few minutes, she was put through to her boss in Washington.

Stephie told him what Kim had revealed and said, "Chief, I can't believe it."

At the National Security Agency, the Director said, "Steph, please promise me. Act as if you know nothing. Play a role until you get back here to Washington. Don't confront Ben.

Please, for our sake, don't say a word. I know it's going to be difficult."

"You said the last time I called he might have had something to do with that scary incident in Montevideo when it looked like people were coming after me. A similar incident may have happened in Ushuaia yesterday, but I may just have imagined something. A short man . . ."

"We don't know anything for sure about that yet. We're aware of people watching you. But please, for the few days remaining, just play along. Say nothing to Ben or anyone else. Promise me, Stephanie."

"God, I'll try, but I hope you're not jerking me around on this. One more betrayal in my life, and I'm going to go off the deep end."

"Trust me. This will work out. We're going to take good care of you. I promise you."

43

On Monday aboard the *Global Quest*, the nine table-mates, dressed warmly, were posing for one of the ship's photographers as they stood on the windy stern deck with Cape Horn in the background. Stephie had a hard time smiling, but some of the others were mugging for the camera. Kim was looking toward Stephie, an anxious look on her face. Ben knelt in front of the group, holding a lifebuoy with the ship's name emblazoned on it.

While they were out on deck, a familiar voice came over the P.A. from the bridge. "This is Captain Marchland, your trusty skipper. Yes indeed. We are positioned opposite Cape Horn at the very tip of South America. For hundreds of years before the Panama Canal was built many a ship was wrecked trying to round this spit of land. The California Gold Rush of the 1840s significantly increased traffic round this treacherous point.

"The weather here today, the near gale force winds, is but a tiny sample of the murderous weather conditions you encounter here . . . Hmm, the cruise director has informed me that Jackpot Bingo has reached four-thousand dollars, so be sure to play this afternoon. And don't forget the line dancing. A person in my position does become a shill to shipboard commerce. Apparently the mundane and the historic collide once again aboard this ship as we continue making our memorable journey."

As the nine tablemates dispersed, Stephie and Ben happened to pass Ann and the Lewises. Ann was peering through binoculars. The Smarmy Man was nearby. Ben saw him and gave him a wide berth.

Later, Ben and Stephie had afternoon tea in the Lido restaurant.

Ben said, "Steph, you've been awfully quiet."

"I still haven't gotten over my adventure in the Falklands."

"You never did fill me in on how you got by there for two nights."

"Oh, just muddled through, probably the same way you did aboard ship while I was gone."

"When we get to Punta Arenas, I'm going to that penguin colony with you."

"You don't have to."

"To come all this way without seeing at least one penguin colony would be criminal."

"Why, Ben, at least I know irony is alive and well and living aboard the *Global Quest*."

A half-hour later, Ben sneaked off to Ann's cabin. Ann was not as responsive as before. She was more distant, quieter, passive. Ben tried to advance, but she rebutted him.

Ben said, "Don't get like Stephie, Ann."

"What does that mean?"

"She has this cold fish act she puts on."

"Probably gets sick of being poked, plunked, pecker-pecked, and molested by you. When we get to Punta Arenas, I'm going to the penguin rookery. I haven't seen a penguin yet."

"Okay, hon, I may be going with Stephanie."

"Does that mean I can't go?"

"Of course not. I want you to see everything."

"Is there any meaning to it when you switch from Steph to Stephie to Stephanie? Are those degrees of caring?"

"Trying to psychoanalyze me again?"

"Heaven forbid. You're not that hard to figure out. Sometimes I think of you as a huge erect penis looking for an orifice rather than as an honest-to-goodness person. Ben, you're a con man, a sexual confidence man. A con man, who instead of chasing the big buck, is chasing, please pardon my profanity, the big fuck. It's compulsive and obsessive with you. I bet Stephie has figured that out by now. I guess Hillary Rodham Clinton has, too, but both Hillary and Stephie decided their long-term goals were somehow allied with keeping the marriage going.

"Hey, faithfulness and fidelity aren't everything, Ben. There are a lot of other things in a marriage that keep it going. For all I know, you're giving Stephie just enough sex to keep her satisfied and enough other compensations to make it worth her while. I've had a few opportunities to observe her on this trip. One time I was five or six deck chairs away from her while we were both reading. She writes a lot. She seems to me to be fairly content, kind of placid, certainly not the long suffering wife."

"Hon, don't be mean."

"Hell, I've got to be a wiseass sometimes. This whole adventure ain't easy, you know. It ain't easy being me. And, God knows, it must be difficult being you. See you on deck, babe."

She left the cabin with an unhappy cruiser ensconced there.

44

The next morning, a Tuesday, the ship was docked at a pier in Punta Arenas. Stephie, Ben, Kim, Doug, and the Rilleaus stood by a tour bus, waiting for the command to board. Stephie moved closer to the Rilleaus, trying to ignore Ben and Kim. My God, I feel like Ben and Kim are radioactive.

After the bus got rolling, the tour guide, Xavier, said, "Punta Arenas, our city of over one hundred thousand, is your ship's first stop in Chile. We are located on the Straits of Magellan in Tierra del Fuego, Land of Fire, which gets its name from its many volcanoes. It's an archipelago. We, the Chileans, control two-thirds, and the Argentineans have the rest."

The group toured a walled cemetery with elaborate mausoleums and monuments, a dimly lit anthropology museum, and the busy central plaza with many shoppers.

That afternoon, the group was brought to the parking lot of the Seno Otway penguin colony where they joined with other bus groups from the ship. Hundreds of passengers were strung out in a long line trudging along the dunes above the beach and the ocean. It looked like an army of colorfully and warmly dressed refugees heading for new homes.

Many of the old timers were having difficulty. Stephie walked ahead of Ben, who was coughing and blowing his nose. Stretched out in the long line behind them were some of their tablemates. Eddie, the host, was assisting Katie and Ruthie. Ann and the Lewises were farther back. A short distance behind Ann was the Smarmy Man, who had his camera out and was taking photos of people of interest to him.

Sandy trails led around fenced-off bluffs and hillocks where the penguin burrows were located. Penguins were standing by the trail, going in and out of their burrows or marching back and forth to the beach.

A large group of passengers hurried to the wooden platforms overlooking the beach where hundreds of penguins
entered or left the water.

Stephie stopped and sat in front of three penguins who
looked at her with curiosity. She always carried Mike's stone
with her. She took it from her pocket and stared at it, wondering if she and her lover would ever get together again. In
her mind she was using the word *lover* in her thoughts about
Mike.

Near a fenced area, Ben was trying to take a telescopic
close-up picture of two penguins. He got too close to one
penguin with his long extended lens. The bird made hissing
noises and started to show aggressive behavior. Ben backed
off quickly, chastened.

He joined Stephie and said, "I see what you mean. These
penguins are fascinating."

Stephie said sharply, "Too bad you were so distracted on
this trip to see them before."

Ben looked at her, puzzled by her sharp tone.

The penguin colony was tiny compared to the one Stephie
had seen at Punta Tombo.

That night as the ship cut through the waves, the pool
deck was brightly lit with hanging lights. Many passengers
were partying in cowboy and cowgirl outfits. Ann was wearing a clever Western costume she had brought for the cruise.
Stephie and Ben were wearing jeans and flannel shirts.

Ben said, "I finally got to see your penguins."

Stephie answered, "Yeah, it took you long enough."

The two joined the line-dancing and, for a few minutes,
managed to look like a functioning married couple. Later,
Kim reluctantly danced with the Smarmy Man.

45

The showroom aboard ship was full on Wednesday morning. Tony was speaking.

"Cruisers, tomorrow morning we'll be mooring in the Puerto Montt harbor and tendering you ashore. It's a beautiful Chilean city with a huge wooden cathedral. Along the waterfront are fascinating markets and some very good seafood restaurants. Hundreds of stalls line the harbor street with great bargains, amazingly low prices for bottles of luscious Chilean wine, and some great buys on leathers and souvenirs."

The video behind him projected the harbor market, the wooden cathedral, and picturesque villages, lakes, and mountains.

Tony said, "On one of the tours outside of town, we bring you to the pretty lakeside resort of Frutillar. You'll think you're in Austria or Bavaria with the Alpine-style buildings. You'll see a real snowcapped volcano as a backdrop."

Tony started walking around the stage, looking in the audience. "Stephie, Stephanie, are you here?"

She raised her hand.

He said, "Steph, no penguins for you here, so go to Frutillar instead. Ladies and gentlemen, this dame is so in love with penguins she deliberately missed the ship in the Falklands and stayed over there so she would have a couple of extra nights with her beloved birds. Now that's dedication for you."

Stephie was embarrassed by Tony's reference to her overnights in Port Stanley.

Tony returned to the center of the stage, saying, "After Puerto Montt, we dock in the port city of Valparaiso, That's where you'll disembark. Some of you will be real glad about that. I hear all that hacking and sneezing. From Valparaiso, we'll be taking you by bus to Santiago, Chile's capital. A couple of hours through beautiful countryside with vineyards and orchards, tunnels through the mountains.

"When we get to Santiago, we'll offer all-day tours of the city with lunch at a fine restaurant. After lunch, you'll be taken to a modern air-conditioned convention center where you can wait in climate-controlled comfort for your late night flights."

In Ann's cabin that afternoon, Ben was standing, looking out the window while Ann polished her nails.

He said, "I'm going to tell Steph I won't be going on any tours in Puerto Montt. I'm going to say I'm staying aboard because I feel my cold is getting worse. You and I will be able to get together."

"I don't want to catch your damn cold. Buster, you're going to be on your own. I'm sick of being cooped up in this brig while you get your jollies. Enough is enough. I'm going ashore. I'm going to take that tour to Frutillar. I like Alpine villages. I might even meet a sexy gnome there. You keep your fever. I've got a severe case of cabin fever."

"Ann, I wish you would keep me company."

"Play with yourself. Tomorrow I'm going on tour, and right now I'm going dancing with some geezers."

"You have a mean streak sometimes, you know that."

"Oh, is that what it's called."

She left him sitting on the bed. *Cripes, she's getting to be worse than a wife and a fucking expensive diversion too.*

46

The next morning, Thursday, in their cabin, Stephie was all dressed for her day's outing. Ben was in bed, his nose red from sneezing and sniffling.

He said, "Steph, I'm sorry, you'll have to do Puerto Montt on your own. I've picked up this cold or flu that everybody aboard seems to have. I feel lousy."

"Pay it no mind. I'm perfectly capable of going on my own. Drink plenty of fluids, take two aspirin, and get plenty of rest. I kinda like going it alone. Bye. Take care of that cold. Don't give it to me. Give it to someone else."

Boy, these women can be real bitches.

She headed out the door.

In Puerto Montt, Stephie climbed off the ship's tender and headed for the line of buses. She looked at her tour ticket and went to Bus Number Three. She boarded and took a seat by the window.

Ann got off the tender shortly after Stephie. She headed for Bus Number Two. Sue Swanson, the land tour director, met her at the door.

"I'm sorry, Miss. This bus is having engine trouble. Would you please take Bus Number Three instead?"

Ann headed for Bus Number Three, climbed aboard, and saw two empty seats, one next to the gnarled old woman with a cane, the other next to Stephie. She approached the old woman's seat. The woman said, "This seat is taken. My husband has the Chilean trots, gringo bingo. He's gone to do a number two, a dump."

Ann hesitated, was almost ready to leave the bus to avoid Stephie, when Stephie motioned to her, smiled encouragement, and beckoned her to the vacant seat. Stephie pushed over in her seat to make room for Ann.

Stephie said, "Please, sit here. Glad to have your company. Someone else who isn't collecting Social Security yet. Are you traveling alone?"

"Yes."

Stephie said, "I might as well be traveling alone. My husband always has an excuse for not taking one trip or the other. I've seen you aboard ship with an older couple, haven't I?"

"Yes."

"I thought so. Do you mind traveling alone? Lately I've been doing an awful lot of thinking about traveling by myself. I think I'd be pretty good at it. I do so much on my own anyway. How do you fend for yourself?"

"I met a wonderful couple my first day in the hotel. They're on the cruise. They've been wonderful company for me. Older than me, but great traveling companions."

"Oh, by the way I'm Stephie."

"Glad to meet you. I'm Ann."

"Maybe you heard about me aboard ship? I'm notorious."

Ann looked uneasy, not knowing what Stephie meant.

"I'm the one who got stranded for two nights on the Falklands because of rough seas. Two members of the show cast got left too. The tender was unable to get us back aboard ship."

"I'm sorry you had that terrible experience. Really scary."

"Yes, the seas were unbelievably rough that day, though I heard they were able to get that last tender hauled back aboard. I could never figure out why we couldn't have been hauled back aboard with us in the tender. But, you know, I can't remember a point in my life when so much is seething in my mind. Those two nights made me rethink a lot of things."

"I feel for you being trapped on that island. It must have been terribly frightening."

"Oh, it didn't turn out too badly. Life has a way of compensating. It felt strange to be stranded, but you know there are other ways to be stranded in life, isolated, alienated . . ."

Tears formed in Ann's eyes. She bowed her head, pulled out a Kleenex. Stephie became aware of Ann's discomfort.

"Hey, I'm sorry, Ann. I didn't mean to stir up any bad memories or anything."

Stephie reached over, touched Ann's hand. This upset
Ann more. If Ben had seen this scene of the two women
bonding, he would have realized his days were numbered.

"Ann, a lunch is included in this trip. Would you join me,
please? I'd enjoy your company. I feel as if I know you. I'm
on my own today, and . . ."

"I don't want to spoil your day."

"Please. I need company. You'll do me a real favor."

"Okay, if it wouldn't be too much trouble. It would be nice
to be with a woman close to my age."

"Yes, we can make girl talk."

Ann couldn't avoid smiling at this. She was thinking
ahead to a fun confrontation with Buster.

That afternoon, with a lake and volcano as backdrop,
Stephie and Ann were seated on the patio of an Alpine-style
restaurant.

Ann said, "What a gorgeous view. Stephie, do you feel
lonely at times?"

"Sometimes I feel desolate. I don't know exactly why. You
can be with someone physically, but your psyche and his
can be elsewhere. I'm afraid of distances, of being separated
from people I love. Maybe losing them."

Ann looked across at Stephie, who looked down at her
hands. Stephie didn't know why, but she teared up. Ann hesitated, then moved her hand toward Stephie. They touched.

Stephie said, "This has been a strange day. We've both hit
raw nerves while we've talked with each other. Each one has
stirred up strong feelings in the other. Hey, don't let my ram-
blings bother you. I'm trying to work my way through a lot
of things. Sorry."

Ann looked long and hard at Stephie and said, "Oh, no,
you shouldn't feel sorry. How about another glass of this
great Chilean wine? I think we both need it. A little buzz
won't hurt us. We're not driving. Hell, let's order a bottle and
start kicking some ass. We girls have to stick together."

Stephie said, "Yes. Most guys don't get it."

Late that afternoon in Ann's cabin, Ann and Ben were

seated on the bed. She had distanced herself from him as much as she could.

She said, "There I was face to face with the woman I was betraying. She comforted me. Imagine. Your wife comforting me. Jeez, how's that for turning the tables? She was no longer an abstraction, but a caring human being. A good person. I have talked to her, touched her. The more I see of her, the less of me I like, and the more I've come to dislike you, despise you."

"But, Ann . . ."

"Ssh . . . I never really thought out what I was doing. I was in it for a good time. Now I like her a lot. Stephie was just a name to me. She was in my way, in my path to happiness."

"Please, listen to me . . ."

"Shut up. I'm shagging her husband. How rotten a person I've become. I realize now I was your chattel. You paid me for three weeks of shagging by giving me a free trip. You got a bargain, and I got fucked. When I actually met Stephanie, I realized I was destroying a person who never harmed me."

"Stephie and I are history. She knows that. I know that."

Ben attempted to move closer, to touch her. She rebuffed him, pushed him away.

Ann said, "And, Buster, you and I are history too. You're a generic Buster from now on. Get used to it. We're through. From here on out, you're not welcome in this cabin, and whenever and wherever you see me, if you dare to speak to me, I'll cut you dead. Those are Ann's new rules."

"You can't do that to me."

"Oh, yes, I can. Oh, and I don't give refunds on cruise tickets. You got more than your money's worth. Now get out of *my* cabin. Hit the road, Buster!"

"We have to . . ."

"Get out now before I scream rape. Now!"

Ben rose from the bed and limped from the cabin, defeated, his tail between his legs.

47

It was the morning of the last day at sea, a Friday. The next day, they would be disembarking in Valparaiso. Passengers were busy packing, doing last-minute shopping in the boutiques, and many were trying to medicate their flu-like symptoms. The ship's medical staff was busy.

The decks were not as crowded as usual because some passengers were in bed, staying close to their bathrooms because of diarrhea attacks.

Stephie had little to do. She wanted to avoid Ben. He was in bed sleeping off a hangover, and she didn't want any more declarations from Kim.

She sat in the shade in a deck chair with an open book, but actually she was thinking about options. Mike was very much on her mind, and she had to plan for her future, a future without Ben. Living in the Falklands seemed like a good idea, even though her initial reaction to Stanley was that it was an end-of-the-world place where she'd get cabin fever, but not if she was living and loving with Mike there.

She needed peace and quiet. She had grown weary of her job; she didn't believe all the snooping and surveillance was helping anyone, and the findings were being used for nefarious purposes. She worked for a government she no longer trusted.

She took out her journal.

I felt a sense of menace in Buenos Aires and Montevideo and to a lesser extent in Ushuaia, but I have a more general feeling of unease that there is something dangerous in the air, something not quite right, very indistinct and ill-defined. Ben has been vague and not with it. From what Kim told me, I know why, but he's too abstracted; there's something more on his mind than a girlfriend. It could be as he said, he was coming down with something, a cold, the flu, that bug that seemed to be getting to everyone on the ship.

Maybe I've become a target, maybe something having to do with Uncle Lee's murder. Perhaps what happened to him is coming in like a fog to engulf me and grip me. I would feel a lot safer and happier in the Falklands I think.

At the same time, the glorious loving feeling I have about Mike. The chance for a new life, a new beginning without a cheating husband. With a caring loving man.

She took out Mike's stone and turned it over in her hand. She promised herself that she and Mike would be together again no matter what.

That evening aboard ship, a huge crowd had gathered, awaiting the call for second seating dinner in the four story atrium of the ship. It was a formal dress night, everyone decked out in their finest. People were standing on each atrium deck along the rail of the spiral staircase looking down to the base of the stairs. A three-piece combo was playing a tango. The Rilleaus were dancing in the center of the lower atrium deck along with three other couples. Marge had a bright red evening gown, and Terry, Fred to his Ginger, was in white tie and tails. As the couples finished their dance, the audience erupted into appreciative applause. The Rilleaus bowed gracefully.

In the ship's dining room later that evening, the nine tablemates were seated around the table. Everyone was in a celebratory mood except Ben. Terry Rilleau stood and raised his glass.

He said, "This is our last night aboard ship. Marge and I have danced the nights away and loved it. We watch dance bring people together, and we watch people who won't dance drift apart. God bless all of you, and thank you for making our cruise so enjoyable. And Stephie, dear, you've had a more exciting cruise than the rest of us. May your future life be full of your beloved penguins and true happiness. May you be free of lonesome strandings on strange islands."

Everyone toasted and drank. At the captain's table, Ann had drunk more wine than usual and was enjoying herself.

At the end of the dinner, the lights dimmed and the waiters, busboys, and kitchen staff paraded around the room with the candlelit baked Alaska.

That night, Ben stayed up late, made the rounds of the ship's bars, and drank too much. He had a lot on his mind.

48

On the Promenade Deck Saturday morning, Ann was looking out at the Valparaiso dock watching disembarkation procedures. Ben, looking the worse for wear, nursing a hangover, approached her.

He said, "Ann, I'm going to call you when I get back to Washington."

"No, you're not. If you do, expect a visit from the police. I'll get a restraining order. I'll turn you in as a stalker. We're finished. I'm not going to end up like Stephie."

"I'm going to fight to win you back. You'll see. I'll do anything to get you back."

"Fuck off, Buster!"

Ann turned and stormed away. Ben stood there forlorn, looking desperately lonely.

Later Stephie and Ben were aboard a bus heading up to Santiago from Valparaiso through miles of well-kept orchards and vineyards.

In the early afternoon, they took a funicular railway to the top of San Cristobal in Santiago's main park and stood below a one-hundred-eighteen foot statue of the Virgin Mary.

Stephie and Ben were looking up at the statue when she happened to glance to her left and saw Ann about thirty feet away. She left Ben and walked over to her.

She said, "Hi, Ann."

"Oh, hello, Steph. I've been thinking about you. I enjoyed our lunch together the other day."

"Are you enjoying Santiago?"

"I love it. It's such a modern city. All those skyscrapers."

Ben stared at them, eyes wide, mouth agape.

Stephie said, "That's my husband over there. I just came over to wish you a safe flight back."

"You too."

They touched hands, and Stephie returned to a dumbfounded Ben.

The Santiago convention center was a large sprawling building in a sparsely built area of Santiago. After hours of waiting in discomfort, Stephie and Ben went to the disappointing dinner.

They exited the dining room and walked down the main hallway in the dimly lit convention center, past sullen, flu-ridden, crabby, elderly luxury cruise ship passengers in their wrinkled and sweaty travel clothes. Ben had a persistent cough. Both were tired, grumpy. They passed the old man with a walker and the old woman with a cane. Both were dour and weary.

They approached their little group of shipboard friends. Doug was standing, reading a paperback, his toupee askew and unruly. Kim, seated, was doing a crossword puzzle. The Rilleaus were still dancing, a slow robotic dance, just moving in place.

Marge said, "No, left foot first. One, two, three."

The Kaufeld sisters greeted them. The muffled voice of Sue Swanson came over the loudspeakers.

"All right, I repeat, will those people on United Airlines Flight Nine-Nine-Six bound for Miami, please line up for bus transportation outside the building at this time."

Stephie said to the group of friends, "Well, that's us. Goodbye, everyone."

There were a series of hugs, kisses, and goodbyes. The Rilleaus embraced first Stephie, then Ben.

Kim hugged Stephie, saying, "Steph, please call me in three or four days. We have to talk. Please."

Kim gave Ben short shrift, but Doug shook his hand warmly. The Kaufields hugged them tightly. Ben and Stephie headed for the main entrance. Sandy, waiting for his flight back to England, gave them a thumbs up as they passed him.

The line of passengers waiting for buses stretched down the central walkway. To the right of the walkway was a line of eight black hire cars.

Stephie and Ben were heading toward the bus line.

Ben said, "C'mon, Stephie. The airlines always overbook. Look how long it's taking to load the first bus. This'll take forever. Let's get ahead of this crowd by taking a private car."

"Ben, let's stick with the group. We've got plenty of time. The tour director called the airport and assured everyone they did not overbook."

"I think they're full of shit. How do we know she called at all. C'mon. Let's go."

Usually when they were traveling, Ben had pretty good instincts, and they usually made out well. Worn down by his pestering, she agreed. They started walking away from the line toward the hire cars. The first driver directed them to the third car in the rank of hire cars.

Once they were inside, the car headed out of the convention center onto a major highway at a fast pace. After fifteen minutes, the driver turned off onto a side-road that ran through an industrial area.

Stephie became apprehensive about the dark side-road.

Ben said, "Maybe it's a shortcut."

The hire car approached a line of traffic cones and a van parked halfway in the road. The car was finally forced to stop. The rear and side doors of the van flew open, and Stephie, Ben, and the car's driver faced four men in ski masks with automatic weapons.

The men threw open the car doors, and pulled the driver and two passengers out. Stephie was terrified. She could feel her face covered by a wet cloth. She knew instantly it was chloroform or something that would render her unconscious. She heard Ben cry out. She was losing consciousness, slowly drifting away. She heard voices, an engine starting up.

Bright flashes of light brought her back to consciousness. She blinked; her eyes gradually got used to the flashes. Someone was taking photographs of her. She looked down. Her nude body was draped with a skimpy white cloth that clung around her shoulder and barely covered her pubic area. Strands of rope bound her to a chair.

Her eyelids became heavy; she passed out.

When she came to again, the rope was gone. Her jeans and the rest of her clothes lay on the floor at her feet. The white cloth had fallen to her lap. She quickly dressed. She felt violated, humiliated.

Stephie became aware of her surroundings. She was in a small room with a tile floor and a high ceiling. In the corner of the room was a sink and toilet. The room had no windows, a heavy wooden door, a single light bulb hanging by a cord above her head, a metal cot with a thin lumpy mattress, a chair, and a small pine table. A towel and sheets lay on the table. The walls were stucco, and the only decoration was a wooden crucifix hanging on one wall.

The room was warm with little air movement. She couldn't hear any sounds. She still had her watch, and as she felt in the pocket of her jeans, she could feel Mike's gift stone. She rubbed the smooth stone around in her fingers. Tears came, and she was soon sobbing uncontrollably.

She looked around the room for a camera or listening device but could see none.

She had no idea where she was being kept, whether or not she was still in Chile, whether she was in the city or the country. After a few hours, the door opened, an armed man entered, and then an old woman wearing a floor length skirt. She carried a plate of rice and beans, which she placed on the table. The guard watched Stephie warily while another armed guard stood just outside the door. The old lady and the guards were expressionless. The door slammed behind them as they left.

That night, she lay on the cot, staring at the ceiling. She fingered Mike's stone in her jeans pocket. The bulb remained lit all night.

As the days passed, the food was rice and beans, some beef, some bread, sometimes watery soup, and tea.

She concluded her captors were keeping her in a house in the countryside. It was very quiet. Occasionally she could hear a dog barking, a snatch of music, the mumble of voices, a radio.

One of her captors, a young red-haired woman, was nasty to her. The woman said in fluent English, "Did you know that all the time you were in Buenos Aires and on your cruise, your fucking bastard of a husband had his girlfriend with him? Did you know that? Was it a three-way? Was the son of a bitch cheating on you every chance he got? Where'd you find such a pig, on the Internet?"

Stephie wondered how the woman knew about Ben's girlfriend. Stephie never talked to the woman, never asked her questions.

No one ever harmed her physically. A routine was soon established that did not vary.

The room, she was sure, was on the first floor. Everything was kept fairly clean. The old woman with the same full-length skirt came in every day and cleaned while a man with an automatic weapon stood outside her open door. Her food was usually delivered twice a day by the old woman, but sometimes the nasty woman would bring it in, slam it on the table so liquids spilled while one or two armed men stood outside.

No one told her why she was being held. Sometimes she thought it was for ransom. Sometimes she was sure it had to do with her job. Other times, she thought it was Ben's doing. This idea was reinforced by what the nasty woman minder kept saying about Ben's mistress.

She was never questioned or asked to make a tape or talk on the phone. She remained silent, afraid to agitate her captors. There seemed to be three male guards, the bitchy woman, and the old cleaning woman.

One day the old woman brought her an old tattered housecoat, told her in accented English she was going to wash her jeans and other stuff, then return them. Stephie carefully held onto Mike's stone while she changed into the dress.

She thought constantly of Mike. She loved him totally and

ached to be with him again. Her thoughts about Ben were ambiguous. Sometimes she worried he might have been killed. Sometimes she thought he must be very worried about her. Then she thought he might be involved in her kidnapping. Why had he insisted on taking the hire car? And how could he have had the audacity to fool around with that other woman on the whole trip?

At times, she could hear coming from another room the sounds of a radio or television, occasional arguments, quiet talking, sometimes dogs. Cooking smells wafted in when her door was open.

One afternoon, the tail of a ginger cat slid under her door. The tail moved up and down in a slow, rhythmic pattern. Stephie gently patted and caressed it, and the cat stayed for quite awhile. The cat would return at different times, and sometimes would show up at night. The warm feel of the animal heartened her. It knew she was there. Maybe it was an indoor cat wanting some contact with other creatures. Perhaps other people had been imprisoned in the room, and the cat had welcomed them too.

There was a peephole in the door so her captors could tell where she was when they opened the door. She was afraid they could spy on her when she was on the commode. The guards were sullen but not mean-spirited. They didn't leer at her, make suggestive remarks. They seemed as if they operated under some form of military discipline. She fondled Mike's talisman stone gift for hours at a time.

It was six weeks to the day since the kidnapping had occurred. Two burly unarmed men came into the room. They forced Stephie's arms behind her back and tied them. They put a hood over head so she couldn't see. She was terrified. *This is it. They're taking me out to kill me.*

Standing on either side of her, the men led her out of the house and pushed her to the floor of what she thought was a van. One of the men, none too gently, bound her feet together.

Stephie prayed. Tears filled her eyes. She would never see

Mike again, never be able to experience life.

Later, the van drove up to the driveway of a hospital rear entrance in Santiago. It was a back street with no vehicular or pedestrian traffic. Two men hurried out, opened the back door, and placed Stephie's bound, hooded, and gagged body on the sidewalk. They got back in the van, and it sped off. Stephie lay there for close to an hour, squirming, trying to free herself.

Finally, she heard a car stop. Moments later, a policeman was removing the hood and the gag. He untied the rope around her feet. His partner notified headquarters. She was taken inside the hospital and after doctors examined her, she was interrogated by Chilean authorities. Officers of the State Department, the CIA, the NSA, and the FBI showed up.

The Chilean officials showed her hundreds of pictures. No one was familiar. After two days, she was turned over to U.S. authorities.

49

It was morning at the U.S. Embassy in Santiago, Chile. Two marine guards in dress blue uniforms stood guard at the entrance. A thin and haggard Stephie was led through the gate accompanied by three civilians, who looked very serious and intent on protecting their charge.

A short time later, Stephie sat at a conference table on the fourth floor of the embassy with three men opposite her. One was the Director of the National Security Agency, her boss.

The Director said, "Stephie, I flew down here as soon as I heard about your release."

The Director introduced the man to his right, but he didn't introduce the third man, the Smarmy Man.

He said, "Chuck Garand is with our embassy here. He's been in overall charge of the investigation into your disappearance. You wouldn't have been kidnapped if you hadn't been working for us, so I feel deeply responsible. We're sorry. I'm sorry."

Stephie said, "But why me? I was never questioned by them. They never tried to get any information out of me."

"No, but the information stored in that mind of yours was their bargaining chip. It was the threat of your interrogation they used."

"Please, Chief, I need to know."

The Director sighed and said, "It's complicated, but here goes. Your kidnapping was connected to two men serving sentences for spying in two different countries. A Chilean man, call him Pablo, a leader of the Communist faction here in Chile, was in jail in Russia. For what, we do not know. A Russian operative, call him Ivan, was imprisoned in Israel. Again, for what reason, we just don't know. The Chilean Communists wanted their man, Pablo, back."

The Director was a pipe smoker. He packed his pipe meticulously, killing time, lit it up, and puffed on it furiously to get it going. A pipe is an ideal prop for someone weighing his words and taking his time to impart real or imagined information.

The Director continued, "The Chilean group knew the Russians desperately wanted their guy back from Israel. They hatched a scheme. They kidnapped you, Stephanie Ably-Ranier, whose head is full of what they think is invaluable information. A human disk drive packed with file after file of invaluable secrets."

Stephie said, "We know that's a lot of bullshit. I haven't been working on important classified stuff for years."

"They didn't know that. All they knew was you worked for the NSA."

"But couldn't I have been warned something was in the works?"

"Stephie, remember when you told me about this South American trip, I told you that you could become a target? I never thought this particular thing could happen, but . . ."

"I knew the risks. Go on, tell me about these two men. Ivan and Pablo, the swap . . ."

The Director's pipe had gone out. He tapped it on the table. "A few days after you had been kidnapped, we were approached. You would be released, clean and pure, in other words, uninterrogated. If we would prevail upon Israel to release Ivan, the Russians would give up Pablo. It took a lot of secret negotiating, but that's what happened. Pablo was returned to Chile, and Ivan was returned to Russia. When the exchanges were completed, you were released. In the early days of your disappearance, we didn't have a clue."

Garand entered the conversation. "In the first few days, we were at a loss where to turn. We investigated every avenue, starting with your time in Buenos Aires and your cruise. Your husband was at us every minute. He was distraught and very cooperative."

Stephie said, "Why shouldn't he be cooperative?"

The Director and Garand seemed taken aback, reticent, hesitant.

Garand decided to forge ahead, "Stephie, we did a lot of checking. We had hundreds of agents working on this. With all that manpower, you find out a great deal of information. We began to suspect your husband for complicity in the kidnapping.

Stephie said, "For God's sake, complicity? Why Ben? Why did you mention Ben on the phone when they made that attempt in Montevideo?"

The Director said, "In the past, we've been worried about his philandering, that it could compromise you and us. Frankly, that's why we took you off sensitive and high-classification stuff. On the trip, Ben did a terrible thing. A piggish thing. Your friend on the ship, Kim, told you he was fooling around.

"Stephie, Ben had a woman with him on the whole trip, the entire three weeks. He was seeing her whenever he could sneak away, but he had absolutely nothing to do with the kidnapping. He insisted on that hire car only because he was antsy and was in a hurry to get to the airport."

Stephie stared at him. To have Ben's calumny spelled out by an official was very upsetting. She seemed to fall apart. She crossed her arms on the table and rested her head on her arms. The Director rose, went around to her, put his hands on her shoulders. She wept. After a time, she raised her head.

She said, "Go on. Tell me about it."

"He booked and paid for a room in your hotel in Buenos Aires and for a cabin aboard ship. Her name is Ann Glidden. Here are her photographs."

The Director showed her a folder of photographs.

"Oh, Christ, I met her. We had lunch together in Chile in Fruitillar."

The unintroduced man, the Smarmy Man said, "Who wouldn't fall for her? She's stunning. Every man's wet dream."

The Director said, "Harry, for Christ's sake, shut up. You give sleaze a bad name."

Stephie said, "He was having sex with her, then coming back to me in our room as if nothing had happened?"

Stephie stared out of the window. The men were quiet.

She said, "Kim, of course, warned me on the ship. He's a scumbag. When I was being held in that tiny airless room, I spent time worrying about him, how he was taking this. I was stupid enough to care how he was holding up. That miserable . . ."

The Director said, "They've broken up. He and Ann Glidden. Ann told us she ended it after she met you that day. She realized then what a whorish thing she was doing. Ben is really contrite. I spoke to him just minutes ago. I'm sorry we had to confirm this. Stephie, he's inside the building down the hall. You've got to see him. He's a wreck."

Stephie said, "He's a wreck? What about me? Could any man ever explain a thing like that? What kind of creature did I marry? What sort of bastard would do something like that?"

The Director said, "I wish I could offer you some comfort. Harry here was on the ship keeping track of things for us. The only time you were out of our sight was that two-night stranding in the Falklands, but we knew nothing would happen to you over there in the middle of nowhere."

Stephie smiled and thought to herself, *If only they knew what happened over there. I hope somehow Mike and I can get together, now more than ever.*

She had already called Mike, and he said he was waiting for her. If she didn't come to him, he swore he'd come to her.

The Smarmy Man said, "May I ask Stephie a question?"

The Director said, "Harry, you may not. Just keep your mouth shut please."

"No," said Stephie, "Let him ask whatever he wants."

Harry said, "Stephie, how could a woman who was hired by a spy agency for her intelligence and her acuity, be so dense about a philandering husband?"

The Director was furious. "Harry, for Christ's sake."

"No, let me answer that. Because over the years, I'd grown

not to care about him. He was just a roommate by the time we decided to take the trip. If I had known about Ann, I would have flown home, but nothing he could do would really bother me, because he had fooled around before. He had worn me out, worn me down It's also being book-smart versus being street-smart. I'm naïve and stupid when it comes to real life. He's the fox in the hen house, the fox on the beach killing the weakest penguins and chicks, and I'm the dumb cluck."

Stephie continued, "Why didn't I leave him? Inertia. I hate change. My God, I was just thinking . . . if I hadn't been kidnapped, I never would have known the full extent of his lying and cheating for those three weeks."

The Director said, "He's waiting for you."

"Could you get me a machete. I want to cut his balls off. Pardon me for my crudity, but I'd like to put him out of business permanently."

Stephie unconsciously took Mike's stone talisman from her pocket and stared at it. Her face brightened.

Stephie said, "I have to tell you I've been planning a divorce from the time we left Buenos Aires. I really don't want to see him. I have nothing to say to him that can't be done through my lawyer."

Later, she closed the conference room door behind her. Gaunt, deeply altered, Stephie walked down the long corridor. Ben was approaching her from the end of the hall. She stopped. Ben walked slowly, contritely like a dog that has been caught doing something wrong, his tail between his legs. They stopped about ten feet apart. Her face was frozen in a look of hatred. Each stood still.

He said, "Stephie, thank God you're free. I . . . . Stephie? What . . .?"

He stared at her. He knew from her face his world had collapsed.

"They told you, didn't they? I'm so sorry, Steph. It's over between that woman and me."

"Yes, always *that woman*. It's over between us too. It's

been over for a very long time. All of it is over. I'm so tired of all of this. I feel dead. I've lost all feeling. You, the marriage, us—all of it's over, thank God."

"Steph . . ."

"I'm staying here in Santiago for a few more nights. When I get back to Georgetown, I want you out of the condo until I move my things out. I'm going away. I want you out of my life."

"Stephie, I'm so sorry. I'll . . ."

"Why? Why did you humiliate me? Was I that bad?"

"I was a pig. I was obsessed. I wasn't thinking of you. Only my own gratification. It was all about me, not . . ."

"Get out of here. Get away from me. You're worse than scum."

Stephie turned and walked up the hall. She went back into the conference room. The three men were startled to see her come back in. The Director went around the table, hugged her, eased her into a chair where she dropped her head, and stared at her clasped hands.

The Director said, "You've been through one hell of an ordeal. We're going to take good care of you from now on."

After a few moments, she looked up, was about to say something, when a door at the side of the conference room opened and the dwarfish man entered. He did a quick take when he saw her. Stephie stared at the man and then looked at the Director, her forehead furrowed.

She said, "What is this anyway? This guy was one of the people following me, threatening me. What the hell is he doing here? What's going on?"

The Director said, "Steph, please . . . I can explain."

"No, I get it now. I was set up all along, from the get-go. No, you can't explain anything. God, what a sap I've been. You betrayed me too. My own government, the agency I worked for and trusted and that creep of a husband. All of you! Bastards!"

"Stephanie, you've got this all wrong. You're misinterpreting . . ."

"No, I'm not misinterpreting anything. I think I was part of a scheme that defies the imagination. I knew you people were conniving, but I didn't realize how ruthless you really are."

The Director said, "No, we're going to take good care of you from now on."

Stephie had a new look of determination on her face.

"No, from now on, this woman is going to take care of herself. No agency need apply. I've had enough betrayals to last me for a lifetime."

"But, Steph . . . Please let me explain."

"No, please, everyone, cut the bullshit! Go screw yourselves. All of you."

She rushed out the door, down the stairs, and out of the embassy.

50

The small two-engine jet-prop plane was flying through clouds. Stephie was sitting, staring out the window. She looked better-fed, healthier than she had after her release. She was glad to be free of all the moving-out details in Washington. The plane's lone flight attendant leaned over her.

"Mrs. Ranier, would you like some orange juice?"

"Yes . . . no, make it a screwdriver. And the name is Ms. Ably, not Mrs. Ranier."

"Oh, I'm sorry. We had you listed as Mrs. Ranier."

"No, that was in another world, another lifetime."

When she was nursing her drink, glancing out at the clouds, she could feel determination and strength returning to her mind. Her hand opened and closed on Mike's talisman stone.

From the plane, she could see the endless sea and the horizon. Then the Falklands appeared, then Mike's island, then the town of Stanley, then the penguin rookery at Gypsy Cove, and finally the airport and the terminal building.

The plane landed at the small Port Stanley airport. Stephie walked down the steps to the tarmac and hurried toward the small terminal. The wind was forceful, chilly. Snowflakes floated through the air. Mike ran toward her. Her face lit up; she glowed. They kissed ardently and eagerly and hugged for a long time.

Mike said, "God, I'm a lucky man. When I read about the kidnapping, I thought you were dead."

"In a sense, I think I've been dead for a long time. Now I'm back among the living."

"We're going to be great together. I love you very much, darling."

Stephie held the shiny red stone out to Mike. He laughed.

They headed arm in arm to the terminal building. Belinda, like a giantess, stood there with a big grin on her face, waving at Stephie.

Belinda roared, "I told you he was a keeper."

Afterword

Now that the large oil reserves offshore from the Falklands were being plumbed, it would be a long time before England thought of giving up the islands. Stephie was still there in the Falklands, living and working with Mike. They had a daughter now. They were both contented with their lives and had a solid marriage. Mike published important research in professional journals, while Stephie ran nature tours so travelers could see the penguins on the Falklands and on South Georgia Island with its millions of penguins.

Meanwhile, Ann had been having a long-term relationship with a lawyer in Baltimore.

Ben played the field for awhile. Then, on September 11, 2001, he was on United Airlines Flight 93, which took off from Newark, was hijacked by terrorists, and crashed at Shanksville, Pennsylvania, killing all aboard. It was believed passengers aboard the plane had made a valiant and heroic effort to thwart the terrorists. They had averted it from crashing into either the United States Capitol or the White House.

Stephie did not believe Ben's death was God's will, that he was being punished for any transgressions. As far as their marriage was concerned, he had not done anything evil, merely something distasteful and shabby. At the end, he may have acted bravely on the plane. That would be very much like him.

His death was like her Uncle Lee's, the luck of the draw, fate, if you will. The bouncing ball falling into the slot on the bingo machine. For her, it was the way the world operated, not by any divine plan or divine symmetry, but by chance. God existed, she believed, but He was not involved with who would live, who would die, how, and when. He had bigger fish to fry.

Stephie attended the memorial services for Ben in Washington, D.C. She brought a sprig of heather from the Falklands and placed it with the other flowers in the front of the altar in the church. During the service, she and Ann Glidden sat together, holding hands. Afterwards, they hugged, dried their tears, and went their separate ways.

On her plane trip back to Port Stanley by way of Chile, Stephie thought about the trip to Buenos Aires and the cruise around South America. It had brought out the worst in Ben, but had been a godsend for her, because it had brought Mike into her life. She knew, more than ever, a good man is hard to find. She did not regret her life with Ben, but she did regret she'd been an enabler for so long.

She thought of penguins, the way they tangoed for life as long as both mates managed to survive it all. In human lives, sometimes the daemon got the upper hand, and human beings found themselves adrift in a world of complex relationships, foundering, being abandoned on real or imaginary islands.

She had brought Mike's stone with her as she always did. She took it out, held it tightly in her palm, and gave thanks for her answered prayers.

Clawed Back from the Dead

In this fast-moving novel John F. Rooney has brought back his series detective Denny Delaney from *Nine Lives Too Many* for a chill and thrill, manic roller coaster ride. A serial killer is on the loose, and he is trying to shut down the making of the movie *Nine Lives, Two Men* that is based upon Denny's match-up with the arch-terrorist Felix the Cat.

Everyone related in any way to the movie is a target in the line of fire. This suspense thriller careens and caroms as it follows a mad assassin. Be prepared to be enthralled with action aplenty as the killer hits his murderous stride. If Denny didn't know better, and if he hadn't killed the evil monster himself, he would think that Felix the Cat was the perpetrator again rampaging, creating havoc and chaos.

Rooney has pulled out all the stops on this one as a murderer conducts a personal vendetta against his perceived enemies in the film industry. The killer seems to be in a race against time as he creates his swath of death. Yet even amid this grim narrative, Rooney is able to inject humor and create memorable characters whose humanity is endearing to readers.

This book helps to round out the portrait of Denny as we see him interacting with his family: his wife Monny, his father, a retired and admired cop, and his brave mother who is standing beside her husband as he battles cancer.

Get ready for a big surprise!

Nine Lives Too Many

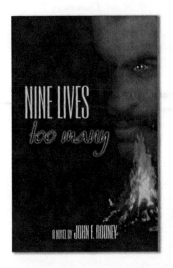

This is a violent and unsettling novel about terrorists, a cautionary tale, but also the deeply moving personal story of a conflicted police detective.

Felix the Cat, only nominally Muslim, but fanatically anti-American and anti-Israeli, is terrorizing New York City and Washington, D.C., with a series of bombings. This third-rate screenwriter plants a deadly bomb which kills and maims hundreds in the Main Concourse of Grand Central Station. The FBI seems in suspicious haste to label it a suicide bombing.

Grand Central Station is Detective Sergeant Denny Delaney's turf. Minutes before the attack Denny has been suspended because his drinking is interfering with his duties. His wife Monny has left him. After Denny barely misses getting killed in the bombing, he examines the terminal's surveillance tapes with his wheelchair-bound, attractive coworker Terry, and he and she realize that this is not the work of a suicide bomber. The bomber has walked away unscathed. After Nine-Eleven Denny had been on TDY with the FBI, and he has made a connection to that duty and the bomber. By threatening to reveal what he knows, Denny gets reinstated to FBI duty so he can work the case.

The novel cascades through a series of suspenseful actions: FBI raids, firefights, ambushes, and attempts on the lives of investigators. Felix, the failed screenwriter, sets up a cinematic conflict between antagonist and protagonist by telephoning Denny. They begin a series of cat-and-mouse, insightful colloquies as Felix's deadly acts of violence proliferate, one for each of his nine lives.

After the Grand Central devastation, nowhere and no one is safe including the streets of New York, the Broadway theater district, the White House, cruise ships, hotels, beaches, and bridges.

Denny has to battle Felix and his alcoholism. Will he be able to win in his inner and outer struggles and defeat a terrorist monster?

The Daemon in Our Dreams

Three strangers in different parts of the world each has three nightmares in which a young Indian man stares menacingly at them. The dreams invoke funeral pyres, glaring skulls and feral beasts. On a land and sea tour from Singapore to the Taj Mahal these three people, Dr. Lee Ably, Fran Carr, and Paul Rowan, separately begin to see the threatening dream daemon in real life, in real time. They have given him a name—Ramesh—but cannot find a reason for his pursuit of them. And how does he get from place to place to materialize before them?

The suspense builds as one after the other of the three travelers is confronted by Ramesh in exotic places. They watch in horror as their daemon changes and evolves in successive sightings into a more deadly foe.

When the trip nears its end, the three think they have found surcease in England, but an Indian hijra message causes them to think otherwise.

In a London hotel lounge three assassinations take place. The assassin appears to be the dream daemon. Why has all of this happened? What ties these three people and their ghostly interloper to one another?

We are drawn into this eerie and insightful story as the book's narrative drive propels and impels readers deeper into the labyrinth. It's an unforgettable tale of human beings facing ominous futures.

The Rice Queen Spy

Philip Croft, a master spy for Her Majesty's secret service, MI6, was cruelly outed and tortured for his homosexuality. All his adult life he was a dedicated rice queen—partial only to Asian men. In his life he had three lovers and a few brief encounters. He was a gentle man and a gentleman, a member of private clubs, a man of privilege, who was betrayed by some of his friends—not for being gay, but for being too decent and naïve.

This novel traces Philip's life and his loves, and is a triumphant testimony to a gay man's passage from mid-life to old age. Brushes with death and derring-do followed him even into his elder years. He was able to keep his dignity and live a full life while briefly thumbing his nose at his former superiors by opening a gay sauna in London. Being a rice queen was his preference, but living a fulfilled life was his destiny.

Readers of the author's suspense novel *The Daemon in Our Dreams* will recall that Paul Rowan visited Philip Croft in his London home and told him about his eerie encounters with the dream-daemon Ramesh. In the later pages of this book we see Paul Rowan's fate through the perspective of Philip and his lover Robin.

This book breathes life into a gay man who served his country through deception, and though his country punished him for his personal deception, he became the victor rather than the victim.

Printed in the United States
136432LV00005B/1/P